D0199818

DISCARD

NORA & KETTLE

A PAPER STARS NOVEL

LAUREN NICOLLE TAYLOR

NORA & KETTLE

ISBN: 978-1-63422-135-1

Copyright ©2015 Lauren Taylor

All rights reserved.

Cover Design by: Marya Heiman

Interior Format by: Courtney Nuckels

Editing by: Cynthia Shepp

For more information about our content disclosure, please utilize the QR code above with your smart phone or visit us at www.cleanteenpublishing.com.

*WARNING: This novel contains realistic portrayals of domestic violence.

TO JOHN & JEANNE FOR FINDING
HOPE IN A LOST PLACE.

1

WINGS

IF I HAD WINGS, THEY WOULD BE BLACK, THIN, AND FEATHERED. NOT A FLAT COLOR... BUT IRIDESCENT. SHINING WITH HUES OF PURPLE, GREEN, AND BLUE. CATCHING THE LIGHT WITH THE BAREST FINGERTIPS. AND WHEN I NEEDED, I COULD FOLD INTO THE DARKEST SHADOWS AND HIDE.

This time between the dark and the dawn is mine. I roll from my bed and slip quietly across the floor, avoiding the creaks in a shadowy dance no one will ever see. My ears tune to the nonexistent noises around me and I sigh, ghostlike, with relief. Because in this time, he sleeps.

A snap of a memory flashes through my mind and body as I feel the sharp, short cracks delivered this time. *This* time.

I ease the dresser drawer out, holding my breath as tiny splinters catch the sides, and reach underneath the lace and silk to the boys' pants hidden beneath. Quickly, I slide them on, my bruises objecting as I bend to fasten them. Tucking the ends of my nightdress into the waist, I pad to the window.

Across from our brownstone, one light shines dimly through a dirty window. Someone leaving for or returning from a shift; a refrigerator light; something simple and easy. I crinkle my nose and think, *Of all the hundreds of people who live in that apartment building, how is it that only one solitary light shines?* I quirk my lips into an unsure smile, a new split stinging as it stretches apart. This is why it is *my* time.

Bending and flexing my legs, I take a deep breath and push the window ajar. It protests, groaning as I push my torso out and use my back to push it up. Settling on the windowsill, I close it down, pulling a small comb from my pocket and wedging it in the gap so I can get back in.

Perched like a bat ready to launch into the night, my eyes dart to the corner of the building, to the rickety fire escape that would be much easier to climb. A car light bends over the gaps in the iron and fans out like the punch in a comic book. *Wham!* I snigger to myself, the laugh seeming foreign, jarring. I'm not supposed to laugh. I'm a sad girl, with a sad life.

But it is *my* life, and tonight… I'm going to fly.

I face my window and grasp the drainpipe that runs the length of the building. Staring up at the sky for a moment, I search out my destination. The one error in the building, which grates on him, invites me. One beam they forgot to trim sits out from the wall like a pirate ship plank. I dig my bare toes into the worn spaces between the bricks and climb.

I'm a shadow taped to the wall, scaling the pipe in solid but fast movements. Breathing hard and forgetting everything. The sky and the stars hang around just for me. They cling to the fading darkness, and I let them spark my senses. The night air closes in like the wings of a crow, folding over, protecting and gifting me something I lack. I pass the window of our sleeping neighbors and shake my head. They won't hear me.

I breathe in deeply. Car exhaust films the air but it lightens, sweetens, as I climb. Overhead, the plank casts a cool shadow over the building, lengthening as the moon starts to dip away and the sun coaxes the sky into pinks and oranges. *My* time is only minutes. *My* mind is only on the hands pulling me up and the legs stabilizing me.

I dig my toes into the brackets holding the pipe. It cuts in, but my skin is toughening through scars criss-crossing over other scars. I throw my head back, my hair wisping and sticking to my cheeks. Sweat makes my grip slippery. It takes more concentration, more strength to hold on, but that's why I like it. This risk sends flickers through my heart; pinprick lights like the points of a star. It keeps something beating that could be dead, should be dead. But I can't let it.

I won't.

The pipe trembles under my weight, the screws wriggle in their brackets, and I hold tighter. Moving faster up, up, up, until I reach the beam. I link my hands together around the plank, the dry wood soaking up some of my sweat.

This part, the upside-down part… I love.

I hug the beam and creep my feet up the wall until I can wrap my legs around it, swinging like a raccoon on a telephone wire. My head drops down and I stare out at the inverted city, the skyscrapers hanging from the earth like stalactites, dripping their lights into the clouds and piercing the sky. One shake and the people would spill from their locked-in positions, sprinkling like pepper into the atmosphere.

Just float away.

Light as air… I want to be a speck carried by the wind.

My hair swings in coils and clumps on either side of my eyes, and my head starts to beat like a drum full of water from too much blood. I work my way around until I'm right way up, lying stomach to beam.

I push back to sitting, my legs dangling, my chest filled to bursting with cleaner air, the flames of sunrise singeing the top of my head.

If I had wings… They'd need to be strong enough…

Closing my eyes as the round edge of the sun pokes above the horizon, I spread my arms wide. I let the small breeze flutter under my limbs, cool my skin, and free my hair.

If I had wings, I could fly.

2
ACCIDENTS

Paths are usually stamped-out, well-defined things.
They're like that for a reason. They point toward a way
through. They are hope in a lost place.
My path is patchy, indeterminate, and young. Thousands
of feet have not walked this path. Although, sadly, I
know some have.

The sun splits the willowy curtains into strands of green and cream, dancing over each other with the breeze. Groggily, I blink and watch the delicate performance, unwilling to move and waiting for the pain to set in. Branches tap out a Morse-code message on the window. I flinch, mistaking it for sharp knuckles rapping on my door. A dull ache courses through my stomach and pins itself to my back, wishing me good morning.

I carefully straighten under the covers, pointing my toes and testing my limbs. I'm okay. These wounds are ordinary. Nothing I haven't dealt with before.

Through the narrow crack of my bedroom door sails the ordinary clatter of the morning—spoons rattling in empty bowls as they are thrown in the sink and a copper kettle whistling, high-pitched and impatient. That new Perry Como song plays on the radio, my mother's humming sounding like nails on a chalk-board in my sore head. I wait. Sure enough, halfway through the song, his controlled, sharp-as-icepicks footsteps cross the kitchen and the radio squeals across the bands to classical music. I clasp my head with both hands at the squeal and then the twanging violins.

I want to sleep. I need to sleep. I won't get to sleep.

"Nora!" my mother screams, matching the sound of the kettle with its impatient trill. Her loud voice pushes its way between the fingers holding my head together and vibrates inside my skull. "I need you downstairs and ready for school in five minutes!" I can almost see her pointing sharply at the tiles as if I should material-ize that instant right where she's indicating.

I release my hands from my ears and lay them in my lap, palms upward. Everything I do is slow because my body is trying to avoid the pain. I want to tell it not to bother, swallowing dryly at the state of my wrists. Fingernail impressions separate the thin veins that run across my pale skin. I pull the sleeves of my nightdress down and tie the ribbons tightly over the marks.

A loud groan rumbles up the stairs. "Ugh! Nora, I'm not kidding. We're going to be late… again." For someone so small, she can bellow like an overweight opera singer.

I sigh, pull the downy covers over my head, and am clouded in darkness. *Just a few more minutes.* I am afforded none as a scrawny, angular weight lands on top of me. Knees like shelf brackets dig into my ribs.

"Nora, Nora, Nora… Get up." My name piles one on top of another without a breath in between. Thin fingers clamp onto my arms and shake.

I pull away. "All right," I mumble, my voice muffled by the heavy quilt.

"Nora. Nora. Noraaaaaa." Because she can't hear me, Frankie's poking continues. It feels like she's taken two forks from downstairs and is jamming them into my sides. I curl down the covers carefully, squinting at all the lights she switched on when she entered my room.

Frankie shuffles back and smiles, gummy, three teeth missing. Her hearing aid is in her open palm. "Can you help me put thissss in, Noraaaaaaa?" she says, her Ss hissing through the gap. I sit up and tuck her long, straight hair, which is the color of autumn leaves, behind her ear. She giggles and rasps, a slight wheeze in her defective chest. Bobbing her head back and forth, she sings some unintelligible song as I wrangle with her hair and constant movement.

I clamp my hand down on top of her head. "Hold still, Frankie," I plead through gritted, fuzzy teeth.

She lurches forward just to make it more difficult, but I manage to slip the aid into her tiny, peaches-and-cream-colored ear. I position the headband my mother lovingly wound with pink satin ribbon. The aid whining itches my teeth as I grab her clothes and still her while clipping the little black box onto her sash. Smiling, she glances up at me with dark blue eyes, yellow streaks streaming from the irises like the rays of the sun. "Tanks!" she whispers and licks my hand.

"Oh yuck, Frankie!" I roll my eyes and watch my ferrety little sister bound out of the room and tear down the hall, sounding more like an elephant than a seven-year-old.

The bathroom door slams. I know I'm going to be waiting a while so I slip down into the bed and cross my arms over my chest, resting like I'm lying in a coffin. The warm air and street noises flowing through the window tell me I'm going to be sweating in a long-sleeved, high-necked dress, but I don't have another option.

My mother's holler coasts over the dark brown banister and hits my ears again. "We're going to be laaate!" Her voice is shrill and getting shriller.

I hear a plate slam down on the counter. Heavy footsteps approach, darker and more electric than a storm cloud.

"I'll get her," my father says loudly, knowing all he needs to do is threaten. I hold still, out of stubbornness, out of fear, I don't know, but I wait until I hear him slowly and deliberately stomping up the stairs. One, two, three…

I stay clamped still until he's at the top and then I scramble out of bed, grabbing my clothes from yesterday off the back of a chair and scurrying to the door. My heart pounds hard for the moments it takes to remember that Frankie is in the bathroom, and then it steadies. Because my heart has a memory. It understands the pattern, and it prepares me.

I gingerly nudge my door further ajar with my foot to reveal him standing proud, gripping the bannister and looking like a painting of one of our long-dead relatives. His eyes are an oily swirl of an amber brush. Not a man, a figment, and definitely not a father.

He gives me a flat, unimpressed smile and says, "Good girl," as he tracks my movements. My gaze connects with his for a moment before I have to look away. In his eyes are the reflections of the beating I didn't know how to stop, and even though my heart remembers, the rest of me would like to forget.

I pad down the hall, eyes down, hands clasped, just like a *good girl* should, toward the bathroom door. He turns, clicking his heels sharply, and takes one step down. A *good girl*. I snort at the comment and he hesitates, one foot hovering in midair. I sense the angry electricity charging his bones and tightening his fists.

I knock on the bathroom door, gently at first, but quickening with every bad thought that enters my mind. He wouldn't. Not with Mother just downstairs. I stare at the carpet and nervously blow air through pursed lips.

The boards of the stairs creak, always in the same place, and he pushes his weight down on it—testing, warning, and playing with my nerves. My mouth tastes metallic, and my hands pump nervously.

"Christopher, let me..." my mother shouts from the foyer, her voice edged in trepidation. The top of her head nods up and down over a tailored jacket and an unfashionably long skirt. She is graced with the same autumn-leaved hair color as Frankie. Her clothes may be dated, but she still looks beautiful. I sigh stiffly and tuck my slightly frizzy, dirty-blond hair behind my unfortunately prominent ears. My father watches me, his eyes crinkling in disgust with my every movement. I have his ears, nose, and hair... and he can't stand it. I wish I could scrub out my face and start again. Not because it would protect me, but because it would mean I wouldn't see him in my reflection.

My eyes round as he takes a threatening step in my direction, fury building in his arms, coursing down into his fingers that clench into solidity. I feel them even though they're yards away. I know how each fist feels as it strikes my skin. *Knuckled like clam shells and as hard as rocks.* I grab my stomach, nausea and pain swirling together inside, and tap on the door more urgently. "Frankie, open the door," I plead. I give him a sideways glance, and there's a sickening look of satisfaction playing across his face because he likes to see me afraid.

The door cracks and I get a glimpse of Frankie pulling her underpants up while walking away. She grins at me as she flushes the toilet, and then shudders when she sees Father's shadow growing behind me. I watch her shrivel before him, and I armor myself.

Footsteps hurry up the stairs with the swish of thick material batting at slender legs.

I turn, breathing in the word *shield*.

My mother climbs anxiously, her waned eyes on my father, her hands out in front as she rushes. Brittle hope rises, and I wonder if she's actually going to say something this time. If she's going to say *stop*.

"Christopher," she pants just before she reaches the top stair, her lip curling on the 'pher' part as she blows a loose strand of hair from her eyes. It floats up and lands back over her delicate brow. "It's fine," she says as she takes another step up, her long skirt trapping her leather heels and snagging her feet. "I…"

A loud siren wails outside. My mother's attention abruptly snaps to the long, arch window over the landing, her face crossed with the black line shadows of the frame and the morning sun.

A collection of events. Each on its own is harmless. But together, one after the other, they change the world.

Startled and off balance, her hands grab at the air in front of her. Her eyes close and she falls backward. My father reaches out, but there's endless space between them.

"Rebecca!" he sort of sighs and screams because he's helpless. His voice is sucked away by the shocking sight of her body plunging downwards and her legs kicking like she's riding an invisible bicycle. The shattering sound of her breath knocking from her lungs with every crack on the hardwood stairs pounds us both with airy hammers.

It's just air. Air and tumbling. Pulling down, down, down. And as her body breaks, so does my very thin thread of safety.

There's beauty in the fall, the weightlessness, the gravity fighting against the will. The curve of her body is a thin stream. And for one ridiculous, far-fetched moment, I believe she will fly. But there is no magic in my life. This world offers no pixie dust to lift our feet from the floor. So I watch her non-flight with detached horror and know that any chance I had just fluttered to the floor like a released pack of cards.

The landing is ugly. It's hard and final. Weight catches up and she skids across the tiles in her slippery skirt. Her hair flounces out of its pinned updo, too much life to the curls bouncing over an ashen face. The view of her lying there spins up from the ground and hits me square in the chest. The pain is bigger than anything I've ever imagined. It keeps pushing, prying, trying to open me up right here in the hall.

Frankie shoves on the door, and my palm snaps to the panel to block her way. "I thought ya needed to go, Nora. Nora, let me out." Her voice is panicky, high-pitched. She is unaware what exactly is wrong but she knows something is.

I brace the door as little, freckled fingers curl around the outside.

Shouldn't it be slow when your world changes? It's not my experience. It's fast as lightning and stings as much. She was at the top of the stairs, alive, talking. A flush to her creamy skin from exertion. Now she lies on the black-and-white tiles of the entry hall, her body angled all wrong. Her mouth open. Her eyes still closed.

That hard, tumbleweed of reality is still pushing against my chest, trying to get me to release something. I pull at my clothes like they're strangling me. *I can't breathe.*

There were no words. There was no time. I didn't get to say anything, barely opened my mouth before it was over.

It's over.

I take a heaped breath in and hold it. My lungs bursting with numbing pain.

I turn to see my father perched at the top of the stairs, staring at me mutely for several seconds, the wail of more sirens gathering seeming otherworldly. The sky screaming for a take back. We move our eyes millimeter by millimeter to the body at the bottom of the stairs, neither one really wanting to see what we already know. Frankie's tiny fists pound on the door like a heartbeat. "Nora, what's wrong?"

Everything.
Everything.
Realization is heavy and it adds weights to my father's shoulders until he sinks to his knees in a knight's stance, mangled sobs heaving from his chest.

I think, *He won't move.*

I think, *He should run down and help her.*

I know it won't do any good.

She looks like one of Frankie's dolls, a frozen sculpture, robbed of life, of grace. I almost expect her face to be cracked, shattered inwards like she was in fact shaped from porcelain. But she looks untouched. She looks like she was arranged this way, a mannequin that was never alive.

My father rotates slowly, still crouching, dirty-blond hair falling over his forehead. Hate waves creep toward me, pulling me to him. It's a look I'm already very used to, but it darkens with every breath he takes.

Eyes half measured with tears and steely hatred, he whispers, "This is your fault," and something inside me breaks, painfully pulled open with strong hands that hurt again and again. It's my heart, my armor, my survival, all shattering and crashing to the floor.

Gently, I pry Frankie's fingers from the bathroom door and close it carefully, ignoring her pleas. I don't want her to see this. She can't see this. *Oh God, she can't see this.* Panic winds my breath tighter. I turn my back to the bathroom door, look up at the ceiling, which seems black and swirling with empty stars, and I scream.

3

SUPER

I like the way the metal of the fire escape creaks beneath my feet. The precariousness of it. It's grating, rusty, and totally man-made. Ordinary people constructed these parts of the building for a practical purpose, and the outside is decorated with that commonality. It drags down the grandness of the stately brownstones, down closer to my level—in the dirt and oily puddles. But mostly, I like the promise of fresh air. The view from the top of a grimy building, an immaculate brownstone, or a department store is the same if you lift your eyes. Just sky, nothing else. When I'm up here, I can pretend. I can forget the outstretched hands, the hungry eyes, and the bellies that are never quite full. I can forget that five nights out of seven, I sleep wedged between a dumpster and a sewer pipe. Pretend that I can't hear and feel the toilet flush every time one of *them* uses the bathroom.

This is my time to be alone. I don't need long, but minutes where my mind can relax are precious.

Rocking back and forth on the platform, I put my hands on my hips and sigh, reminding myself that I'm luckier than most down there.

I swing my slightly too-big sneakers up over the concrete lip of the building and land with a thud on the roof. Dirt, leaves, and rubbish swish across the tiled surface. The pigeons don't flee; they simply shuffle to a safer distance, huddling in a circle like they're plotting something. A tunnel of warm air hits me in the face. It's too warm. I put my hand up like I can touch it, scanning the sky and wondering where it came from. Rolling my shoulders, I feel a warm chill. It's something odd and wrong that causes my skin to prickle, and my hair to fray and stand on end. It's like anger rising. Steam pushing the lid of a pot up with frantic bubbling.

My nostrils burn. Singe. A smoky cloud slaps my eyes.

Fire.

I squint through the growing smoke, the black soot casting old pictures in front of my eyes. *A small, blackened hearth in a flimsy, tar-papered building. Hands covered in calluses and needle pricks held out to warm themselves. The letters U and S not meaning what I thought they meant. Not 'us'. Not us. Only them.*

My head falls and I close my eyes, hearing the words, seeing the characters I've almost forgotten how to write, flaring black behind my eyelids. *Head down. Prove your loyalty. Show respect.*

Across the alley, the low-cost apartment building shudders with a chorus of screams and shouts as what was once a peaceful morning erupts into chaos. I snap back to the present and search the breaking structure before me.

Halfway down the apartment block, the fire escape groans and I watch as a mother, her baby tucked unceremoniously under her arm, scrambles down the metal rungs, her husband right behind her. Thick, black smoke physically shoves them from their home.

She glances up at me briefly, opening her mouth but then closing it as her husband pushes her roughly in the back. Her eyes, her whole body, become focused on putting one frightened foot in front of the next.

I start toward the edge of the brownstone I'm on, realizing there's nothing I can do from here. Taking a slice of the sky for later, I swallow what's left of my peace, leaving an empty, unsatisfied feeling in the hollow of my stomach.

I breathe in deeply, wanting that taste of fresh air but savoring only acrid smoke. My ears are punctured by the gathering clamor of noise and panic. Plumes of blinding smoke pours from the windows of the apartments above as now, the fire really means business. The family carefully picks their way down the fire escape way too slowly. I pause, waiting for the sirens and lights.

It takes just five seconds for the first siren to scream.

Gripping the rails, I watch as a piece of charred cardboard floats lazily on the breeze, winding its way up into the sky like a spirit.

One long scream howls through the morning air and I turn to its origin, behind me in the brownstone. Confused, my head snaps back to the apartment building just as the cardboard shivers and disintegrates before my eyes, becoming part of the steady cloud that's piping into the sky. The scream is crammed with pain and loss and all the things I know so well.

If I had time, I'd wonder why it is coming from the building not on fire. But I don't have time. And wondering is for suckers. I blink, cough, and shake my head. I have to get out of here before the authorities arrive.

I jump over the roof barrier and land unsteadily on the metal staircase, wobbling and nearly falling straight over the edge. I hear Kin's voice before I see his tiny form in the alley, shadowed by the smoke.

"They're here!" he shouts with a hint of humor to his voice, like he enjoys the running. I want to roll my eyes but they burn from the smoke, and I settle for grunting.

Taking three steps at a time, I plummet through the levels of the building as fast as I can. My lungs burn and I can't tell if it's from lack of air or from the foul smoke that's fast filling the atmosphere. The family keeps pace with me, floor by floor, and I watch them, distracted. My feet catch on a step and I hit the next platform hard, my cheek planting on the metal, my eyes on the couple and child. They are two floors from the ground when the mother stops. She doubles over and coughs uncontrollably. Holding her chest with her spare hand, she shakes her head 'no' to the father. She passes the baby to her husband.

Heat is building behind the thin, glass windows, the structure buckling above, my reflection vibrating like the surface of a bubble.

It's so delicate. Our skin, our life. We're held together by the thinnest of membranes.

The husband snatches the child to his chest and starts down, moving around her while she catches her breath. Not waiting. *Don't wait.* The window explodes and shatters as he screams in panic. Like a waterfall we follow; the baby screams, I scream, and the mother screams as she is pelted with glass. The father hunches over the child protectively, his thick jacket shielding him.

I can't hear over the sirens and shrieks. But I see the silent exchange, the mother telling the father to go on without her, his reluctant nod as he kisses her, clasps the baby tighter, and leaves. I grimace. They are so close that I can almost touch them. The mother lies still but for a burst of coughing as smoke wraps around her body like a blanket.

From below, Kin cups his hands around his mouth and yells, "Jump down!"

I shake my head.

To hell with it.

I walk away from the edge and press my back to the ruddy, red brick wall, cursing at my cramped position. A four-step run up is probably not enough.

"Not… that…" I hear Kin initially shout and then his voice peters out, "…way," as I press off the platform and launch at the opposite building, my hands outstretched, my eyes watering from the smoke.

The mother lies wilted on the platform.

I land with a metallic thump, missing her limp arm by a millimeter. She is cut to shreds by the glass, but she's still breathing.

Below us, the husband sobs. Safely on the ground, he stoops, unsure of whether to lay his baby in the filthy alley and climb back up or take the child to safety. Smoke soon obscures my view of them and they disappear.

I squat down and talk to the woman through my

pulled-up shirt. "It's going to be okay, lady. Just put your arm over my shoulder and I'll get you to the ground."

She mumbles incoherently but she manages to stumble to her feet. I pull her to my back and half run, half fall down the last two flights of stairs. Her blood seeps through my clothing and her hold on me loosens. I grit my teeth and drag her out of the alley and into the street, while the husband frantically talks at me in Spanish. I honestly can't tell if he's happy or angry or what, only that he's beyond upset and talking at a mile a minute.

I lay his wife down on the sidewalk as carefully as I can, and the husband bends down to kiss her. I think he's happy. He motions to the crowd of emergency vehicles that have swarmed around the base of the building, and I know this is my cue. Coughing tarry junk from my lungs, I hover in the shadow between the buildings, slightly dazed with my hands on my hips. I just want to make sure they see her.

Kin's strong arm claps onto my shoulder and drags me deeper in to the shadows. We peel around the corner, and he shoves me against the wall.

"What the hell, man?" he asks as he quickly checks me over for injuries, patting my body down like a cop frisking a pickpocket. "You're not a super hero. You can't pull stunts like that!" He sighs, releases my shirt, and steps back. "You do realize you can't fly, right?"

I shrug and grin, swiping my hand over my face, which comes away black and sooty. Coughing again, I feel the smoke coating my lungs. "I came pretty close." I wink. "Besides, what was I supposed to do—leave her to die?"

Kin steps back from me, opens his mouth to say something, and then pauses, his dark brows knotted. He's having a moment. I can tell. He's trying to decide whether to be big brother or friend. "Yes. It's what *they* would have done if it were you." Big brother, then. I shake my head even though I know he's probably right. "You're nothing to them." He points at my cap pulled low over my eyes. "You hide your face... why? Because showing them, reminding them of who *you* are and what *they* did, makes them feel bad. Or," he says, shaking a long, dark finger at me. "They think you're the enemy. Either way, they just want to pretend we don't exist." He winces at the words. He doesn't like talking to me this way, I can tell. He needn't bother. I know what people think I am. I don't need reminding.

"Don't talk like that," I growl. "We're Kings, you and I." I pump my fist to the air.

Kin's head slowly dips. "Sure we are. Kings of the Alley, Kings of the Dumpsters!"

I shrug. The sirens are still winding round and round. A red light runs across the wall and disappears repeatedly. Firemen unravel their hoses and attempt to put out the fire.

"We really need to get out of here." Kin's dark eyes are darting and counting all the possible escape routes. "Be invisible, remember?"

"I remember," I say craning my neck to make sure the mother is getting medical attention. I made the rules after all. Kin pushes his sleeves up his hard arms that have seen too much labor for a seventeen-year-old and turns away.

I stall.

A slippered foot appears at the corner, the velvet shining under a thin stream of sunlight. It's coming out of the building I just jumped from, the building that the unholy scream came from five minutes ago. A teenage girl in pretty, expensive-looking clothes hovers at the edge of the crowd. She doesn't flee like the others, the sensible people who can see the building might possibly collapse into the street. It's like she's tied to the bricks. Each step seems painful. Her sandy hair flies all over the place, beating her spine like a fan. Her shoulders pull in, and they shudder. Fascinated, I take a step forward, then an annoyed hand grabs the back of my shirt and yanks me back.

"I think we've risked our lives enough for one day, Superman," Kin mutters as he overpowers me into a headlock. "Leave the pretty, rich chick to grieve over her wasted morning."

I blink, and she disappears behind the fleeing families. "You're right. Let's go home," I say, elbowing him.

"Home? Ha! Good one," he says sarcastically.

I don't respond.

4
AFTER

We follow a stretcher covered in a white sheet, mountains and hills of cloth that can't be my mother—*it can't*—as it wheels out of the foyer doors. After what they're calling 'The Accident,' we were evacuated from our building because of the fire next door. I carried Frankie down the stairs, holding her head against my shoulder to shield her from the scene, and we left Mother there, cold and alone, returning only when it was deemed safe.

I think I had hoped when we stepped back inside, she wouldn't be there, but she was of course. She hadn't moved, because she's dead. The words catch in the back of my throat. *She's dead.* Now the trolley squeaks on the highly polished tiles, carrying something that's supposed to be her.

When the paramedics get to the brass doors, they shove the stretcher feet first into the glass, the whole bed bouncing as it goes over the threshold. I expect a gasp, arms to flap up in shock. Nothing.

I watch our reflections in the shiny surrounds of the door, long, languid beings with stretched faces. Another world. I glance at the sheet. I imagine lying there, my feet tucked in at the ends, my face clothed in heavy cotton, and I can't breathe. Bringing a tightened fist to my chest, I suck in a breath as best I can although it feels as if I've swallowed a lump of coal. I have to keep it together. There's a small child wrapped around my legs, and she needs me.

When they get to the stairs, the wheels fold up so they can carry it down. I cock my head to the side, wondering if she's heavy. It seems like she should be heavier, like she's set in concrete now, a statue.

Outside, the air should be fresh, clean, but it's charred and wet. I look to my right at the burned-out apartment building. Maybe I should be looking to blame someone, the person who started the fire perhaps, but my mind is frozen, as blank as the confused expressions of the crowd watching a casualty being wheeled out of the wrong building.

They slide her into an ambulance. I rock back and lurch forward, an arm stretched toward the open doors. "I'm going with her," I squeak. Clearing my throat, I say, "Please. Let me go with her." My eyes search for any sympathetic face, but no one looks at me. They're all looking to my father for answers.

His hand clamps down on my shoulder and shirks me backward. Frankie's skirts fly up in a gust of wind as she struggles to hold onto me. *Don't let go.*

"No," he utters under his breath. "Get in the car." He does it carefully, controlled-like, so it looks like I tripped as he flings me at the sleek, black car waiting to take us to the hospital.

"Where are we going?" Frankie asks innocently as she shuffles to the middle of the backseat.

I slide in next to her and pat her glinting, gold-and-crimson hair. Her head is on fire and I'm about to douse those flames, squash her little soul until she's just a smoldering pile of crumpled ashes. My voice catches in my throat, humming and spinning.

Father is talking to the paramedics outside so I take this opportunity to tell Frankie in a way I can control, before he takes a hammer to the truth and slams her with it.

Deep breath, heart on fire, heart trodden and bleeding.

"Frankie, Mommy had an accident," I start, each word stinging.

"I know." She nods solemnly. And I get the sense she also knows what I'm about to say.

I straighten my dress and gaze at my shoes, slippers. I rub my feet together, hoping he doesn't notice that I forgot to change my shoes.

"She's…" My lip is doing this quivering thing, and I don't know how to stop it. I bite down on them for a moment, my eyes on my father, who is rounding the car and about to step into the passenger seat.

"Mommy is dead," Frankie says matter-of-factly, her small hands clasped in her lap, her little legs pumping round and round like she's paddling in a pool.

"Do you understand what that means, Frankie?" I ask, my eyes wet. I wipe my nose on the back of my hand.

She shakes her head and sighs. "Like Grandma. Sleepin' and not never wakin' up."

She's jiggling in her seat, a ball of uncontainable energy. I nod. "Yes, Mommy can't wake up. But it also means you and I need to stick together. It means that even though Mommy's not here anymore, I am."

I try to still her agitation, laying my arm across

her legs, knowing how he'll be if he sees her bouncing around in the backseat like this. "Please Frankie, try to calm down."

"Where did she go?" she asks innocently, and I hear our driver choke back a sob.

I don't know. I don't know. I don't know. I'm waging a battle with my own panic here, and I have to win. I have to protect her.

"I'm not sure, Frankie," I reply. "But I know that wherever she is, there's no hurt or sadness. Mommy is at peace." I really want to believe that's true.

Frankie grabs the two front headrests, swinging back and forth like a monkey. "That's good then," she says, staring out the front window, her eyes, her brain, now focused on the commotion outside of this car. "Look at the firemen." She points, grinning, and I think I might scream again. This is too hard, and I don't know what I'm supposed to do.

I pat her arm. "Please Frankie, sit still," I say again. I want to just let her be herself, but I can't. Not here.

The car door snaps open and slams shut as my father smoothly takes his place in the passenger seat up front. "Mount View Hospital," he growls at Sally, our driver.

"I'm real sorry for your loss, Mister Deere," Sally whispers. She even almost touches his arm, but when he turns away from her and barks, "Mount View," she retracts her hand and places it shakily on the steering wheel.

Her large, brown eyes blink sympathetically at us in the rearview mirror.

"What'd ya lose, Deddy?" Frankie blurts before I

31

can stop her. Sally tenses, holding her breath. We both hold our breaths.

I brace myself for shouting, for a hand to whip out and slap her. My arm is already in front of her face as a barrier. But all he does is turn to us for one second, his eyes darker than malice, and then he crumples.

He lays his head on the dashboard and weeps.

The car swings into traffic and we roll away from it all, following an ambulance whose lights are as dead and dulled as my heart.

Sally drops us at the entrance and drives away. The hospital has always looked more like a castle than a state-of-the-art healing center. Its old, red brick walls crumble at the corners, dripping with ivy. Dark, barred windows glare down at us, absorbing the sunlight. I shiver as we walk under its beckoning shadow.

We follow our father's sharp, certain footsteps to the reception desk, and I'm swallowed by a memory.

Metal bangs against metal, people ask so many questions, different questions, and then the same ones over and over. I run a hand through my hair, effectively smearing Frankie's blood all over my face.

I was here four years ago. My eyes graze over the wide entrance hall, the grand arches, and the colored tiled floor. My mother's anxious voice echoes, ghostly, through these hallways, and I shudder. *"Who cares how it happened? Just help her, please,"* she cries desperately.

"She fell down the stairs, she fell down the stairs, she... fell," my mother coached me as we drove like demons toward the hospital. She put a hand on my shoulder. "Say it again."

Her eyes churned with regret and fear.

My voice cracked, and she flinched. "She fell… she fell down the stairs," I whispered, my head down, my sister's broken body curled into almost nothing beside me. Blood poured from her ears.

I laugh maniacally at the memory. The lie I had to tell that had now come true for my mother. And then I instantly feel sick. I fist the cloth at my stomach and run to the nearest bin, hurling nothing but water. Sweat beads on my skin and I waver as I stumble back to my father, who is staring at me with furious eyes. Frankie stands lost, leaning from leg to leg like she might run out of here. She might be better off.

She doesn't remember. She was only three.

His low talking to the nurse is a bare mumble over the noise of my vivid memory.

My mother tears into this space, her face white with fear, my sister limp in her arms. Fluorescent lights light up the green marker Frankie had decorated her entire body with. Almost angry-looking, marks all up her arms and legs, her normally light eyebrows now a mossy green, a fantastic curly moustache drawn over her upper lip.

That was her crime—being three and believing she had the right to behave like a three-year-old.

He deafened her and attempted to silence her. Boxed her ears to the point where one was useless and the other barely worked.

They take Frankie to a trauma room and then a solid looking nurse pulls me away from the curtain and over to the vending machines. She cups her hand to my face, wiping some of the blood from my forehead with a neatly folded square of gauze.

"Are you all right, dear? Are you injured?" she whispers.

I cross my arms over my chest defensively, the bruises already starting to show on my skin from where he'd gripped my wrist to stop me from reaching her. "I'm fine," I lie.

The nurse tips her head at an angle and gazes at me curiously, her eyes raking over my nightdress, my knees knocking, my body shivering. "What really happened tonight? You can tell me. You can trust me," she says.

My lips lie. My brain tells me to do what my mother asked. My fear wins. My face blanketed in false calm, I say, "She fell down the stairs," without slipping once. Each word feels false, without meaning, strung together to make a lie.

The nurse's shoulders slump. She sighs deeply and shakes her head.

When she walks away I slide to the floor, leaning my back against the cherry red vending machine, the rattling refrigerator lulling me into numbness.

I was thirteen then. Things are different now. Now we are on our own.

My father beckons us with one stern finger. "The police have some questions and then you'll be allowed to see her to say a brief goodbye," he orders.

I nod stiffly and pull Frankie to my side. She's holding me up as much as I'm supporting her.

He puts a hand to the small of my back and steers us down the hall. His fist wants to burrow to my spine for embarrassing him, I can tell, but he holds back for now. We walk slowly, following a bustling, flustered nurse. She stops at a door, opens it to check if anyone's inside, and then ushers us in. The plaque on the door reads "Mourning Room". I gulp at the stale, disinfected air. Everything feels dense and hollow at the same time.

"If you'd like to take a seat, a pastor will be here shortly," she says somberly.

My father puts his hand up. "That won't be necessary, Sister."

She looks like she's about to object but the look my father gives her is pure shadow, and she quickly leaves.

Five minutes later, two police officers enter the room. It is fast. There's nothing much to say. She fell. My father and I confirm each other's stories, our maid already made a statement at home. It's over. The police officer mutters something about insurance on the way out, but my brain has left the building. I'm now waiting to see my mother. To say goodbye.

How do I even do that?

5
HOME

I t's funny how I always feel lighter, almost like I'm flying, as I head home, even though I'm descending into a dark, dank kind of place.

I whistle as we wind our way through slimy alleyways stinking of trash and other unnamable things. Ignoring the smells, I plunge my nose into the bag of groceries I'm carrying; fresh bread and crisp-skinned apples reward me. Kin gives me irritated, sideways glances as I whistle. I'm only doing it to annoy him, and it's working.

"Will you *quit* it?" he snaps.

I flick his hat from his head, and it lands in a puddle. He swears, going to punch me in the guts. I swerve and he stumbles, almost head-butting a big, green dumpster. "Ha! Serves you right," I say triumphantly.

He growls and gives me the silent treatment the rest of the way to the station.

It's peak hour, the best time to get home. We fold ourselves into the swarms of people huddling shoulder to shoulder, pushing their way through the turnstiles. We line up at side-by-side turnstiles, wait for the person in front to produce a ticket, and then press too close to them, slipping through. We both apologize and run off before they can respond.

It's a weird, quiet noise that rumbles through the

underground space. People moving, thudding into each other by accident. No one really talks, but this many people crammed together just make noise, a chorus of bodies and breathing. I like it. It's life, messy and complicated, getting mixed up together. This place forces rich and poor to mingle. Down here, we're all just people trying to get home. I grin at the thought and catch Kin rolling his eyes at me.

We line up at the platform, looking like we're about to jump on the next car, but as soon as people swarm around the door, Kin and I step backward, kicking an old, wooden door with our heels. It slowly gives way, and we slip into darkness.

As I turn and rake my hands over the cool stones of this dark tunnel, peace hums over me. The moss whispers home. The stones seep comfort.

Kin breaks the silence. "How long has it been this time?"

"Three days too long," I reply, slapping out at his tall, slim form in the dark. My hand connects with his back. His ribs jut out like ladder rungs.

"But you made it count didn't you, superhero?" he teases.

"I made some money if that's what you mean."

"Yeah, sure. That's what I mean." He groans. "You know, if you skimmed a bit off the top, even if you crammed a few packets of those cookies down your pants, we really would be eating like kings tonight."

I hoist the bag of groceries tighter to my chest. "That's not how we do things anymore. You know that. Right? We're better than that."

Kin snorts and spits on the ground. "Yeah, yeah.

For seventeen, you're a self-righteous lil' bastard." He reaches out to pat my head, and I duck away from his shadow.

"Kin, you are only a couple of months older than me."

He grunts.

"Now, answer me this—will we eat tonight?" I ask.

No answer.

"Will we eat tonight?" I croon.

"Will you shut up?" he croons back.

"Kin," I say with a descending tone to my voice.

"All right, all right. Yes, we will eat tonight, and yes, we didn't steal. Blah, blah, blah." I smile at his half-hearted whining.

"Good man!" I chirp, my feet slapping against the dirty water running through this abandoned passage.

We come to the second door. Golden light tries to escape through the cracks in the wood.

Kin mutters under his breath, "You shouldn't bug me so much. I'm much bigger and stronger than you."

"Yeah, but this is my place. I found it. I called dibs. You wanna live here, then you do it by my rules." I puff up my chest, smiling. Kidding around. But there's truth to what I say. I lean against the wall, remembering the fear that drove me into this tunnel, the desperation as I plunged between the legs of commuters and fell through the door. I still feel that pack of sweets digging into my palm, the shuddering terror at the thought of being dragged back to detention or worse, the orphanage. Finding the tunnel was a sign or something. It was a refuge.

We knock on the door in a secret way. Things move and rattle on the other side, and it creaks open. Cat-like green eyes and a broad smile greets me. Keeper runs a dirty hand through her black hair and chomps her teeth like a piranha. "Food!" she yells. She snatches the grocery bag from my hand and runs to the others, throwing random items into greedy hands.

Wrappers scrunch in dirty fingers and eager eyes glance up at Kin and me for permission to start. "Easy. That has to last us a few days." They tear into the wrappers but eat slowly, taking small bites and rolling down the tops of the packets to keep for later.

My family of homeless children, the Kings of the subway, eat quietly, fight over who gets to eat what, and play.

I snatch a cracker from Krow's hand and nibble. He glances up at me. "Is that all you're going to have, Kettle?"

I shrug. "I ate on the way here."

Kin elbows me in the ribs and whispers, "Liar," so only I can hear him.

I shrug again and leave the group, running my hands over the stacked stones, raising my eyes to the ceiling and marveling at the arch over our heads. Every stone is in perfect balance. Some people might see sandy, discolored rocks, but when I look at this haven, I see gold. I see a palace. The iron chandeliers hanging from the ceiling, though unlit most of the time, still hold an air of grace to them. The way the candlelight flickers and reflects off the green tiles that pattern parts of the walls and ceiling is a tapestry.

I collapse on a dusty cushion and sigh. The candle sitting on an old cable drum next to me wavers with my breath.

It's good to be home.

6

GOODBYE

Keep me, I breathe. I know it's impossible but… wherever you're going, keep me with you.

I'm staring at my feet. The velvet looks battered and dirty, layers of hospital dirt creeping up my heels. My toes push up at the ends.

They lead me down a waxy hall, pink spotted with black mixed with dried blood creates the carpet on which I walk. Frankie's tiny shoes step in line with mine. I can't look up. If I make eye contact with one more sorry face, my own will melt away. I could drown this whole hospital in tears. Because this is very suddenly becoming too real. This is not a dream I had. This is not a mistake. My mother is dead.

She fell, she fell, she fell.

I will never see her again.

I clutch Frankie closer to my side and look at my reflection in the heels of my father's shiny shoes. We are wisps of children, ghost-like and hungry looking.

The nurse gestures to the elevator, presses the button, and gives me an I'm-so-sorry look, which I manage to catch under a curtain of my own hair. I nod.

"The morgue is on Basement Level Two," she says. "Someone will meet you at reception."

The doors open, and my father strides inside. He sniffs. This is harder for him than he would like either of us to see. I don't want to see him like this either. It makes me wonder about him in a way I can't. The idea that he loves, loses, and feels sadness is too much for me.

When the doors close, my father clears his throat and speaks, his voice dry and wooden, "Girls, I want you to behave respectably. Keep your goodbyes brief and control your emotions."

Frankie steps forward out of my grasp, and I see my father's fist clench at his side. "What does re-spect-a-bubble mean, Deddy?"

I pull her back and answer for him. Cupping her chin, I whisper, "It means don't scream and cry. Be polite and do as you're told. Okay?" There's a warning in my eyes, but she's not getting it.

"Will there be toys in the mork?" she asks as she grasps the handrail and swings from it, lifting her knees to her chest.

"Toys? Why you... I..." He spins around and grabs at her, but I step in front. His knuckles connect with the top of my ribs, which would have been her head, sending icy splinters of pain radiating up my shoulder. I stumble back and then straighten.

"She's sorry, Father. She doesn't understand," I say, attempting to diffuse and trying really hard not to reach for the throbbing new injury he's given me. I need to shield her. "I'll make sure she behaves respectably. I promise." I bow my head, a small tear squeezing from the corner of my eye.

He seems to remember himself, remember where

he is, and irons out his shirt with his flattened palms carefully. He turns his back to me, but I can see his wobbly form and furious expression in the elevator doors. "Right. Good. Make sure you do."

Swallowing, I hold out my hand to my sister, wishing so hard this wasn't happening and understanding what my life will be like now.

The elevator chimes, and we step out. Before I've taken two steps, my father kneels down at Frankie's eye level. He puts his hand on her shoulder and smiles. She smiles back. "Daddy didn't mean to scare you, darling." He touches her hair, tucks it behind her ear, and sighs deeply. I shudder. "You look so much like Rebecca. You'll grow up to be a beautiful woman one day, sweetheart."

Frankie curtsies. "Thank you, Deddy."

"Are you the Deere family?" A young voice inquires.

"We are," my father replies.

Minus one. We are the Deere family minus one.

Father goes in first, flanked by a man in a white coat and a police officer. He is in there longer than I expected. Something about identifying the body. When he comes out, he sweeps his long arm around us both and hugs us awkwardly while the police officer watches.

"Can I take my girls home now, Officer?" he asks impatiently, with not much of a veil over his irritated tone.

"Wait." I step forward. "I thought you said I

could…?" He's eyeing me hard, and I know I'm going to pay for it later, but I need to see her.

"I decided it's no place for a young lady," he answers shaking his head. "It won't do you any good."

"Please, Father?"

With everyone watching, my father concedes. "Suit yourself. But I warned you." There are two meanings to that warning—one pretends to care, the other is a ready fist. I bow my head, not even wanting to look at the punishments lurking in his eyes.

"Thank you, Father," I say to the ground.

I silently follow the police officer through two doors. Bluish lights glow overhead and the cold seeps deep, deep, deep into my bones.

We come to a bank of metal drawers, and the police officer speaks, "Are you sure you want to do this, Miss Deere?" his tone wary.

"I'm sure."

I'm not sure at all as I watch his hairy hand grasp the drawer at knee height. I kneel down opposite him and wait. He flexes his fingers and tugs on the drawer quite forcefully. It opens just one foot with a metallic, grating screech. A face covered in a white sheet stares at the ceiling.

He shakily pulls back the sheet so I can see her and winces when I gasp. Putting a hand to my mouth, I try to shove the scream that wants to escape back inside. I look up at him, my vision blurred by tears. "Can you give me a moment alone, please?" I whisper.

"I can't leave you alone in here," he says kindly. "But I can give you some space." He takes five echoing footsteps backward, crosses his arms, and leans against the door. He stares up, searching the ceiling and seeming to count the perforations in the white tiles.

I turn my back to him and hunch over my mother's stony face. Every line seems sharper, her sculpted cheekbones, her fair but long, thick lashes. Her red hair fans out around her head like a crown. I lift a finger to touch her, but I'm scared. Scared she'll move, scared she won't. Knowing she can't.

Her face has been washed of makeup; it's clean, natural. She is beautiful. She was...

A tear sweeps my face and lands on her cheek. I take a small breath. "I'm sorry." I reach out with one brave finger and wipe the tear from her quiet expression. Her skin is ice cold. I place an open palm on her hair, and her head rocks away from me like it's made of hollow wood. Sickness, nausea creeps up my spine. "Please," I murmur through trembling lips. "Please Mommy, don't go."

Please.

7

KETTLE FAMILY

Time is hard to tell when the lights flicker on and off with a mind of their own, but the frigid air makes me suspect it's nearly dawn. One day, they'll stop working all together as the wires erode from lack of maintenance.

I scrape my eyelids of sleep and grit, propping myself up on my elbows. The sound of snoring kids is intermittently drowned out by subway cars whooshing through tunnels. No one stirs. The rattle of wheels over tracks is a lullaby, comforting, reassuring.

Two nights home and now I have to leave again.

I sigh loudly and collect my gear. Keeper's small voice penetrates the hazy light. "You going already?" she whispers as she wipes the back of her hand under her runny nose. I crawl over sleeping bodies and touch her forehead. She feels a little clammy, a little too warm.

"You feeling okay, Keeps?" I ask softly.

She nods her head and coughs into her palm. "Just a cold," she says and smiles for me. Her big, green eyes blink, red rimmed. "Mubbee I got allergies?" she asks.

I sling an arm around her slim shoulders and laugh, pulling her to me. "Maybe. Just take it easy today. Make sure everyone cleans up before lunchtime, eh?" She scribbles notes in a frayed pad of paper I gave her six months ago, licking the tip of the pen every now

45

and then.

The corners of her mouth are stained with black ink when she grins and nods. "Yes sir, Kettle." She sniffs again, and I hand her a handkerchief from my pocket. She nuzzles into my chest, almost purring just like a cat.

"I don't need anyone getting sick, okay?" I warn with a wink.

She coughs, trying to cover it by stooping over. Her black hair falls over her face in one solid lump. I light a candle and peer at the watch nailed to the rocks behind me. I've only got about half an hour.

"Keeps?" She swings around, hair hanging over her eyes and in her mouth. "Come here, let me show you something." She shuffles closer, looking a little scared. I pull out a hairbrush from the bag I brought home last night. "This is a hairbrush." She squints at it, waiting for it to do something. "It's for your hair, so it's not so, um, hard to manage…" She tips her head to the side, looking for all intents and purposes like a puppy about to have its first bath. She's our first and only girl resident. "Come sit in front of me." I pat the ground gently, and she slides backward. "Don't be scared. I'm not going to hurt you," I reassure, although I'm not one hundred percent sure that's true. "Keeps, what did I say when you came to live here, when you became a King?"

"Dat I could stay as long as I wanted and dat you would keep me safe," she replies warily.

I grip the brush firmly in my hand and gesture to the section of cold stone in front of my crossed legs. "Do you believe that's true?"

She scrunches her eyes shut and says, "Yes." Crawling over to sit in front of me, she turns her mound of thick, black hair my way.

I raise the brush to her head, place it in her hair, and make a liar of myself.

The boys cover their ears to shield themselves from her caterwauling.

"Throw her back," Krow mutters, scowling, which only makes her scream louder.

She bends her head back every time I run the brush through and screeches like I'm actually scalping her. The brush snags in the dirty clumps, and I can't pull it through. I've said sorry about a hundred times but now that I've started, I feel like I need to finish it. She needs to look less like a street urchin and more like a child on her way to school if we're going to remain inconspicuous.

On the hundredth and fiftieth scream, Kin finally storms over. He gets up in her face, and I think he's going to tell her to shut up. It's what I should have done, but I feel at a loss on how to deal with a ten-year-old girl who thinks I'm torturing her.

"Keeper, what would you like me to do? I can cut it all off or you can let us clean it up. Right now you look like a drowned rat wearing a dead cat toupee. Do you want to look like a drowned rat with a bad hairpiece?" Kin says.

She shakes her head and whimpers. Then she whispers, "I wanna look like that." She points to the catalogue I've been teaching some of them to read from. A sweet girl with long brown hair in two plaits on either side of her head smiles thinly at us, her eyes round and blue, her ribbons frozen in mid-swing.

Both Kin and I stare at each other and gulp. Then Kin puffs out his chest, swears, and laughs. "If you can rescue women from burning buildings, together we can surely plait a ten-year-old girl's hair."

The boys snicker. "Shh!" I snap and then look to Kin. "Here you do this side and I'll take the other." We separate her hair into two uneven handfuls and go to work. With my mouth pressed tight, I start, with one eye on the photo we're trying to replicate. The other eye is watching Kin try to plait hair with his giant paws. I swear he's starting to sweat. I snort, gripping her hair so it doesn't fall out.

Kin's face jerks to mine. "What?"

I look down at the ground, my eyes watering. "Um, nothing…"

Kin holds his twisted clump of hair tightly, a concentrated, almost cross-eyed look on his face. "What?"

A laugh escapes my mouth, and all the boys join in. "I can't watch you. My God. It's like watching a bear try to peel a plastic banana!"

Kin sighs in exasperation but refuses to give up, a small smile creeping into his stern expression. "Yeah well, you're surprisingly good at this. Anything you wanna tell us?"

Laughter fills the rocky space. It's warm and bright, scrubbing the walls of grime and filling my heart.

When we're finally done, I grip my plait tightly in my fingers, searching for something to tie it with. Krow steps forward and begrudgingly hands me two bread bag ties, which I wind around the ends. I push Keeps gently in the back. "There. That wasn't so bad, was it?"

Turning around, she gives me a look of 'you're kidding, right?' and scampers to the mirror. She frowns when she meets her reflection. Her whole face is now visible, smooshed cheeks and pinchy little ears. She looks cute. She tips her head down, and one large lump falls over her eyes. I remember the gift I bought that I was saving for her King birthday. Fishing around in the paper bag, I retrieve two red clips with white polka dots on them. Keeps stares at herself like she doesn't know it's her face. I sweep her fringe back and clip it in place. She touches it lightly, like I've just put a diamond tiara on her head.

She smiles sweetly, her dark lips brimming with teeth. "I think you should cut it off. I'm a King, not a queen," she states proudly.

I stall in shock, and then my heart does that proud, pumping-strong thing. Kin slaps my back, and I stumble forward. Keeps draws in a sharp breath as I fall and begins coughing uncontrollably.

"We're going to be late," Kin says, extending a long arm in my direction, his eyes sliding to the coughing girl sitting delicately on a faded purple cushion. "We'll think about the haircut."

I smile at her. "Think about it some more, Keeps. You might miss it when it's gone."

Her determined eyes tell me otherwise. Her sallow, sweaty skin worries me.

We leave the boys and… girl… with instructions and head to work.

8
STRANGE

Silence frightens me. In the silence is plotting, planning, and waiting. Silence is death. In his silence lies pure malevolence.

Frankie kicks and bucks in her sleep. Her silky, fine hair sprays up my nose as she flips her head back and forth on the pillow like a carnival clown. I humph and shuffle to the edge of the bed. She follows me, even in her sleep, inching over and plastering her sweaty body to my back, clinging like a marsupial to its mother.

I shudder as the last few nights roll over me in a cloudless nightmare. Mother. That is my role now. Mother and shield.

The door creaks open a crack and I close my eyes, holding my breath and clamming up so I'm still as a stone, silent under an ocean. Appearing unconscious is my only defense. Because I'm not technically doing anything wrong, he has no flimsy excuse to strike me. I feel his shadow falling over my curled-up form, cold and heavy as a thick military blanket. But then it's tugged away and I breathe freer when I hear his footsteps retire to the den.

That's where he sleeps now. Their bedroom is an

untouched shrine to Rebecca Deere. The bed messily made, a silk dressing gown lying lonely across the foot of the bed. Three pairs of shoes toppled around the large dressing mirror.

I wait until I hear the thump of his defeated body hit the red velvet sofa and then try to relax.

Sleep is uneasy.

How can you sleep when a threat hangs over you like a chandelier clipped of all but one stubborn wire? Soon, glass will shatter, iron will graze, and electricity will burn.

I wake in confusion as I have the last two mornings. My brain still reaches out for noises that no longer exist—my mother's radio blasting and her loud stomping rumbling through the corridor. It's like someone scooped up the life of this house, shoved it in a sack, and threw it off the Humblestone Bridge.

My hand shoots sideways, searching for Frankie's warm body beside me. Her wriggly worm movements are absent. I jolt up from my bed and run out, my heart squeezing in panic. I don't have time for a dressing gown or slippers as I throw open the door and tear down the stairs, trying hard not to close my eyes as I grip the bannister. I can't leave them alone together.

I hit the cold tiles, stepping around where *she* landed like I might sink through the floor, and make my way to the kitchen. Listening for voices—plates smashing, crying. Instead, I hear my father laugh.

I halt in the doorway, pressing my fingers into the dark brown frame. I count the bumps and carvings in the architraves, my toes balling under. My fingers catch on a rough part, and a splinter digs into my skin.

"Ouch," I whisper.

A chair pulls back, and I hear footsteps. I squeeze my finger, and one drop of blood rises like a bubble on the tip. Staring at it with morbid fascination, I turn it this way and that, waiting for the surface tension to break and blood to run down my skin.

My father's jolly face peers around the cabinet I was hiding behind. "Good morning, Nora," he exclaims brightly, frighteningly. I take a step back from this dancing mask of a face.

Marie, our maid, sighs deeply, and Frankie squeals from the table. "Mornin'. Mornin!"

My hand darts behind my back as he approaches, and one strong eyebrow rises in curiosity at my quick movement. Scents of vanilla and butter crawl across the kitchen, and I smile. Pancakes.

My father stands over me, hands lazily resting behind his back, trying his best to look nonchalant. His necktie hangs from his throat like a curtain cord. "What are you hiding, Nora? Show me what's behind your back, please," he says sternly but with lightness in his voice.

I stare down at his shiny shoes, and then back up to his face. His expression remains impassive. Timidly, I hold out the bleeding finger. He tenderly takes it in his hand, brushing the blood away with his thumb and shakes his head. "That looks painful, darling." He glances up at me, eyes as earnest and round as a puppy dog he would ordinarily grip at the scruff of the neck, and says, "Will you allow me to remove it?"

I nod, dumbstruck by his sudden kindness.

Frankie's rusk-like voice spills out around a mouthful of macerated pancakes and cream. "You better hurry up coz I'm gunna gobble up all the pancakes!" Lumps of half-chewed food fall onto her plate as she beams. I wait for the snap, the shoulders to pull back, and the hand to come flying at her face. I mentally measure the distance between us in alarm when I realize I won't make it in time.

But my father remains calm, although I can see his jaw winding tighter and tighter like Frankie's chattering toy monkey. He opens his mouth and a lighter-than-air laugh floats through the kitchen. He's still gripping my wrist as he drags me to the butcher's block that sits next to the kitchen table. Usually we eat in the dining room, but there's nothing usual about this situation or his demeanor.

"Marie, do you have a sewing kit?" he asks over his shoulder at our dull housemaid, who's busily pretending to wash dishes.

She jumps, her hand to her chest. "Yes, Mister Deere," she squeaks and scurries from the room, her long, black skirt swishing like a magic broom.

We wait in silence, him pinning my wrist to the stained chessboard wood, animal blood and fat spotting all colors of disgusting, and me staring out the side window. From here, I see nine squares of beautiful. Each frame the size of a photograph. Gold blossoms, fastened to spindly branch fingers, gleam in the morning sun. Smiling dreamily, I think about walking to school and collecting handfuls as I go.

Marie returns and shakily places her sewing kit on

the block. Frankie jumps from her chair and stands on her tiptoes, leaning over my shoulder to get a better look.

"Ick!" Frankie remarks.

I feel a prick and realize he's already started digging at my skin with the needle, a greedy, concentrated look on his face like he's seeking treasure. "Nora, I've decided to withdraw you both from school," he states as he pierces my skin. "I've hired a tutor who will work with you and your sister full time, Monday through Saturday morning." I feel the locks turning as he talks, the bolts of his control sliding neatly into place. "I hope you can understand how I feel. After losing your mother, I want to keep you both close... safe from harm as best I can." He wiggles the needle and then holds it up. One tiny, blood-dipped piece of wood the size of a grain of rice. "Ah! Got it!" he says, proudly holding it up to the light. He then flicks it to the floor like my last scrap of freedom and smiles.

I pull my hand back and nurse it in the other. "But..."

He methodically cleans the needle and places it back in the case without looking at me once. "No arguments," he says, dusting his hands off on his tailored brown pants. "Marie? Call the handyman and get him to sand back the door and give it another coat of lacquer. We don't need any more injuries, now do we?"

Marie shakes her pretty, plump head too fast, gazing at the floor. "No sir."

In one graceful movement, he sweeps his briefcase from the floor, lays his jacket over his arm, and presses his lips to the top of Frankie's head. She rocks on her heels, hands behind her back, and looks up to smile at him. "Have fun judging people, Deddy."

He opens his mouth to correct her but instead, he gives her a tight-lipped smile. Counselor Deere strolls to the front door. I watch him edge around where she fell too, feeling the gaping ache of missing her widening in my heart.

"You better eat your breakfast quickly, Miss Nora. The tutor will be here at nine," Marie urges, pushing a plate heaped with pancakes, syrup, and cream toward me.

Frankie jumps up onto the stool beside mine, teeters like a tenpin, and eyes my pancakes with her tongue in the corner of her mouth. "Can I have some of yers?" she asks pleadingly like she's starving. To add to the drama, she clasps her hands together like she's praying

"How many have you had?" I ask incredulously.

"Five!" She holds up her tiny, white hand, wriggling her fingers and giggling.

I laugh. The sound and feel is like Christmas baubles tapping against each other. I hold my chest, feeling like it's wrong to laugh when Mother only died a few days ago. Frankie still gazes up at me expectantly.

I fork a pancake and plop it on her chipped bunny plate. The only one she'll eat from. "Oh, all right. Here you go!"

She picks it up in her fingers like a cookie and bites before I can stop her. "Frankie…" I sigh as she takes another one, rolls it up, and puts it in her dressing gown pocket.

She pats it once and whispers, "I'm saving this one

for Mommy."

Marie sniffles and wipes her eyes with her apron.

I don't know what to say, so I just wrap an arm around her and rest my chin on the top of her head. She gives me a squeeze with her sticky hands.

Never still for long, it only takes a few seconds for her to start rattling around and buzzing like a fly in a bottle.

I feel lost as I walk back upstairs to change. The swirly handrail is clamped in my hands as I trudge up each carpeted step, my toes touching the brass weights pressing the rug into the corners. Cool autumn sunshine lights the landing. A few leaves leap from trees and swing gently back and forth to the ground. I think about what it would be like to be tiny and ride the leaf like a surfboard to the ground. My arms push out from my sides as I pretend to ride the wind. When I realize what I'm doing, I stare down at my feet, embarrassed. But then, no one's here to watch me anyway.

I lean back on the railing, feeling my clothes slip on the waxy wood. Staring out the window, I wonder what Father is up to. Where did this sudden kindness sprout from? I want to believe that Mother's death has given him new perspective but I just can't believe it. A growing winter spreads in my heart at the prospect of being trapped in this house with him. And without her.

I move faster up the stairs, the memory of my mother flying over my head like a ghost. It's still too fresh to linger and I quickly wash and dress.

Just as I'm fastening the last button of my dress, a

knock at the door disturbs me. I tighten my belt and carry my shoes in my hand to the top of the stairs. My eyes close slowly as I consider the fact that no one is around and before I can talk myself out of it, I throw my shoes to the ground floor with a "thwack", mount the rail, and let go. I shoot down like a greased marble, my breath still held at the top with my stomach. My hand reaches out to stop me, but I'm already at the bottom and have run out of handrail. I grasp the air as I slip off the end and fly toward the front door. My bottom hits the lower panel with a thud, and I let out a hysterical, panicky laugh putting my hand to my chest as my heart tries to escape. When I knock the back of my head on the door, I giggle.

A sharp knock vibrates through my head, and I search the ground floor for Marie. Then I hear her wrangling Frankie into a dress upstairs.

"Er, hello?" a muffled voice comes from the other side.

My voice is much higher than it should be when I answer, "Just a minute."

I jump up to grab my shoes, putting them on as I walk. When I reach the door, I hover, my cheeks hot, my breath still shaky from my ride. I gulp and open it, expecting a strict-looking, middle-aged woman. Instead, I'm confronted with a young man, sharply dressed in a light gray suit, his hair combed back in greased waves. He smiles nervously as I step back from the entrance.

He moves forward, his hand outstretched in greeting, and nervously stutters, "Are you Miss Deere? Err. I mean, Nora Deere?"

I frown. "My father's already left for court."

"Yes, yes, I know," he says. "I, um, I'm Douglas Inkham," he says, still holding his hand out to me. I retreat. "Your mother sent me."

I freeze, a strangling hope pushing at my feet and propelling me forward. Feeling flustered, I gesture grandly to the coat rack. "Would you like hang up your coat?" I ask, lips trembling. He nods and hangs his hat up as well.

We step into the foyer and I hear a creak above my head. The bannister shudders as Frankie shakes it manically from above. "Nora, look!" Frankie and Marie stand at the top of the stairs, Frankie, too close to the edge, swings her skirts back and forth. She's wearing a Sunday dress, a sweet silk flower tucked into her headband.

Our eyes go to them and then back to each other.

"My mother couldn't have sent you," I say flatly, quietly. "She's dead."

Mr. Inkham fumbles with his case and stares at the floor. "I know, Miss Deere. And I'm terribly sorry for your loss. But your mother's sad passing is why I am here."

Curious eyes follow me from the upstairs platform.

"Marie! Take Frankie to her room to change," I order. "That dress is inappropriate for school hours."

Marie drags a protesting Frankie back to her room with a "Humph".

"I need to speak with you, urgently. Privately." His eyes are intense. Dark. They look like they've seen things I don't want to know about.

I gulp, nod, and try to pretend I'm grown up enough to handle what's coming. "Please follow me,

Mr. Inkham." I gesture and lead him to the sitting room at the front of the house, echoes of Frankie ducking Marie and Marie's frustration becoming quieter and quieter as we step down the hall.

KETTLE

9

WORK

I gaze down at my rough fingers. The pads are like sandpaper. There are calluses, parts of my skin that seem to be permanently blackened now. Those fingers just braided a ten-year-old girl's hair. I laugh as we leave the light and slosh through the dark tunnel to the door to the subway platform.

Kin's deep voice rumbles through the cavern. "What's so funny?"

I shrug though he probably can't see me. "Nothin'."

We hold our caps in our hands and fit them just as we reach the door. I press an eye to the crack in the wood and wait for the next train. In the flurry where everyone is getting on and off, that's when we make our exit.

The rickety whoosh of the subway sends stale air through the gaps, and we count. "Three, two, one…"

We slip out, close the door behind us, and meld with the crowd.

We become another clothed head in a sea of bobbing ones. Some are the lucky ones on their way to work. Everyone with a responsibility they probably can't handle.

We climb up and then down again, weaving our way through the tunnels to the platform we need. We know we're nearly there well before we arrive as men have started to push and shove to get on the next car. You can feel the desperation, the need. No one wants to be late. If you're late, you don't get picked. It's a tumbleweed of bad timing from that point on, which leads to an empty wallet, a bare pantry, and hollow stomachs.

Kin parts the crowd easily due to his immense size, grabbing heads and yanking them back until we're at the front. I stick close. The train pulls up and the front-runners hold the others back like a fence, working together so they don't end up falling onto the tracks. When the doors open, we're lifted by the sheer force of the men behind us onto the first car. I sigh with relief once we're in.

It's strange, because after all that pushing and fighting, it's now a forty-minute ride to the end of the line, the aggression drains out, and we wait. Men become respectful again for a short time. They relax as best they can and prepare for the sprint. Kin casually folds his arms across his chest, pulls his cap over his eyes, and rests.

The men twitch and fidget. They rock on their heels and sway with the train. They avoid eye contact because unlike me, they think it's bad form to be friendly with the guy you're about to elbow in the face. I don't mind so much. We're all in this together. *Kind of.*

We're all pretty familiar now anyway. We're each other's competition and once chosen for the other side, we are each other's workmates. It's a strange relationship. Inside, we rely on the men around us to keep us safe. Outside, they will knock you out without thinking twice.

An old man slumps against his seat, his face less

taut with adrenaline and testosterone than the rest of us. He rolls an unlit cigarette idly between his fingers, twirling it tight as a bandage. Gazing up at me from legs spread wide, his milky eyes crinkle happily. Slowly, he lifts his shirt up and winks. I try to turn away from the flasher, but we're wedged in. My eyes fall on his pale stomach, covered in gray hairs, and I understand. Then I lift my own shirt to show the same diamond-shaped bruises that crisscross my skin. He lets his drop, as do I, and we exchange a nod. He's a front-runner. May not look like much, but those marks mean he's made it to the front recently and more than once.

Kin's sharp tongue lashes out at both of us. "Put it away. No one wants to see that, old man." A crumpled laugh ripples through the huddled men. It's slight. Our minds are on the next few minutes.

The train lurches to a stop and bodies press against the door. Men flex their arms and barricade their bodies. Kin stands tall next to me, and I stay close to his side. The old man lights up his cigarette and crosses his legs casually. I have the urge to tell him to get up, get up and fight if he wants to make it through, but then that would be one more man I'd have to grapple with. When the doors slide open, I lose him anyway. I'm sucked into the flow, pressure pushing us forward like a dam suddenly breaking.

It's comical the way we all run-walk. We sprint through the large spaces, bottlenecking at the narrow ones, and then we are forced to walk when we go up the stairs, through the turnstiles, and up the stairs again.

I take them three at a time, my elbows out, jabbing

anyone who tries to pull me down. My breath flares through my chest as my face hits the cold fall air. Whitish light hits our eyes, and the smell of seagull shit and salty water floods our senses. A hundred men's footsteps pounding the pavement is the chorus of determination. They will only pick forty. I have to be in that forty.

There are few women on the street. They've learned not to be in the way of this multi-footed, anger-fueled monster that scurries toward the docks possessed. Eyes full of dollar signs and stomachs that churn with hunger.

The cobblestones are pressed neatly into the road. Slammed down hard and smoothed by so many feet and so many heavy vehicles. We spread out. Each man taking what they think is the best route. Kin and I head straight down the center. It's thicker with bodies, but it's quicker. *We're* quicker and younger.

I dart and slide between people, moving lithely like a dancer. Kin just knocks men out the way. The dull, cyclone-wire fence surrounding the dock seems to shudder as we approach.

Someone grabs the collar of my jacket and jerks me back. I fall, tumbling several men like milk bottles in my wake. The man I'm essentially sitting on snatches at my hair, his hand wet with oil from the black puddle he fell in. It slips uselessly from his hands. I jump up, give him a smirk, and keep running, preparing for the pain.

It's like running full force into a brick wall—a writhing, huffing, puffing wall of frenzied men. We are five men deep in the crowd when the sirens sound.

"You ready?" Kin asks, as if I have a choice.

"Sure," I say, rolling my shoulders.

He holds his interlocked hands out, crouching, his forehead resting on the back of the man in front. I step up awkwardly, fighting for space in the crush. "One, two, three…" He launches me forward and I dive into the sea of bodies, kicking one guy lightly in the head and almost pulling someone's ear off as I land. But I'm in front and Kin's pushing people aside like they're made of corkwood.

"We're hiring forty men today. Please behave in an orderly fashion as we open the gates to count," the man with the speaker grunts sarcastically. He knows there's no order to this. He's counting on it. The men who get through are the strongest, the most determined, and the most hardworking. It's what they want.

Men with guns in their belts stand on either side of the ten-foot-high, sliding gate. They have a twist to their faces, enjoying the small power they have over the rest of us. I'm being squashed like a flower between two books now as the men surge forward, aching to get through the small, man-sized gap they'll make in a few seconds.

Two armed men bang on the fence hollowly, guns in hand. "Back off," they warn as desperate bodies squish against the wire. There's no controlling them. There's only the push, sweat, and sea air.

The gates start to rattle open, hard knuckles gripping the edges, ready to slam it closed once they reach their count. Arms go first, then heads and bodies slide through the gap like some sort of reverse birth. I don't even need to fight that hard, I'm carried along with the crowd. I hear the number twenty called out as I pass, my forearms ripping as I'm batted back and forth against the sharp ends of the wire. Kin is two men behind me and gives me a wink. The rest pour fluidly past like grain poured from a sack, and then some men assist the guards in shutting the gate. Fingers are crushed. A face is slammed with the butt of a gun. I turn back and glance at the sad and angry faces left behind. I can't smile about my fortune because it means I cheated others out of theirs. I turn away before I make a decision I'll regret, like giving up my place. We all need it as much as the other. There is no story more or less pathetic. We wouldn't be here otherwise.

Dragging gravel beside me with his wrinkled toes is the old man from the train. Kin laughs as he slaps the man on the back. "You made it through, old man. Good for you!"

He shakes his head and spits on the ground, a chewed cigarette hanging from his lip. "Yeah, we just won the worst prize on the planet. Back breaking labor for minimum wage," I snap, rolling my eyes at Kin's chipper demeanor. It's not as easy for me to ignore the hopelessness of the ones trapped on the other side who won't get to feed their families tonight.

Kin shrugs and kicks stones as we near the water. "These were your rules, Kettle. I'm just trying to play nice like you asked me to." The black water swallows the stones without a sound, sinking into silty darkness.

He pulls his cap low over his eyes and rubs the back of his neck. I watch his broad back shift away from me, and I know I'm probably going to get the silent treatment for the rest of the day.

My eyes search the sky. Gray clouds hang heavy over the water, edging inland slowly. The breeze is salt, fish, and rusting metal flavored. I lick the corner of my mouth and head to the sign-in station, my feet thudding against damp jetty sleepers.

I slap Kin on the head as I pass him, and he swears at me.

The old man coughs and turns his gray face toward me. His eyes narrow as he really takes in our dark skin and Kin's almost black eyes. "You two brothers?"

Kin scoffs.

I smile at the old man and shake my head. "I'm far too handsome to be related to that ape in a hat."

Kin forgets he's mad at me and speaks, "Yeah, we're brothers. He's the smart one and I'm the much smarter, pretty one with the good hair."

The old man is looking like he's sorry he asked and picks up his pace. His gait is fresh and speedy, and I realize the frail old man stuff was an act. I smile, impressed at his deception.

The shadows of crane arms cut our path, and I gulp in anticipation.

"Ready to fly?" Kin asks, wiggling his dark brows.

I don't answer, thinking good thoughts.

10
UNEXPECTED

M ister Black, the supervisor, ambles over, his black, squiggly hair bouncing under his hard hat, his white shirt hanging out past his jacket cuffs. "Kettle, you're up, boy," he orders gruffly, tossing me a hardhat and a bright yellow vest covered in greasy stains. His voice is tired, whiny, and full of impatience at his current circumstance.

He hands me one large, rusty hook the size of my head. It sinks in my arms. His severe frown is compromised by the frosted look of his beard and moustache, salt-crusted from working near the sea all day, every day. I clasp my hand around the metal. It's reassuring. It's so heavy, so solid that it edges out the small fear I harbor in my heart. I'm not even sure fear is the right word; it's more of a small ball that spins and builds to a rush. It's rough-edged, but it doesn't hurt. It's what pushes me up, makes me crave the sky.

My eyes lift. The sky is veiled in tattered lace, clouds so thin they seem to be part of the blue. I grin. I want to believe the sky has something for me. That it isn't empty. That it's full.

Black jerks a finger in the direction of the first container, red and dented. "Hook it up, ride it over, set it down," he says as he twirls around so his back is to me. His hair flies out from his face, and I have to clamp down my lips to stop from whistling at him.

I nod, though he can't see me. I know the drill.

Moving fast across the cracked concrete, I scurry up the side of the shipping container, the metal dimpling and rebounding as I land on the roof. I crouch down, fingers spread, ready to grab the thick chains that will sail down from the sky. One of the chains is missing a hook. It swings more loosely, unsafely, and I don't want to think too hard about how it happened. The chains land on the metal roof with a clang, sweeping and dragging like a giant, teasing necklace as I try to catch the hooks and attach them to the anchors. I screw the replacement hook in, tighten it, and couple it to the last anchor point. My eyes scan the oil-streaked ground for Kin, but there's no proud head amongst all the others that count the cracks running like dried-up veins along the floor. I shrug. He must be working in another area, and he's probably sulking.

No one looks at me as the container lurches from the ground; their heads are down or on the next job.

I clamp my hand around one of the thick chains. It's instantly stained orange, but my skin has always been copper colored so you'd barely notice. I center myself and hold tight as we lift into the air.

Metal makes a strange sound when it's fighting against gravity. It protests, it whines, and groans. I rise past the levels of colored containers stacked on the docks. Piled high like giant sugar cubes, full of things I'll never see, nor have. Things I don't really want either. I know how precious my freedom is, my independence. It's enough.

I keep to my knees as the crane swings over the

water, one hand holding the chain, the other keeping my hat on my head as the cold blast of wind coming off the water hits me in the chest. I don't hold the hat to my head for my own safety, though. If I lose it, it gets docked from my pay. If I fell from up here the only part of me that would survive, ironically, would be the hat.

I puff out my chest, breathing in deeply. This is the part I love—this small window of time between leaving the ground and setting down on the ship. Through that window, I can fly. My hair flares back from my face, my cheeks sting with cold, brackish air. Fear leaves me, and I am *free*.

I crow like a rooster as the container lifts higher, wanting to crook my elbows and spread my wings, but it's too dangerous to let go. It swings in the wind, seeming like a feather and not tons of steel. A few men glance up to find the source of the noise, shielding their eyes with their hands. Their confused faces make me grin, my lips basted with salt, my eyes fighting to stay open against the wind.

I spread my toes in my shoes, trying to act like glue as the floating metal box bears down on the ship. I've seen men tossed, like foam from the waves, from their container at landing. That's why this job pays more. It's the most hazardous.

The top of the container I'm supposed to set down on approaches fast. I plant every part of me to the roof as the crane driver angles, adjusts, and finally drops me with a loud, metallic bang. My whole body springs up at impact and I am thrown to the side, my legs swinging over the edge momentarily. I dig in, my fingernails scratching into the paint, sending up flecks of red and manage to pull myself back up. My heart jams for a second, and then beats wildly, jumping all over the place at another near death.

Kin has complained to the bosses about the lack of harnesses and safety gear, but he forgets who he's talking to. He has this sense of entitlement that I don't have. Maybe that comes from having a family and parents who valued you, I don't know. I don't know anything about what that might feel like.

I'm still planted to the roof of the container, thinking about the small hole in my life that can't be filled, when I hear the groan of the next container getting closer. I blink, jolt up, and remember we're getting paid cash, no questions asked. They cut corners, but we're not supposed to exist. Our welfare is a low priority as there are so many others begging to take our place. These feelings are ones I better understand. They are the patches of fabric that make up my orphan skin.

A horn sounds, which is my cue to unhook the chains and clamber down the giant steps made of metal boxes. I do it swiftly, jumping down as I see the shadow of the next container bearing down on me from above. Squeezing into the gap between two of them, I breathe one quick breath before bolting down the other levels as fast as I can. Each container set down is another coin in my pocket.

As I jump and squeeze my way down to the ship's deck, I think about Kin. I think about whether he's right that stealing would be easier. It would probably be safer. But even though this kind of work is on the dodgy side of legal, I'm not likely to get caught. *I can't get caught.*

Images swirl in my head. Memories I keep stuffed in the back rooms under a grubby kimono and slash-black characters.

Kin and I have done our time. I remember the threats that prison would be far worse, and from the looks in their hard, hateful eyes, I believed it. Nothing is worth my freedom. I have scars inside and out that remind me every day. So does Kin.

The vibration of heavy metal slamming against itself rumbles through my body, and I hurry down the last couple of levels until I hit the deck. The counter hands me a card at the bridge, which I pocket.

I jog down the plank, smiling, as I get ready to go again.

Twenty more containers and the horn blares loudly.

"Take a half-hour break, men," Black yells as he limps to his little glass cubicle, tucked into the side of the giant warehouse.

I glance down at his flipper-like foot. He uses it as a warning, flapping it in front of the new guys to scare them. And the way he smiles, mouth full of metal-capped teeth, I think he enjoys it quite a lot.

"Squashed flat!" he'd squawked when I first arrived here. His hand slapped down on the white trestle table, and he held his foot out for everyone to see. "Keep your arms and legs tight to yer body, don't linger, and don't freeze up."

I grab two sandwiches and a can of soda off the lunch table, elbowing another man out of the way for the last one. He grabs at my neck but only manages to catch my collar. He mutters a word I'm very used to hearing as I shake off his grasp. I don't turn around. There's no point in engaging, no point in telling him I'm not what he says I am, because I don't have an answer for exactly what I am. I walk away quickly and go looking for Kin.

My worn sneakers splash up muddy puddles as I wind my way through the bones of an unfinished ship. Abandoned after the war, it rises out of the shallows like the ribs of a giant sea creature. After seven years, people have forgotten about the frantic building that happened here. The shadows cut across my olive arm and I'm reminded that even after seven years, some things are still the same. Some things don't degrade, don't wash away like the small waves that slap at the framework, slowly eating away at the metal and feeding the barnacles that stick to it. The sea and its allies are trying to gradually pull it apart and drag it into the water. Soon, it will win.

I see Kin's dark head above the level of some old drums stacked against each other at the end of the slip. His strong, dark arm rises up, he scratches his head, and then he laughs. I lift my hand and pause. He's talking to someone.

I move behind the wreckage of discarded metal and wood, creeping closer so I can eavesdrop.

"You're so pretty," he whispers. My face twists in disgust and astonishment at how he managed to find a girl out here on the docks. I cover my mouth, trying to stop the snigger that wants to come out at the thought of what kind of girl could be 'found' down at the docks. "What's a gorgeous girl like you doing out here? You're too good for this place," Kin croons.

I lean closer, my eyes kind of scrunched shut because I don't want to see Kin kissing some girl, but I also want to know what he's up to.

"Here," he urges. "Take some of my lunch. I know, I know, but look at you, I can see your ribs through your fur."

My eyes snap open and I draw in a breath, choking on a laugh. A minute meow is followed by a swearing, truly embarrassed Kin, standing over me with a tabby kitten tucked under his arm. His cheeks flush pink, and then he glances protectively at the animal curled into his elbow.

"Oh my God, Kin," I manage through my chuckling. "I thought you were talking to a girl."

The sight of my large friend holding a kitten so gently and self-consciously, carefully like it's made of china, is too much for me and I collapse backward, tears in my eyes. He reaches out with his spare hand and clips my ear.

"Stop laughing," he growls. He sets her down on a rotted crate. Her paws touch the damp wood for a second before he picks her up again. "You scared her." He brings the fur ball to his cheek, his eyes full of affection for the, quite possibly, disease-ridden creature.

I laugh, holding my ribs. "Kin with a pet. I never thought I'd see it. It's so, it's so…"

Kin strokes the creature's head, and it purrs. "So, what?" he asks, taking a threatening step toward me.

I'm struggling to think of something that isn't going to upset him more, so I swallow my laugh and calm myself. "So what's her name?" I ask carefully, avoiding his crimson face and furious, dark eyes.

"Tiger Lily," he says, placing her gently on the ground and handing her a pinch of tuna fish from his sandwich.

I didn't think I was capable of giggling, but I do. I giggle until my stomach hurts, and Kin has stalked away from me. Watching him as I shove dry, choking-hazard-like bread into my mouth, I wash it down with sugary soda. He crouches down and holds a welcoming palm to the kitten, revealing this softer side of him I'd always kind of suspected might be in there somewhere.

The wide-mouthed siren wails, and we both turn our heads in the same direction. Kin pats the little cat and murmurs, "See you tomorrow, Tiger Lily," and then we sprint shoulder to shoulder toward the cranes.

11
THE PRIZE

THE HOUSE IS TOO QUIET. IT'S LIKE WHEN SHE LEFT, SHE TOOK THE SOUND WITH HER. EVERYONE PADS ALONG THE FLOORS LIKE THEY'RE AFRAID OF WAKING A DEMON IN THE BASEMENT. WE'RE STUCK IN THIS EMPTY SPACE, A VOID CARVED OUT SO DEEP, SO FINAL, THERE'S NOTHING LEFT TO DO BUT HUG THE EDGES AND TRY NOT TO FALL IN.

Mr. Inkham's loud footsteps disturb the unholy peace this house has settled into, and I can't decide whether I like it or not.

He follows me down the short, dark hallway and into the sitting room, hovering in the doorway as I fling open the curtains. Light floods the stale room, lifting the floral patterns from the sofas and highlighting the dust that flies through the air in streams.

I gesture to the dusty pink sofa, edged in ropey brown timber. "Please take a seat," I say formally. I sit opposite him and fold my hands in my lap, then at my sides, finally scratching my nose for something to do. "Er, do you want something to eat or drink?" I offer.

Mr. Inkham shakes his head, a flop of dark brown hair curling over his eyebrow. "No thank you, Miss Deere." He peers out the window, watching the featherbone clouds sift through the sky. He seems uneasy and is doing the same awkward movements with his hands that I am. "I need to keep this brief," he says, his eyes tracking a couple walking down the street arm in arm. Leaves fall in the woman's hair, and the man lovingly picks them out of her bun.

I rub my tired eyes and sigh. "Keep what brief? Mr. Inkham, why are you here?" I lean forward, sunlight hitting my face. I blink, still gazing up and out the window. *I want to fall into the sky, lay my bones against the clouds, and rest.* Just for a moment, I'd like to rest. I lean back and press a hand to my heart. An ache pushes between my fingers.

He bends down and fumbles through his briefcase, pulling out a small stack of papers. "As you well know, your mother came from a very wealthy family."

I nod my head, though I didn't know. This is the first I've heard of it, but then I never put any thought into how my parents supported themselves. Thinking about the fact that my father is a public defender and how we live, I guess it makes sense that the money came from her. Mr. Inkham raises an eyebrow at my stilted reaction. "Your mother had a large amount of family money that upon her death was to go to her husband, er, your father…" I realize my shoulders have sagged, my head is hanging by a thread, and I try to force myself to sit up straight. "Your mother came to me at the beginning of the year and asked me to change her will. She requested that most of her inheritance, save a sufficient living allowance, be put into yours and your sister's name for you to claim either when you marry or turn twenty-one, whichever comes first." He delicately hands a piece of paper to me. I take it like it may disintegrate in my grasp. He points with his index finger to an amount of money so large my jaw actually drops.

"All this will be mine?" I stammer, underlining the number again and again with my eyes. It glows red, a prize... a price.

He leans back in the chair and smiles sadly. "Yes, it will be yours and your sister's. Half to you when you turn twenty-one, and the other half to her when she does the same."

My feet curl under as I form the question, "Does my father know about this?" The paper feels poisonous, slicing my fingertips. A reward I can't claim may as well be punishment.

Mr. Inkham shakes his head slowly as he contemplates his answer. "No, not yet, but his lawyers have contacted me. I won't be able to delay them finding out for very long. I'm sorry." He acts like he knows.

It's struggling to sink in. The information is looking for a hiding place in my head and failing. "So my father will get none of her fortune save a living allowance?"

He crosses his legs, uncrosses them, and pats his hair down. "That is correct, Miss Deere."

It makes me smile although it shouldn't. His anger is going to shake the walls of this house when he finds out. My voice quivers a little when I ask, "What do you need from me, a signature?"

Mr. Inkham leans forward and places a soft hand over my jittery fingers. I withdraw sharply. His eyes warm when they regard me, and he gives a small nod. "I don't need anything from you, dear. I just came here to prepare you for what's ahead, to war..." He averts his eyes and doesn't finish. His mouth is suddenly hard and sucked in, a bitter taste on his tongue.

Warn me. You came here to warn me.

He packs the papers away and clasps his case.

"Is there anything else?" I lean forward in my chair, my starved eyes ready to swallow the room. I'm hoping for a letter, a note, anything that might explain her reasons. Honestly, I'm looking for an apology.

"I'm sorry, Miss Deere. I truly am. Your mother, she was..." Again, he doesn't finish. He's holding secrets in his mouth, words that keep pummeling his lips to get out.

A tear is working its way out of my eye. I'm battered with the truth. I don't understand what's happening, and there is no way to get any answers. I lift my face to the ceiling in an attempt to stop the overwhelmed feelings from pouring out of my eyes. The plaster roses on the ceiling seem to crawl out from the middle of the room like spiders, and I want to grab at a leg and pull it from the plaster. I want to find a hole and pull myself through. Climb up, up, up, into the dust and spider webs.

"So what do I do?" I ask, still looking at the bumps and buds of a hundred tiny, plaster roses instead of his horribly sympathetic face.

A hand goes to my shoulder. "Just take care of yourself. Survive, endure, for three more years..."

"What about my sister?" I think of Frankie alone in this house with him, and my dress suddenly feels like it's strangling me. I tug at the collar. "She's still so young."

There's hope in his expression. His cheeks raise

and he talks to me like an equal, like someone who might matter or at least, matter one day. "When you're financially independent, you can petition for custody. And if you choose to do that, I will help you file the necessary motions."

Oh, I'll do it…

"Three years," I whisper to my lap. My fingers count, one, two, three, tapping a silent prayer against an empty window. *It's so long.*

He stands, reaching into his pocket and handing me a black card embossed with white writing. "Three years. Then you call me."

I hold the card in my fingers, folding it over once so it looks like a tiny tent I want to shelter under. "Or marry…" I whisper to my hand.

Mr. Inkham stops midstride, light cutting across his tailored pants so they look faded and old. He turns toward me, his eyes full of warning. "It is an option but, please, don't rush into anything. You don't want to end up in a more… er…" he searches for words that don't exist and comes up with, *"compromising situation* than you already are."

Got it. All men are dangerous.

I stand, straighten like a rod, and almost stamp my foot as I say, "My priority is my sister's welfare. I'm no fool, and I will not make any decision lightly. What happens to me affects her too. I will do whatever necessary to keep her safe."

"Fair words," he concedes and then he pauses, rapping his fingers lightly on the surface of his worn leather case. "There is one thing you should try to remember, something you can hold onto, look forward to."

I eye him warily, leaning back on my heels. "What's that, Mr. Inkham?"

"Happiness," he states with neither a smile nor a frown on his face. He is neutral, flat, like he's offered me a cup of tea.

The word is a slap in the face. It's too much to hope for. Too far-fetched.

I laugh sourly. "Any chance of happiness tumbled down the stairs and shattered to pieces with my mother."

His eyes widen in shock, but he quickly composes himself, allowing me to pass through and walk him to the exit in silence.

"Good luck, Miss Deere," he says grimly as he waits at the front door. He places his hat loosely on his head and steps outside, leaving me with a promise, a future three years forward, and a thousand days out of my reach.

Survive...
        Happiness...

The two words are oceans apart.
An impossible couple.

12

ORDINARY LIFE

I sigh dramatically, and Kin jabs at me with his spare hand. "Do we have to eat here every day?" I complain as I throw my sandwich in the air and catch it. *Down by the water, the sad shadows of a ghost ship hovering over us.* I would have thought this kind of reminder was enough to put him off hanging around here.

Kin rolls his eyes. "You should be thankful we've managed to get in this many days in a row. Not that I like working this hard, but the money makes it almost worth it." He shoves some food in his mouth, chewing carefully and swallowing before he continues. "I am starting to miss home though. How long has it been this time?" He flicks crumbs from his mouth.

I press my toe into the sludgy, tiger-striped sand, and flick a piece at one of the steel uprights still fighting gravity and the sea. It lands with a plop, slipping down and back into the water. "Four days..." I say, turning and pointing at him accusingly with my rust-colored finger. "Hey! You said *home*."

Kin shrugs and mutters, "Shut up."

I smirk and wade to the other side of the ship and up onto the dock, sitting down with my back against a stack of sleepers. Kin gallops over, slapping water toward me on purpose as he jumps up to join me. I shield my face but end up drenched in briny water anyway.

He collapses at my side and opens another sandwich, fishy smells releasing from their packaging. I screw up my nose and make a gagging noise.

"Enough with the tuna!" I say, waving my hand in front of my face. "You're starting to smell like a can of week-old cat food."

"Our people do love seafood," he says proudly, his high cheekbones seeming to stick out even prouder.

I roll my eyes. "What people? Cat people?" I say sarcastically.

Kin ignores me but I can see his nostrils flare as he looks left and right, holding a piece of his sandwich out in front of him and shaking it.

A meow sounds out of place amongst the sloshing waves and seagulls cackling. Tiger Lily sidles up to Kin, rubbing her body against his leg. "She won't eat anything else," he says dotingly as he feeds her with one hand and pats her with the other. She purrs.

She tries to rub against my leg and I shift it, tempted to push her into the water. "You need to stop wasting your food on that thing," I growl, pointing. "Look, she's getting fat."

He picks her up under her arms and smiles, almost touching his nose to hers.

"Ugh!"

"You're not fat. You're just growing, aren't you, Lils?" he says to the squish-faced ball of fur.

I arch an eyebrow, but there's nothing I can say. He never listens to me anyway.

"This looks good," I say to Kin, pointing down the

alley between two buildings in opposition to each other. A burnt-out, 'affordable housing' project next to a luxurious, historical brownstone. It still smells faintly of smoke, but it should be quieter than the average alley as there's no one in the apartment building and I'm banking on the brownstone residents keeping to their side.

"I think you're confusing good with dirty and unsanitary," Kin quips, narrowing his eyes. He rolls his shoulders and starts in on the conversation I hoped we could avoid. "I can't believe you stopped me today, Kettle. That man, if you can even call him that, was being a jerk."

I sigh. "He just bumped your shoulder. You need to learn when to walk away."

Kin shakes his head like he's so disappointed in me. "You heard what he said. The word he used."

I purse my lips. "It doesn't matter. You need to ignore it. It's not worth getting in a fight."

"Then what is? How far do we let them take it before we say something?" he asks, his voice getting stronger, more agitated. We've stopped on the corner, and people are starting to stare. I grab his shirtsleeve, and he shrugs me off. My eyes dart around, checking for men in dark blue or green, gold stars sparkling on their lapels.

I glare up at him, trying to warn him with my eyes. "Really far, Kin. Really, really far."

I jerk my head toward the alley, and Kin stalks ahead of me. This fight will go nowhere, and he knows it. I wait a few seconds before following, making sure no one's looking in our direction. Lamps are flicking on, the dark swarming over the buildings and dripping down the walls. My bones ache inside my salt-crusted, slightly sunburned skin. The walls from the two buildings lean close to each other over the alley. Kin stands right in the center with his hands on his hips, his shadow lengthening as the sun begins to set. I look up. I won't get to see it tonight. Too risky. Maybe sunrise...

Kin shouts, "Dumpster or cardboard box?"

I approach him quickly, hoping he'll quiet down.

His temper has flared and burnt out already, and he smiles at me as I throw a soft punch to his shoulder. "Who am I kidding?" He laughs. "There's no cardboard box."

I laugh, though it's not funny. I'm thinking of home. The Kings. The golden light dancing on sandy walls.

13
FIELD TRIP

It's been three weeks since Mr. Inkham visited and gave me the incomprehensible news. Since then, my father and I have slipped into a monotonous, but safe pattern. Avoidance. He leaves early, returns late. He's working on something important, and we do our best not to run into each other.

The foyer tiles are wearing down, skirting where she landed. We're digging a line in, carving a path around the shape of her body.

"Nora, are you listening to me?" Miss Candace, our tutor, swipes a hand in front of my face, a warm breeze heavy with perfume fluttering up my nose. A small, sticky claw clamps over my wrist and shakes me.

"Nora, we get to leave the house today. Field trip! Field Trip!" Frankie shouts, toppling her chair and galloping around the playroom with her ruler between her legs. I wince, still expecting tempers to flare and voices to rise to the rafters, but Miss Candace's bosom jiggles with bubbling laughter as her eyes follow Frankie tearing around the small room that is now our classroom.

"Now that's enthusiasm," she says, tapping her heart like the laughter has stolen her breath. She bends over my desk and tries to connect with my eyes. "Do you think you can muster some energy and enthusiasm to go to the zoo with us today, Miss Nora?"

I nod, trying to lighten my expression, brighten my eyes. Watching Frankie makes me smile, and I haven't been out of the house in days, at least not out the front door.

"Yes, Miss Candace," I reply, trying to shake the deadness from my face when I look into her raisin-like eyes.

She gives a sharp clap and I jump, my heart sputtering before remembering that here is a safe place, a safe person. "Wonderful! Girls, get your coats and hats." She rumbles out the room and tromps down the stairs. They creak under her weight as her short, bobbed hair bounces up and down with *enthusiasm*. Frankie runs all the way down the stairs and then back up, her energy exploding out of her socks. When Miss Candace reaches the bottom, she walks straight through, not around. My eyes sting and I sniff, wiping a tear away with my sleeve. She doesn't know. It's not her fault.

Miss Candace opens the foyer door and leans her sizable rump against it, wrestling with Frankie as she puts one arm in her coat backward. She sighs, but she doesn't scold. Her patience is infinite.

A swish of leaves greets us at the slate step. I pause, pinned to the edge like a pigeon, my toes bending over. I gaze down at the crunchy, yellow leaves battling to get into the house and shake my head, warning them. *You don't want to go in there.*

Frankie climbs the brick guardrail of the stairs and tiptoes to the bottom, holding her hands out and jumping like she can fly. I'm still stuck on the step, my ashy-blonde hair curtaining my eyes. A hand wraps around my arm, and I flinch.

Miss Candace lets go as suddenly as she grabbed me, as if she's afraid I'll bite her. "Sorry dear, I didn't mean to scare you. But shall we get going?" The concern in her eyes is like arms outstretched to a sinking boat. I want to, want to, *want* to take them, but I can't. I've got to tread the water on my own.

Coated men storm down the shadowed paths underneath large oaks that are slowly molting. A homeless man drags a pram full of his belongings across the road, his face squished and angry. People sidestep him, and one woman hurries across the road when she sees him approaching. I raise an eyebrow; people are often scared of the wrong things. They don't realize that sometimes, the menace lives in the lavish brownstone, sips expensive scotch, and defends laws they have no intention of abiding in their own home. Once upon a time, this man who grips the handles of a dilapidated pram so tightly had a different life. One that he lost or had taken from him. People don't see. They don't want to.

"Where's the car? Where's Sally?" I ask, taking one step down to follow Frankie, who I know is about to ask the homeless man what's in his pram.

Miss Candace slings her purse crossways over her body and snorts, puffs of steam flowing from her nostrils like a racehorse. "We're walking. We're going to experience the city," she says, tilting her chin at the old man with the pram. He tips his cap to her and shuffles along, and my affection for her grows. "Miss Frances, hold your sister's hand."

Frankie grabs my hand and swings from it, almost popping my shoulder out of its socket. When she grips my wrist tightly, I wince, quickly pulling my cardigan sleeve over my fingers. One kind, narrowed eye glances my way before turning down the street and ordering us to march.

Despite our street being wide, the brownstones lean in as if they're trying to touch foreheads, leaving little room for light. Old trees line the sidewalk and dance with each other in the wind, holding hands and caroling for the world to skip the winter that's coming. We hurry past the burned-out apartment block next door. It's the first of many as you round the corner. The richer neighbors lament their presence and the effect the poorer folk that live in them have on the 'value' of the area. My family was never among the complainers. I remember the first time someone tried to get the building license for the one next to us revoked. The way my father's temper had flared, opened, and swallowed every negative attitude. It confused me to see his anger used for good. It didn't work in my head... like oil and water trying to mix. But then, he is a contradiction, a campaigner for those less fortunate, yet unable to afford his children the same consideration. It causes conflict in me I don't want to be there. An itchy feeling I'd like to scratch out. I want to hate him. I don't want there to be room for any other feeling.

Glancing up at the broken windows as we walk, I smell the old smoke clinging to the walls.

I used to love watching the families and listening to the trills and rolling of different languages clashing against common English.

I smile as I tread faster down the street, listening to crunching leaves under my feet and enjoying the feeling of dirt satisfyingly staining my new shoes. The upper-crust residents won't win this one. They are outnumbered. The cleanup has already begun, and repairs will follow. Something flutters in my chest at the thought of new families moving in, new noises and smells wafting across the gap between us. I frown when I remember how out of reach they are to me.

We round the corner and the streets become narrower, busier, and dirtier. Life is opening up as shop fronts bloom, umbrellas rise, and canvas awnings are propped up. I pull Frankie closer. She's playing with her aid. "Do you need it turned down, Frankie?" I ask, cupping her face with my hands so she can see my lips as I talk.

She blinks at me, screws up her tiny pink nose, and nods. Tapping her ear once, she says, "Too many people talkin' at the same time. It's too noisy. Ah, can't hear propply."

I kneel down and adjust it for her. "Better?"

"Batter!"

I scruff her hair up, and she wriggles under my touch. Miss Candace turns around, her face already flushed from walking one block. "First—coffee."

We wait outside while Miss Candace enters a bar to get a cup of coffee. Frankie stands in front of me and plays with my skirt. I keep my hands pressed down against my thighs to stop her from showing the whole street my underwear and lean against the window of a cake shop, my eyes absently climbing the yellow windows of hundreds of apartments. My mind wanders through kitchens, my finger drags across someone's dusty dresser. Sometimes I wish, like Alice, I could climb through a window, through a mirror, and into another world.

A crowd of people pours from the subway entrance across the road, hundreds of hatted heads spreading like a stain over the pavement. Cars honk and stop, and I anxiously play with the button of my cardigan while keeping the restless seven-year-old pinned to my leg. I knock a heel nervously against the black tiles that line the shop window.

Men approach me from across the road and I cast my eyes down, the button in my fingers coming loose and falling to the ground.

Frankie goes to grab it, and I pull her back. "Leave it. It's dirty," I snap.

A large hand scoops the button up, and I follow the hand down a long arm to a handsome face. The young man holds the button between his finger and thumb and smiles. "Did you drop this, Miss?" he asks, arching dark eyebrows at me.

I shake my head. "No."

He places his hand against the window over my head and leans in. I can feel the blood rushing to my face. "No? I swear I just saw you drop it."

His casual expression is at odds with the way he's flexing his arms above me. He's a full head taller than I am. Shrinking into the window behind me, I glance up at him with the sun spreading behind his face and burning my eyes. "I…"

A snap makes him jump away and I realize Frankie has grabbed his suspender, pulled it back, and let it go.

She giggles as he dramatically staggers back, holding his heart. Another young man, his cap pulled down over his eyes, slaps the back of the taller one's head and grunts, "That'll teach you to bother girls who are way out of your league."

They both laugh and turn away from me. I relax slightly, but then the shorter one turns back suddenly and marches toward me with purpose. He takes my hand gently and opens my fingers, placing the button into my palm, his eyes still hidden. "Sorry about him, Miss." His voice is dark, like his skin, a smoothly poured consistency to it that warms the tips of my ears. Before I can answer or pull away like I should, he's disappeared into the crowd.

Frankie pulls my skirt around her shoulders like a cape and laughs huskily. "That was funny!"

A bell rings by my head. "What was funny, little Miss Frances?" Miss Candace asks as she steps into the colder air, a new flush to her face.

"I pinged a man who took Nora's butten," she answers, placing her hands on her hips and giving us a self-satisfied grin.

"What on earth! Pinged?" Miss Candace splutters.

I cover my mouth and let out a quick laugh. It escapes my chest like a desperate dove trying to hit the clouds. "Yes. She pinged him real good."

Miss Candace relaxes her shoulders and smiles, her red lipstick lining the bottom of her teeth like she bit into a candle. "Very well, girls. Follow me."

The further we get from home, from the piles of

brick that seem mortared with blood and tears, the better I feel. My chest opens to the brisk breeze, my feet step lighter, and the smile I'm wearing feels less false and forced.

Giant, wrought iron gates are set open, inviting us into the large, green park that is freckled with autumn leaves chasing each other across paths and irritating the groundskeepers. The scrape of a rake against gravel grabs my attention, and I turn my attention to the noise.

I hear Frankie asking Miss Candace a question, "Can we, can we, Miss, please?"

The reason for the question sits like a giant, stone potato in front of my eyes, as tall as a tree, wide and leaning. My smile turns from almost genuine to a complete grin. This rock is begging to be climbed.

Miss Candace's breathy voice permits me. "Of course, young Deere. This park is meant for exploring, discovering, and adventure."

Frankie's thumping footsteps pummel the earth behind and she pulls up next to me just as I reach out and touch the giant monolith, feeling its surface for footholds and dips.

I look back at Miss Candace for reassurance. She simply waves her hand at me as if to say, 'go on,' plops herself on a park bench, and lights a cigarette.

Frankie scratches at the rock, trying to find a place to get up, and fails. "Nora, can you help me?" she whines.

I pat her head and heft myself up to the first ledge. "No way. If you can't do it yourself, then you're not ready. If you're going to climb safely, it has to be your own way."

She gives me a rather nasty glare and moves around to the other side. "Fine then," she mutters, though with Frankie, it always sounds one decibel short of yelling. I shrug and climb.

It's harder in a skirt and dress shoes, and I lose my footing a few times. I like the slipping and almost falling though. It does this electrifying thing to my heart, glazes it in a sparking, thrilling feeling.

I reach the top and sit down on the scooped-out plateau, my hands behind me avoiding the small pools of stagnant water breeding mosquitoes and algae. From here, I can see the whole park, sprouting out of the middle of this busy city, the tops of the evergreen trees looking like broccoli, thick and dense. The deciduous plants huddle together in patches of woods, desperate to stay warm against the coming cold. I breathe in and sigh out the large amounts of stress that have been sticking to my insides. *I could stay here forever.*

"Nora. Nora." Frankie jumps up and down, throwing herself at the rock's surface in frustration. I look down and notice the park bench is empty.

"Miss Frances! Look at your dress. Where's your sister?" Miss Candace's voice sounds slightly panicked as she walks around the rock twice.

Frankie gazes up at me, and I put my finger to my lips to stop her from telling Miss Candace where I am. Her eyes sparkle with the mischief that always seems to be there, and then she giggles.

"Miss Nora!" Miss Candace shouts out. Then she whispers to herself, her head tipping as she holds her chest, "Well done, Candace, you've lost a child on your very first field trip." Her bob shakes back and forth as she scolds herself.

I decide I've played with her long enough and scamper down the opposite side to the ground. Walking casually toward her, I play innocent. "Did you call me, Miss?" I ask sweetly.

She jumps with surprise. "Where were you?"

I blink. "I was right here."

Miss Candace purses her lips.

Frankie puts her hands on her hips and frowns. Poking her skinny finger at me, she says, "No, you weren't." She points to the top of the rock. "You were up there."

Miss Candace's eyes follow Frankie's finger and widen. "Nora! I'm all for exploring, but that's dangerous. You could have fallen. I meant for you to investigate, not scale the memorials."

Frankie grabs Miss Candace by the elbow and gives her a very serious look before saying, "It's okay, Miss. Nora's a dear devil."

I snort and cover my mouth. "Do you mean to say daredevil, Frankie?"

Miss Candace's expression has relaxed somewhat. Now we're both looking down on Frankie, who's twisting and twirling the skirt of her dress with a dark, dark look of annoyance on her face.

"No, I meant what I said. I'm always meaning what I say. You're a dear devil. You're a Deere and you're a devil," she says, reaching out and pinching my arm hard.

"Ouch!" I pull my arm to my chest. "*You're* the little devil," I accuse her.

Miss Candace steps between us. "That's enough,

girls. Let's go get our tickets."

She holds Frankie's hand and keeps us separated until we get to the ticket booth at the entrance for the zoo.

I collapse on the bed, kick my shoes off, peel my stockings from my aching legs, and smile a smile that fills the entire room.

This day.

This day sucked me back to childhood. It reminded me of swinging pigtails and stuffed monsters. It took me to a time when a lion's roar was an excuse to cling closer to my mother's leg. When I had all the protection and didn't need any. I *needed* this day. And so did my sister.

I think it was Miss Candace's gift to us both. And even if we can't do it again, I'm going to store it away, wrap it, and then unwrap it. It will be a new gift every time I remember.

Frankie fell asleep on the subway ride home, and Miss Candace and I took turns carrying her. She's snoring loudly and sleeping soundly in the room next to mine.

Stars are fighting for a place in the sky against the clouds. I get into my nightdress quickly and kick my clothes into a pile by the door. My stomach gurgles happily from all the unhealthy food we ate today as I curl into bed. I'm holding this serene feeling close to my heart. Needing it to last a few more moments before it slips away, evaporates like steam and floats into the sky.

14

BEGINNING

Cotton candy sticks to my fingers. It winds around my hands, dyeing my skin pink. The smell is so deliciously artificial, so sweet and simple, that it brings tears to my eyes. I bring my nose to the fluffy cloud of sugar and inhale. The breath gets caught in my throat and I inhale again, startled by the feeling. I can't breathe. I'm choking. Choking on a pink cloud. I cough, putting my hands to my neck. I try to cough again, but nothing moves. I mouth *help me* soundlessly.

My eyes fly open.

Darkness presses down on me, and a weight leans against my windpipe. My eyes flick to the window. I imagine small rectangles of golden light shining in the night like invitations and witnesses, though only hollow, broken-glassed holes stare back at me. I reach for them, my arms shaking, a tear caught in the creases of my eyelids.

"You knew and you didn't tell me," he whispers darkly, dragging my oxygen-starved body from the bed, to my feet, and then releasing me. I stumble as I drag in a breath as quietly as I can. I can't wake Frankie. My knees knock as I brace myself against the wall. "You sad, pathetic little girl. Did you honestly think you could keep this from me?"

My head drops, my mind still catching up, still

caught in cotton candy. "Keep what from you?" I manage, my voice squeezed of sound like my windpipe now has a permanent kink in it.

I can barely see him in the dark room, but I hear the deep, frustrated breath in. It's wrapping around me like a snake constricting and squeezing. I feel the disgust in his footsteps, sharp, stabbing at the floorboards. He darts and grabs my arm, gripping so tightly that I know his handprint will be tattooed on my skin by tomorrow. "You come with me. Now!"

Like I have a choice.

He yanks hard. Every movement is punctuation to his hatred of me, to his unending anger that it was her and not me.

The hall is lit by a single lamp, and it flickers and dances happily against the wallpaper. My heart beats along with every flick and my body starts trapping itself against the pain. I fold in and in like a note passed around the classroom.

When I trip on the rug, he doesn't even stop, just tugs upwards on my arm hard. I bite down on my lip to stop from crying. He won't spare Frankie if she comes out of her room, and she won't be able to take another beating.

I can.

I can do this.

The study door is kicked open, and I'm swung into the room like a discarded doll. I land, palms flat on the hard floor, the polished boards reflecting the golden spines of hundreds of books. Books that educated a man, yet failed to teach him how to be one.

He looms over me, hands on his hips. His striped

pajamas and slippers softening him into a lie I can't believe, because there's a darkness in him, a clawing, scrabbling darkness deep within. He casts no shadow. He swallowed the unwilling likeness years ago, and now it coats every organ in his body with blackness.

"What were you trying to achieve?" he spits.

I shuffle backward on my bottom and prop myself up on my elbows, trying to think what to say, how to diffuse him. There's nothing.

"I wasn't trying to 'achieve' anything. I'm sorry, Father," I say. "I thought Mister Inkham would inform you of the changes."

His eyes widen at the name, but he doesn't respond to my words. He's stuck on the speech he wants to give. The punishment he's holding in his clenched fists.

"Do you think it's acceptable to lie to your father? To entertain strange men in my home when I'm not present?" he starts. Raking a hand through his ash-blond hair, he pauses. "I don't know why I bother…"

He takes a step toward me, our feet just touching, and I'm frozen. I want to run. I want to scream for help. Fight back. But I can't overpower him and I can't leave Frankie alone with him.

"Please, Father. I'm sorry. I didn't know what he was calling for until it was…"

A dark whir like a giant batwing comes at the side of my face with such force that my teeth feel as if they're escaping through my cheek. The words, the futile words, are knocked from my mouth. I should have learned by now. But I always try.

"Get up!" he snaps, nursing his hand like it hurt him too. I scramble to my feet and start for the door.

"Stop." He swiftly closes it and turns, his face shadowed in violence. "Get the belt from the desk drawer."

I abide.

What did Mr. Inkham say? *Survive, endure, for three more years…*

Disappear. Sink down, down, down. Go somewhere he can't find you. Hide.

I can do this. I have to.

"You're nothing like her," he says with the first crack. "You're of no value to me." The words are a cloud floating away as I cocoon myself, pull down the shutters, and wait for it to be over.

My back is broken. Split apart. I pull myself up from the study floor only to collapse back down again. The clock reads three am. My skin reads lashes of the belt. Wet blood cools my wounds. It's the smallest relief. Gathering my strength, I stand. I need to clean myself up before morning.

In the bathroom, I don't look at my reflection. I can't stand to see her. I can't argue with the fear, the sadness in her eyes. It shouldn't be like this. But it is. I sigh and dab at my back as best I can, tearing up my nightdress and throwing it in the bin by the sink.

As pink water runs down the bathtub drain, I think of his words. "You're of no value to me." He may think he has me pinned. That he has clipped my wings and broken my spirit, but he's wrong. My value is in my love for my sister. My value is growing with every day I live.

Drying myself, I dress in my day clothes, the cloth

sticking to my back. I grimace at the thought of changing at the end of the day.

Poking my head out of the door, I pad down the hall. I can hear him breathing heavily and when I get to the end, I can see one leg hanging over the armchair in the den. Stepping back, I head to their bedroom.

Each toe stamps out a message. I'm a million thoughts, but only one seems to be propelling me forward. I creep into my mother's room, the room they shared, and close the door behind me.

He doesn't come in here, coward that he is. This room is stuffed full of memories and stopped up like a cork in a bottle. Nothing new can escape.

My hand grazes the brass bed; a layer of dust floats up and sits on the moonbeams that stream through the window. I lightly kiss her personal items with my touch. They feel cold, dead. Cautiously, I move to her dresser, sliding open the stiff drawers and sifting through all her combs, clips, and brushes.

I touch each crystal, each shining silver and gold piece, until I have the one I want. It's my favorite. A simple comb with a small ship glued to it. The ship is dull pewter and it sits, not in waves, but on a cloud, diamanté stars clustered around the tops of the sails. I sigh as if to breathe life into those sails and clutch the small comb in my hand.

I came here to steal. To take something of hers, something that held *value* in his eyes, and remove it. It's a pointless crime really. He'll never know it's missing. But it gives me some very small sense of control, the size of the head of a pin, but it's something. I tuck the comb into my sleeve and turn to leave the room.

A small breeze tickles my legs, teasing the silk scarves hanging from the bedpost, and I pause.

I start to cycle through the possibilities and punishments that will occur if he finds the comb on me or in my room, and I shudder. I can't give him any more reason to hurt me. Tiptoeing back to the dresser, I pull the comb from my sleeve. It glints, almost winking at me under the white light of the moon. I do have one other option.

I creep across the floorboards to the window, each creak making me flinch, and ease up the sash, leaving enough room for me to ease my torso out. My torn-up back scrapes against the frame. I let out a whimper but as I lean out, curving to the side so I can clear the fire escape, the cool night air is a respite to my burning skin. My arm punches out, comb in hand, and I release it. As I hear it clink in the alley, it makes me smile. I don't search for it. I don't look down. I retract my arm, put my hand on my chest, and breathe a sigh of satisfaction. Maybe this way part of her will reach beyond the prison of these walls.

He's trying to rob me of my freedom, my confidence and self-respect. I'm just going to plain rob him.

15

TRUST AND FAIRY DUST

"I'm tired of sleeping in the alley, Kettle. We've earned a lot of bread this week. Wouldn't you like to take a hot shower and sleep in a real bed for once?" Kin asks after swallowing a large mouthful of hot dog and mustard-soaked bun. He's so loud when he eats that I can hear the cartoon-like gulp. He likes to think he has good manners, but years on the street have etched them out to more of a faded manual.

I shake my head as we walk, crossing my arms against the cold. "Is your head hollow? I swear, I can hear every chomp and chew even though your mouth is closed!"

Kin grins at me and opens his mouth to expose a mashed-up ball of food on his tongue. "Oh yuck!" He proceeds to keep his mouth open and in my face until I say, "Look, a hotel room costs as much as it would to feed us all for days. You know we can't." I try to connect with his annoyed eyes, although I'm finding the open mouth and the looks we're getting just a little distracting.

Kin finally shuts his yap and faces forward.

Suddenly, his arm shoots out and he shoves me, my shoulder hitting a poster with rosy-cheeked kids smiling over a plate of "Vitamin Donuts." I make a mental note to buy them next time I'm at the store.

I rub my shoulder and am about to punch him back when he says, "Sometimes, it's okay to be selfish. Even if it's just once in a blue moon." He's smiling. And I know he'll go along with what I say even if he doubts me. He's annoying, proud, and arrogant, but he's loyal.

"Maybe. But it's only one more night before we can go home," I chirp, hooking my fingers in my belt loops and increasing the pace. Each step is a strain on my aching muscles, but the promise of being home is enough for me to want to rush to a resting place and close my eyes so the next day can come.

The temperature of the air sinks as we walk. Streetlamps flicker on as the sun slips below the level of the high rises, glowing over the blackened stones of the tired buildings that always seem to appear wet even when it's not raining. We step around the crowd, picking our way through like we're playing a game of hopscotch. Kin whistles, and I try to pretend I'm not associated with him.

My bag is pressed close to my hip, the money sitting there like a hot coal that may burn a hole through the canvas. I nervously lay my palm on it and look ahead. Kin knocks his head toward the alley between the burned-out apartment building and the fancy brownstone again. I nod. It's a good spot because there aren't people watching us from above.

He scoots into the alley and heads to the dumpster we slept against last night. The dark in here is almost complete. Just a slice of waxy moonlight that doesn't want to lower itself to come into the alley shows at the two street ends. We curl into the shadows and sink to the hard ground.

Backs against the wall, we prop our elbows up on our knees and gaze at the small rectangle of sky above us.

"Would you like to live up there?" Kin starts, his voice airy and philosophical.

The back of my head rubs against the grimy wall. It doesn't much matter. I've accepted that on these days, I'm filthy. There's nothing I can do about it. Water tumbles past my ears as someone uses the bathroom in the brownstone. "Up there. What? In the sky?"

He slaps my knee and scoffs. "Don't be dumb. I mean, up there in one of those brownstones."

I ignore him, thinking about the sky. How it's temporary. It gives promise, but it also takes it away. That's why I like to be up there, flying through the air on a container… but it's also why I like to land.

Kin nudges me. "Hey! Are you even listening to me?"

My eyes droop heavily like they're hooked to weights. "Sorry, just tired… No. I don't think I would like to live up there. Besides, we're doing okay, aren't we?"

It's a lie. Of course I would like to live in a proper home, have security, food, warmth. But that's not my life. It's never going to be my life. This is better than where I was before and it's probably all I'm going to get, so it has to be enough for me. I sigh and smile. *It is.*

"One day," Kin whispers. "One day, I'll get up there. Maybe I'll marry that pretty little thing we bumped into at the cake shop…"

I chuckle quietly. "Don't you think she was a little young for you?" I tease, thinking of the lively redheaded girl who snapped his suspenders. She looked like she had firecrackers in her eyes and hands made for mischief. I liked her.

I get a clip over the head for that comment. "Don't be daft. I was talkin' about the blondie. The one with the rosy cheeks and haughty attitude."

I'm about to say, *I don't think she was haughty, just... protective and a little sad,* but I don't feel like sharing what I gained from our brief exchange. I shuffle closer to Kin for warmth as the night really starts to take hold and the stones bleed ice into my back. Let him have his fantasies. "Good luck with that!"

"Luck? I'm too handsome for luck to play any part in our inevitable union." His arms shoot out from his sides, and he starts gesticulating as he winds his way around to some sort of point. "You know what your problem is, Kettle? You..."

I 'mmhmm' and nod and let him prattle on for the next half hour about how I need to relax, I'm too responsible, I need a woman's touch, etc... etc, until he's run out of words. Slowly, his breathing calms and so does mine. I drape our coats over our legs, keep my bag tucked between us, and drift off to sleep.

My dreams are wishes. My nightmares are truths.

There's a song playing in the background. Strings and halos of music hum against rice-paper walls. Her voice is so soft and soothing. Her black hair pinned tightly to the nape of her neck balloons with weight and thickness. She scoops water from a bucket with a wooden ladle and pours it over my head. I shiver before it touches me but smile when I re-

alize it's warm and smells like jasmine. I hold my chubby two-year-old hands out in front of me, giggling as the water pools and pours away.

A sucking sound, like water pulled down the drain, overpowers the music. Rice paper tears. A man yells 'haji'. She grows smaller and smaller, her back rounded and smooth as a stone. She curls into a ball on the floor, bowing and apologizing as I stand there, dripping wet and crying. A towel is thrown around my shivering body and I am gathered up, pressed against the chest of an old man. An angry man. He says nothing but haji—shame—over and over again.

Distance grows and grows. Her cries come from behind a door, behind a car window, and they peter out as I'm driven away.

I wake suddenly. My mouth opens in a silent scream. I rub the back of my neck and feel sweat around my collar despite the cold. Kin snores beside me, rumbling like a dirty motor at my side.

It takes a moment to orient myself, to come back to the real world, the one I've been placed in by authoritative hands. My breath is quick, and I have to remind myself to calm down. These dreams feel like early memories, but they may not be. Maybe they are wishes. An invented past so my brain, my heart, can believe that at some point, someone wanted me.

I remind myself I'm not with *them* anymore. I'm not a prisoner. I am free.

The sound of a window being jimmied above grabs my attention, and I shuffle closer to the dumpster, trying to hide. My eyes cast up the wall of the brownstone.

The moonlight touches a thin, pale arm, outstretched in the air like it's just sampling the weather.

Fingers open like a star, and something drops at my feet. Dirty water splashes into my eyes, and I swallow a curse word. The arm withdraws and I hear the window close out the alley, the person returning to the warm safety of their home. I remain frozen, drips trailing down my face and onto my shirt, waiting for the person to come back, to retrieve what they have lost. I wait for at least an hour, rigid as the stones behind me. They never come back.

I snatch the item to me. In the dull light, I can see it's a comb and I can feel the bumps and ridges of the carvings as I run my finger over it. It's probably expensive. It's probably not something I should have.

I put it in my shirt pocket and rest back, wondering who would drop a treasure from the sky and why?

The dawn light crawls along the road and finally angles its way into the alley last. Kin's eyes blink open as the light hits them. He yawns and stretches, cracking his neck several times. I grit my teeth at the noise, which sounds like beads breaking under someone's foot on ceramic tiles.

"How'd you sleep?" he asks, although I know he's not overly interested.

"Oh, wonderfully!" I snarl sarcastically.

He slaps me on the back too hard, and I sprawl forward. I grab my shirt pocket, my hand over my heart to stop the comb from falling out. Whatever it is, wherever it came from, it feels like I shouldn't share it. It feels personal.

Kin throws back his head and laughs, his dark eyes

glinting in the weak light. "Sometimes I forget how tiny you are!" he mocks. Then he holds out his hand. "Gimme some money for breakfast. I assume you're going up there for your alone time." He rolls his eyes and smirks like I'm doing something elicit up there.

I frown and hand him a dollar bill. "Don't be long," I warn as I glance up at the fire escape clinging to the burned-out building.

He flips me off as he walks away.

I avoid the brownstone, wary of the person inside who might be looking for their comb and regretting their decision. Quickly, I clamber to the top of the building, the escape croaking quietly as I swing around each corner and scamper up. By the time I reach the top, my hands are blackened from the soot residue caused by the fire. I wipe my hands on my pants and sit cross-legged on the roof, the odd pigeon cooing behind me for company.

Pulling out the comb, I take a good look. I was wrong. It's not expensive. It's costume jewelry. I think maybe they were just throwing out something old they didn't want.

Despite that, I keep it. And I keep it to myself.

16

HIDE ME

Acool hand swipes the back of my neck. I quietly moan in pain when the hand lightly touches the skin between my shoulder blades and withdraws at my whimper.

"Frankie, let me sleep," I mumble into my pillow.

A throat clears, and I stiffen. "Nora, let me look at your face," he says with genuine concern, confusing but not unfamiliar.

I gingerly flip over, holding my weight up with my arms so my back doesn't touch the mattress. Bedraggled and exhausted, I look up at my father, the picture of regret and sympathy. He reaches out to touch my face, and I jerk away. "Don't," I whisper.

"I'm sorry," he says, tears made of poison slipping from his hazel eyes. "You understand, don't you? I lost control and even though it was partly your fault for keeping the truth from me, I'm the grown up. I should have handled it better…" He leans in, and I lean away. "Nora, it won't happen again."

I nod, my hair falling over the cheek that burns from the slap he gave me last night. "I understand," I answer blankly.

He takes my hair between his fingers and tries to tame it over the bruise. "You'll keep this between us, won't you? You know if you tell anyone, it will ruin our family, our reputation. We need to stick together. If not for ourselves, at least for Frances. Her needs are most important." He's squeezing my wrist too hard now, the charm on my bracelet digging into my skin.

"I'll do what I must, Father." My mouth feels twisted with anger, and his twitches with irritation as he releases my hand.

"Wear your hair how I showed you," he mutters.

"Yes, Father," I reply icily.

"So we understand each other?" he asks a little warily, but with anger ready to break the surface tension of his temperament as he steps back from my bed.

I can hear Miss Candace stomping up the stairs. I nod and as he turns his back to me, I whisper just loud enough for him to hear, "As long as I live, I will never understand you."

I can see his legs pushing into the floor, his anger radiating from his body in sharp, zigzagging lines, but he doesn't turn. He doesn't have time to hurt me right now.

I breathe out and take a deep, dragging breath in as he leaves, not realizing I'd been holding it.

I do my hair as I've been told, curling it over my cheek as best I can and using my mother's makeup to cover the rest. I don't change again. My clothes are stuck to my back, and I can't bear to pull them from my wounds.

17

KETTLE
GUARDIAN

We wait for the morning bustle to settle before heading home—a large bag of groceries in each arm. I am nervous and excited to get back there. It's like unwrapping a gift. Sometimes you're thrilled with what you find, other times you're disappointed and it's not what you wanted. I'm the unofficial leader of this group, but it's a free and easy kind of camp, which is how we like it. It cycles and changes all the time.

A few months ago, I came home and found Keeps had been added to the Kings. Her tiny, undernourished body had been found right in front of the train station. That was more like getting a gift you don't know what to do with.

I think back to the time when we returned to an empty tunnel and shudder. I've lost many family members to the cold, to the sharp reflexes of a beat cop, to hunger. I've had many people taken away from me too.

I pat the two packs of Vitamin Donuts in my bag, hoping they'll give Keep and the others a boost. Shaking my head, I touch my forehead to the top of the box. *I don't know what I'm doing.*

Kin strides ahead, his tall shoulders plowing through the crowd that's pouring out of the ground like a bulldozer made of people. He turns to me with a serious expression, bodies streaming around him like water, and jerks his head to the entrance.

I follow him down. When I see a cop, I keep my head down and my cap low. I'm better at sinking into the crowd than Kin. He's too proud, too unapologetic about who he is. I grunt as someone hits me in the chest as they're trying to exit. If I were Kin, the guy would have got a shove.

We pay for once. When there are fewer people, it's too hard to skip over unnoticed. And satisfyingly, we have money in our pockets today.

The attendant sees me struggling to push the bar across with my arms full and steps out of his glass box. I grip the bags tighter and try not to look guilty, still pressing my legs into the bars that won't budge. He squashes his hat down over unruly curls, looking like a fat clown and waddling like he's wearing clown shoes. In one hand, he holds a rolled-up newspaper. The headline brings acid creeping up my throat. "West meets East: JAs Still Struggling to Recover after Relocation."

A worn voice echoes in my head. *If they push us any further away, we will be walking into the sea.*

The attendant glances at my burdened arms and reaches out as I try again to push through. "Wait!" he cries out, his voice higher than I would have expected.

I get ready to drop the bags and run.

He holds out his free hand and plucks one bag from my arms. "Let me help you, young man." He takes the other bag, rests it on the stall, and uses a key to unjam the arm. When I get through, he hands the bags back to me.

I make the mistake of looking up into his eyes as he says, "Have a nice day…?" His tone rises at the end so it sounds like a question. Surprise registers on his face, and he glances down at the paper in his hand for a brief moment. Is he embarrassed? Scared? I can hardly tell, but he's definitely uncomfortable.

"Thank you, sir," I mumble as I quicken my pace.

Kin's waiting for me at the platform, his dark eyes shrouded in concern. "What happened up there?" he asks, covering his mouth as he speaks.

"Nothing that hasn't happened a thousand times before," I snap, thinking of all the curious looks and then the ones of unmasked hatred that have been thrown my way since I came here.

"It's because you look so guilty all the time, like you're ashamed of your face, your heritage…" he starts, and I kick him sharply in the shins.

"Not. Now." For once, he actually shuts his smirking mouth as we wait for the next train. He doesn't get it. I'm not like him. My only *heritage* is being passed, unwanted, from one place to another.

We count to three again. I'm not sure why we do it. Maybe we're steeling ourselves, taking a breath before we're crushed by needy arms and surrounded by curious, hungry faces. My eyes sweep left to right. The platform is deserted. We step through the door.

The familiar lap of dirty water around my ankles is comforting. I listen for other sounds—the giggles of the younger ones and the swearing and sighing from the older boys, but I can only hear Kin as he stomps loudly through the tunnel ahead of me.

We walk in silence until we're closer to the next door. Soft murmurs drip through the wooden panels, and I sigh with relief. Then I hear a sound I really don't want to—a wet cough.

Kin and I exchange a worried glance. His lips harden in anticipation. I transfer the bags to one arm, awkwardly balancing one on my uplifted knee, and knock the secret knock. Scuffling and voices pulse through the door, and I hear Krow say, "Keeps, they're here. It's going to be okay now."

More coughing followed by wheezing, gasping breaths. My heart backs away from my ribs. *She's sick. She can't be sick.*

Black braids sprout from under a pile of blankets. They jiggle slightly with her breathing. Kin drops his bags and calls the others away. He doesn't check on her. He's scared. He's avoiding.

I bend down near her head and watch. Her tiny, normally copper-toned face is a pale, sickly cream color. Her eyes are closed and she shivers in little bursts like someone's prodding her with a bare wire. I reach out and put the back of my hand to her forehead. It's a memory of something someone did to me long ago. She is burning hot.

Suddenly, she moans and brings her knees to her chest, slowly rolling back and forth. I stand and make eye contact with Kin, shaking my head. He frowns.

"Krow, how long has she been like this?" I ask, standing over the lanky, fourteen-year-old boy with crumbs stuck to his jaw.

"'Bout a day. We did like you said. Cleaned ourselves up and been scarce. She's been coughing since you left, but she wouldn't wake up yesterday. Well, not propply anyway."

He shoves more food in his mouth and chews noisily, his eyes vaguely concerned. I don't blame him. These kids are used to impermanence, illness, and death.

I scan the other boys, trying to think back to the desert, to the towers and red kits with white crosses on them. "Is anyone else feeling unwell?" I ask, scanning the faces. They all vehemently shake their heads. One holds up the box of vitamin donuts and it makes me feel like an idiot. What we have here doesn't work if we get sick.

I squat down and gently shake her shoulder. "Keeps, can you tell me what's wrong? Tell me what hurts?"

She opens one eye a slit and lifts her head from her pillow. A dark stain lies under her head. She whispers through dry lips at the same time as I say, "Your ear?"

"My ear."

I try to force her to drink some water, of which she splutters and swallows about a teaspoon. She grips her pillow like an anchor, her eyes rolling around in dizziness.

I run a hand through my hair and gesture for Kin to come over. "What do we do?" I ask. It's obvious she's really sick, too sick for us to handle on our own.

Kin hovers a few feet back. "We can't do anything." His voice wavers, not quite able to remain emotionless.

"She needs medicine or a doctor or something. I don't know. This is serious, man. She could die if we don't help her." My words spill out fast and frightened. I'm not doing a good job of staying calm, and the other kids are picking up on my panic. One of the younger ones, Kelpie, shuffles closer to me and wraps his arms around my waist.

"S'ok, Keeper, s'ok," he whispers, leaning down to pat her head.

I flinch. "Get away from her," I snap, my heart racing, my brain frantically searching through options. He whimpers, and I think he might cry. "I'm sorry, Kelpie. I just don't want you to get sick too." I pat his head and push him back to the opposite corner of the tunnel where Kin has the others penned in.

I lean down and whisper into Keep's good ear, the one that's not leaking a mixture of blood and pus. "I'll be right back," I say. "You rest." She nods her head and closes her eyes tightly, as if she could retreat to a dream world. A place where horrible things didn't happen to sweet little girls whose only crime was being born to the wrong mother at the wrong time in history.

I walk toward the wall at the back end of the tunnel like it might open up for me. The tumbledown bricks are dusty and sewn together with cobwebs. My shadow grows in front of candlelight until it's broken up over the blocked end of this cave like it's not even attached to my body. Leaning down, I quickly place the comb from my shirt pocket in the small, wooden box by my bed. I jump up and snap the box shut when Kin's hand touches my back.

"We have to take her back," he says sadly. "She

can't stay here."

I laugh bitterly, placing a kettle on our small gas burner. "She's not a broken toaster, Kin. She can't go *back*. There's no *back* to take her to. You're telling me to dump her in the street. Just say it."

I can't do it.

Kin flops onto my pile of cushions, a week's worth of dust pluming up around his legs. He's trying to meet my eyes, but I won't look at him.

"I can't do it, Kin. I'm sorry," I say, pouring the water into a bowl. Keep's coughing bounces off the walls as I quickly wash my face and arms. I move behind the curtain and change.

"You'll get caught," he warns darkly, resignedly, because he knows me. He knows I won't leave her to die.

I poke my head out from behind the curtain, buttoning my shirt as I talk. "She's just a kid. She deserves a chance to grow up."

Kin shrugs.

I pull a clean shirt, my best pants, and good shoes from an old suitcase and lay them on top. "I'll take her to a doctor downtown in the morning. It'll be fine. You can handle things on your own until I get back, can't you?"

His head is in his hands and he sighs deeply. "Sure. Sure thing, Kettle… until you get back."

In the middle of the night, Kelpie howls with fear. I light a match and touch it to the wick of my candle. Faces alight. Wide, tired eyes hone in on Kelpie and his terrified shrieking as he points at Keeps, whose body is rigid one second and flapping about uncontrollably the next.

I don't stall; I don't think. I just jump from my bed, scoop her up, and run.

18

THE START OF A FIRE

It's not hard to remember the first time. The moment my world turned clear upside down and was nailed to the floor is burned into my mind forever.

My mother was pregnant at the time. Frankie was a star in the sky, a twinkle of light that hadn't been brought to earth yet.

I was eight, I think. Eight years old and safe.

Hands seemed softer. They were used for sweeping sawdust or running through hair, filling in paperwork.

My father as a junior lawyer was a very different creature, but ambition drew a shadow out of him that lived with us from the moment he gained his cause.

"Let me help you, Christopher. Can I fill in some of these for you?" my mother asked softly.

A fist hit the desk. "You can't! You're just a housewife. You wouldn't even know what you were reading," my father snapped, his tone unusually frustrated.

I crept toward the study door, curiosity spurring me forward. My mother cleared her throat, her voice holding a bemused tone. "You forget where we met. I'm an educated woman. You shouldn't underestimate me, Christopher. I may surprise you."

Something like a growl emitted from the door. I peeked around the corner to see my father hunched over his desk and my mother standing behind him, her hands on his shoulders, her round belly an obstacle between her and the back of his chair. "Rebecca, leave me alone," my father groaned, his fingers absently rubbing the rim of a half glass of whiskey.

She moved her hand to his head, smoothing his hair down gently. The moment her fingers touched his hair, he flinched, jerkily throwing his shoulders back and spinning to face her. She stepped back, over balanced, but managed to catch her hand on the shelves to her left before she actually fell.

Composing herself, she said calmly, "Clearly, you're overwhelmed at the moment. But there's no need to behave like a child."

My own thoughts: *No child behaves this way.*

I watched him shudder, his whole body rippling with anger as he suddenly stood and came at her. She held firm, her own temper growing.

I scurried back, my back hitting the balustrade, my mouth open wide in fear. My father grasped at her cardigan with both hands, scrunching it in his fists and pulling her to him. She gasped, her feet bending over.

"Don't you ever..." he spat and threw her against the bookcase, several books falling to the ground around her. She made this horrible, hollow thudding sound, and her hand went straight for her stomach.

I wrapped my little fingers around the dark wooden posts behind me, and I screamed in shock at what I was seeing.

My mother's hand reached for me, and then she shook her head. "Nora, no," she whispered. Her words breathless, her face scrunched in pain. But I couldn't stop. He hurt her. She was still hurting. I could see on her face how worried she was for her baby. His head snapped to me, where I was wailing and thrashing like a bird caught in a net.

It was so fast. And I remember thinking it felt just like when he used to throw me over his shoulder and spin me round, laughing and tickling me. But it was stripped of those emotions. Sunlight turned to dark. Bare anger and terror held me now.

He charged, scooped me up, and ran with my limbs jangling and kicking to my bedroom, my mother's weak challenge melting in the air as we moved further away. He squeezed my wrist tightly, his breath coming in bursts like a bull. I just kept screaming, not understanding what he wanted me to do. Not really capable of understanding.

"Be quiet, child," he warned as he stormed down the hall. When I continued to shriek, he stopped walking, pulled me from his shoulder, and held me in front of him, gripping under my arms and shaking me while my legs dangled in the air. "For God's sake, will you *shut up*?"

I gulped, wearing a mask of tears. I quieted down as he shook me again. My lower lip between my teeth.

When he was satisfied I wouldn't scream any longer, he placed me down on the ground. My feet hit the rug, and my anger bloomed out from under me. I could see my mother dragging herself to the door, her eyes so sad.

He put his hands on his hips and stood over me. "Right. Are you going to stop being hysterical now?"

I glared up at him, doing everything wrong, doing all the things I've learned not to do since that day. "You hurt Mommy," I chastised. My mouth had barely closed over my words when his hand came at me, open palmed, a slap so hard I flew into the balustrade.

And that was the end of my childhood, the end of my safety.

I remember thinking that it wasn't happening. That the hot pain that spread from my ear to my mouth wasn't real. Because the trust I put in this man was supposed to be unbreakable. He loved me. He loved my mother. Yet he had just shattered everything with his furious hand.

I was silenced, my eyes darting to my mother, who didn't say a word. Her head dropped down in shame, and she wouldn't look at me. Shock stole any words, any tears I had left in me. He turned away from where I sat, legs sprawled like Raggedy Ann, one hand to my cheek like I could scrub it from my face.

The fury subsided as quickly as it had risen. He approached my mother and offered her a hand, which she took. Those joined hands burned a path for me I've been trying not to follow, but it still pulls me in.

There were 'I'm sorrys' and the phrase 'it will never happen again' and then, too quickly, acceptance. Promises that were just chalk scribbled over deep, deep scars. Promises he was incapable of keeping. But she wanted to believe him. She *loved* him.

Things happened that day that we weren't allowed to talk about ever again. But I'll never forget how tiny he was. How he didn't cry, but my mother made up for his silence with sobs of grief that seemed to want to explode from her chest. She broke. My mother cracked open like a china doll that toppled to the floor. Parts of her never recovered, growing dust under the hallway dresser.

We thought it would never end.

And then there was Frankie.

19

KETTLE

TOO MUCH

I tear down the tunnel, carrying Keeps. Her slack head almost hits the walls of the narrow space, and I have to turn sideways. She's not helping me at all, hanging from my arms like a wet blanket. Water splashes up my pants and soaks them from ankle to knee in black water. So quickly, she has gone from vibrating to limp. Her hands slap against my legs as I run.

She's popsicle sticks, glue and twine, clattering out of kilter.

I can't get caught running through the subway with a dead girl in my arms, and the selfishness of the thought scares me. When I press my head to her chest to check for life, her lungs rattle like there's a bag of marbles rolling around in her ribcage. Her heart still beats but I'm sure, even though I know nothing about such things, that it doesn't sound right. *Not right. Not like it should.*

It's not the same. It's not the same.

A wet cough, a cold night, and thin blankets. She didn't have a chance. Keeper will have a chance. I'll give her one. The words stab at me over and over. I'm trying to make up for something that wasn't my fault. I breathe in, standing behind the gappy wooden door, waiting. Feeling wooden myself.

I think of her little heart struggling to pump, the fever burning the blood in her veins, and I grip her tighter, my ear pressed to the splintered door. I listen for the next train and the flash of lights to pulse through the cracks. When the car pulls away, I quickly exit. The door swings open and stays ajar. Kin's loud footsteps thud from the opening, and his head appears through the dark. He gives me a stern yet resigned look.

"Be careful, brother," he utters as he pulls the door closed.

Careful. I want to laugh.

It's so late that there's no one around except beggars and bugs, neither of which care about what I'm doing. It also means no doctor's practice will be open. It takes me two seconds to decide that I'll have to take her to the hospital.

I can't believe I'm going to do this.

I curse when I look down at my bare feet and my toes purpling from cold, but there's no time to go back and change. I'm not even wearing a coat. The next car pulls up, and I jump on. It slides over the tracks, and I almost lose my balance. Locking my knees, I try to hold strong. I don't want to sit. I want to be ready to run when the doors open again. Keeps shudders in my arms. Her usually olive face is so pale, individual hairs sticking to her forehead like drawn-on wrinkles.

A clearing cough from the only other passenger makes me look up. An older guy sits with a bottle in one hand and a grimace on his face. He stares at me with uncomprehending eyes, clearly drunk, as I stand rigidly by the door. I lean against the pole to steady myself and am ready to bolt as soon as it glides open.

Something tickles my arm and I flinch. The braid

I did, that she kept in for five days, has turned her straight black hair curly. It brushes over my arm with the rhythm of the train. She breathes slower now, air creeping lethargically into her mouth. I don't like it at all. I curse again, and the drunk looks up at me from under his bushy, gray eyebrows.

I practice what I'm going to say when I get there. *I'm her brother. I don't know her social security number; I'm home from boarding school and was babysitting while my parents went away for the weekend.* Keeps is ten years old. No. She'll need a new name. I think of her cat-like, green eyes. Cat. Cate… I pluck the only American surname I can think of from the air—Jackson. Cate Jackson.

The subway door opens and I sprint up the steps, nearly slipping as I reach the top. I'm scared.

I don't want this to be my fault. I knew she was sick and I left her alone for days.

It's my fault.

The sleepy attendant doesn't bother to stop me when I climb awkwardly over the barrier, resting Keep's butt on the metal box while I move through. As I stumble up the incline, the cool air plummets further as I hit the sidewalk. I try to wrap my arms around her tighter. The instinct to keep her warm is so strong despite the fact that she feels like the surface of the sun right now. She moans. *Good. She's alive.*

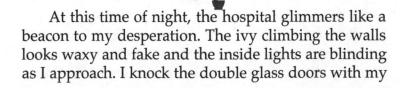

At this time of night, the hospital glimmers like a beacon to my desperation. The ivy climbing the walls looks waxy and fake and the inside lights are blinding as I approach. I knock the double glass doors with my shoulder and stumble into the large reception area, feeling ready to scream.

All eyes are on me. A nurse hurries toward us, her white dress and white stockings shining too brightly under the lights. Her mouth moves and her hands flutter in front of my eyes, but I can't seem to hear her. I shake my head slowly and narrow my eyes as orders pour from the nurse's lips and a bed on wheels appears. Her pale hands shoot out, and Keeps is ripped from my willing arms. They lay her dirty, ragged body down on crisp white sheets and I watch as she's wheeled away from me, unable to do anything. Feeling only guilty relief.

A hand goes to my shoulder, and I try to focus, to listen. "Your sister is very ill. We should call your parents," says the short, blonde nurse. She reminds me of a clothes peg doll, short and sturdy looking.

I don't answer—just stare at her in shock.

I don't know what to do.

I shake my head. *They've* got her now.

"Young man." She shakes me gently. I feel so insubstantial that she could probably knock me over with a flick of her finger. "Do you have a number where we can reach your parents?"

She doesn't have any parents. I was the closest thing… and now…

"I… um…" My hands are outstretched like she's still in my arms. They feel heavy with her lost weight.

She pats my arms and forces them down to my side with some effort. Gesturing to the men's bathroom sign, she says, "Why don't you go splash some water on your face, take a few deep breaths, and then come find me. We've taken her to bed," she glances down at her clipboard, "eighteen in Emergency."

My voice cracks when I say, "Okay… you're going to take care of her, right? She's going to be okay?"

She presses the clipboard to her flat chest and crosses her arms over the top. "This is the best hospital in the state. You did the right thing bringing her here. Don't worry, we will do everything we can to help her." The *right* thing. I try to wear those words because it doesn't feel like the *right thing*. Everything about this feels wrong. "Your parents will be very proud of you."

I pull back from the strange expression that wants to show on my face. The orphan one. The one that reads—parents, what parents? And I enter the bathroom.

Mechanically, I do what the nurse advised. I splash water on my face, take a few deep breaths, and they crush me with guilt. I'm going to have to leave her behind. I can't stay here. I can't answer the questions they're going to ask.

I'm sorry, Keeper. I'm sorry I couldn't look after you.

After a few minutes, I peek out the door and see the nurse is still waiting for me, tapping her foot impatiently and starting to look suspicious. I let the door close, rake my hand through my hair, and look for a way out.

The window is old, rusted, and I push it open easily, small flakes of old paint falling into the basin I'm standing on. I crawl out, feet first, and drop down to the icy pavement like a bomb, sending splinters of pain through my heels. There's something like a tear in my eye, but it never falls.

I blink up at the sky, think of flying, and follow the stars home, each one feeling like a spurred weight pressing into my back.

20
THE LIGHT

Six Months Later

The ache of missing her is slowly being replaced with bruises. And each bruise adds a layer of armor. My skin is thickening. I'm a lizard that can't shed its skin. I just keep growing more scales as times goes by. Soon, I shall be swallowed by them.

Since she died, I have released a comb, a necklace, a silk scarf, a pair of stockings, one high-heeled shoe, a lipstick, two costume rings, three hairclips, and a pair of riding pants into the alley. And each time, I feel a little less human. I feel closer to her, though, because I'm becoming a ghost, someone floating in Neverland.

Two and a half years is too long.

It's after dinner. A rare one where we ate together as a 'family'.

The phone rings. My father gives us a get-out-of-here look, and Frankie and I retreat to the playroom.

It starts out as low tones and mumbles but as minutes pass, he becomes aggravated. I smile as I watch Frankie pulling the hair from one of her dolls. This one isn't about me. Hopefully, he'll get out his aggression during this phone call and have no energy to hunt me down later.

I miss the sky. I want to get out there tonight, but he doesn't sleep like he used to... before. It's harder to sneak out.

"We always knew it was wrong, Karl. Hell, most people knew, but they were too afraid to say anything," I hear him shouting to his partner. "Now that we have a chance to make amends, I'm not changing my mind." He pauses while Karl talks and when he replies, his tone is terse and impatient. "We have a case. They are American citizens. Their only crime is the color of their skin... Yes, I know. But attitudes are changing and even if they weren't, wrong is wrong. They deserve compensation. For God's sake, man. It's been over seven years; the war is over. Besides, many JAs fought for our country, died for our country. I won't let it go... No, I don't agree... It's time for the American government to make it right... No, I don't care how long it takes... Yes, I understand there are these so-called Lost Children to track down too; damn papers have to make a catch-phrase out of everything... I would have run away too if my future had been so uncertain..."

I listen to my father's passionate argument. It is admirable and confusing.

"Go back West? Many of them don't want to or can't, and I don't blame them. They have nothing to go back to... Given a small grant, these hardworking people would contribute greatly to the community. In fact, they already are. Imagine what they could achieve given the chance. You can't strip a person of everything and then expect them to just get on with life like nothing has changed... Look Karl, I don't think most Americans feel that way anymore. Yes, I can meet you though I see no point... Fine, see you in ten minutes."

The phone clangs down violently, and he stomps down the stairs.

Frankie is chewing on her doll's hair now and looks at me with curious, big eyes, her lashes looking like the fraying end of an ear of corn. Delicate and the lightest brown. "What's Deddy talking about? What's a Jay Ay?" she asks, blinking innocently. "What does he mean by Lost Children?"

My heart clenches in my chest and my eyes fly to the window, hoping an answer will be tapped out in the rain pattering on the pane. "JA means Japanese American. During the war, Japanese Americans on the West Coast were put in camps. Lost Children are what the papers are calling the children whose parents passed away, couldn't care for them any longer, or they ran away," I say, pulling her into my lap. She's all sharp angles and anxious bones. She lays her head against my chest, her ear pressed to my collarbone, which is still healing. I breathe in sharply at the pain.

"Are we Lost Children because we don't have a Mommy anymore?" she naively asks.

Yes.

I shake my head. "No, darling, it's not quite the same."

"We've got Deddy," she says so very sadly with a small pale finger on her nose, and I wonder how much she comprehends and senses. Probably more than I give her credit for. More than I want.

I tap her nose too and watch her grow cross-eyed. "Yes. But we also have each other," I whisper, trying to pull her closer but it's like trying to pin down a spider.

She bats at my finger and wiggles in my lap like an eel, kicking her legs for a while, then she squirms out of my grasp. "Love you, Nora Snora." She giggles.

I throw a cushion at the back of her ever-swaying head as she runs across the rug. Love doesn't even cover it.

21

WHAT HAPPENED?

Kelpie kicks my head in his sleep. His long toenails scrape across my face and I grab his ankles together in one hand, trying to swing him around so we're not laying head to toe. Ever since Keeps got sick, he somehow finds his way over to my bed at night. It scared everyone. Even Kin keeps a closer eye on the boys than he used to. *I* even bought a thermometer and some cough syrup. Thankfully no one's been sick, but every time I hear a sniffle or a cough, I jerk out of bed like Count Dracula awakening from his eternal sleep or so Kin tells me.

I pull back the covers and scoop Kelpie up, picking my way over the others and laying him down in his little bed. His eyes flutter open briefly and he whispers, "You going, Kettle?" His young face, still slightly chubby, is smudged with dirt, his blond curls flattened on one side from sleep.

I smooth my hair from my forehead and try to smile. Poor kid, he's younger than Keeps was… *is*… damn it! I take a deep breath and say, "Not til' morning, Kelpie." I go to pat his head but pull back, putting my hand in my pocket. "Get some sleep, kid." He lies down and closes his eyes, his two hands pinching the blanket like bird claws, up under his chin.

My fingers fold over the necklace nestled in my

pocket, the smooth stone cold on my skin. I've stopped wondering why. I don't question. I just catch the things that fall from the window. I want to believe they are for me. I want to think that something good can happen to someone like me. I shake my head as I collapse back on my bed. Checking that everyone's sleeping, I pull it from my pocket, swinging it back and forth between my pulled-up legs. The stone glints darkly, the spikes that radiate out from the center making it look like a black star. I unlock the padlock, lift the lid of my chest just slightly, and then change my mind, slipping it back into my pocket. This one has value.

Morning comes and I haven't slept a wink. Water swashes across from me as Kin washes himself with a bucket of water behind a curtain. I stand, rubbing my eyes and stretching. "Kin, I'm going to meet you at the docks," I say, slipping on shoes and darting out the door before anyone can stop me. On the way out, I ruffle Kelpie's hair. He gives me a gappy grin, his hair standing up stiffly where I just rustled it. *Toothbrushes. I need to check that everyone has toothbrushes.*

I need answers.

I jog up the steps, warm, smelly air hitting me as soon as I touch the pavement. Already the swelter has started to bake the fruit in the stalls and warm the trash in the overflowing cans that line the street. I take shallow breaths, pull my cap over my eyes, and hug the shadows the colorful awnings create.

A few blocks and my eyes find the sign I'm searching for—*Paul's Pawn Shopp*. I think there used to be an e on the end of shopp, but now it just looks like Paul can't spell or has a stutter. I grip the necklace in my pocket and open the door, the bell sounding sickly as I enter.

Paul is sitting on a high stool behind the counter, his grubby face absorbed in a magazine that's not really for public viewing. When I come to the counter, he ignores me and sweeps another page over, licking his finger as he turns it. I swallow my disgust and pull the chain from my pocket, letting it drop to the glass cabinet noisily to startle him from his 'reading'.

Gently laying the magazine across his lap like it's made of silk and lace, he gives me a skeptical look. He's a jellyfish, parts of his cheeks, chin, and brow bulging out and wobbling. He's wearing only a vest with suspenders and the smell coming from his armpits is absolutely horrendous.

"Hello, young man," he says in a most genteel and sophisticated tone, one so at odds with his appearance that I take a step back from the counter in surprise. He bows his head, folds the corner of the magazine down to mark his place, and puts it under the counter. "How can I help you?"

I shift from foot to foot as the swinging metal fans move back and forth like judges shaking their heads at me. Then I stare down at the necklace and remind myself why I'm here. "How much for this?" I ask, jamming some confidence into my voice.

He grasps at it with chubby fingers smudged with ink, and other things I'm trying super hard not to think about, and holds it up between us. Below, encased in glass, watches, jewelry, and lighters with personal inscriptions glare at me dully, trapped and separated from their owners. "Very beautiful piece. Quite old, I'd say. A family heirloom?" he asks me, even though I'm sure he knows it's not mine and probably suspects I stole it.

I nod.

He gently lays it down, the chain of the necklace coiling over the stone like a protective snake. He pulls a notepad from the register and writes down a number. Pushing it across the counter, he waits for an answer as the fans hum and blow body odor around the 'shopp'. I look at the note. It's less than it's worth, but I don't have time to bargain. So I take what is offered.

As I'm leaving, Paul shouts, "Young man, if you have any other family treasures you are willing to part with, please consider my business in the future."

I slip out the door, the heat crashing down on me like a wave, turning back as it closes. "Sorry, that was all I had." He's already picked up his magazine and is re-engrossed. I shove the cash in my pocket and run toward the hospital.

She's like a drawing coming to life in my head, the sharp lines of her face and body, her lack of height and carefully curled blonde hair. She was kind to me that night, and I'm hoping she will be again.

I trip over the curb and onto the lawn in front of the hospital. My hands hit the cool grass that's just been watered, and I take a moment to compose myself. When I lift my head, wheelchair wheels are in front of my face and a nurse stares down at me impatiently.

"Excuse me," she snaps as she pushes a wilting old lady, who's covered in lacy shawls with large, fancy rings barely clinging on to her crusty fingers.

I stand swiftly and mutter, "Sorry, ma'am." I take my cap off and pat down my black, spiky hair. "Sister," I say, reading the title on her name tag. "I wonder if you could help me? I'm looking for a nurse."

She rolls her eyes and makes a point of landing her gaze on the ten other nurses and sisters strolling around on the lawn and paths as they smoke on their breaks or walk patients. "Do you have her name?" she asks, locking the wheelchair and putting her hands disapprovingly on her hips. She's scrutinizing my face as many do. Trying to work me out. I let her eyes roam over my smooth features, my darker-than-normal skin. When she comes to my blue eyes, she stops. I smile, and she doubtfully returns it.

"Regretfully, I don't have a name," I say, shaking my head. I go on to describe the woman as I remember her. The sister listens patiently, rocking the old lady back and forth in her chair like she's settling a baby. "She was about this tall," I say, holding my hand up to my shoulder. "She had short, blonde hair curled under, you know, like a lady." The sister's mouth twitches at that. "She would have been about thirty years old, and um, she was definitely a nurse, not a sister, er, Sister. She was a nice lady. Kind."

"I think you're talking about Sue," she replies after tapping her chin a few times. Her gray eyes crinkle as she searches her memories, and the old woman who seems more like a dressing table groans or snores quietly. "She got married a few months back. Her name is

Sue Alvarez now. Susan Grace Alvarez."

"Alvarez?" I blurt before I can stop myself.

The sister gives me a stern look and shakes her finger at me. "You, of all people, should understand that the world is changing." The old lady snorts in her chair, startled by the louder tone the sister has just used.

I want to say a lot of things in reply, but I hold my tongue. It's changing, but it's too late for me. For Keeps and the others. We're the leftovers of a war everyone wants to forget. People don't want to be reminded. I replace my cap and thank the sister. My watch says I'm not going to make it to the docks in time to get through the gate. Kin is going to kill me.

I pull my cap low again. The sister can say what she wants. People still look at me like they're not sure whether to feel sorry for me or run from me. I am half of *them*, all of me, but the only half they see is the enemy. I scrunch my sweaty hands around the money in my pocket and go get change for the payphone.

When I ask for Susan Grace Alvarez's number, it's given straight away. The world has changed, but not that much and not all at once. There was only one person with her name in the whole directory. I dial the number with shaky fingers, trying to plot in my head what I'll say. When the last number rotates back to its place, it only rings three times before a female voice answers, "Hello, Sue speaking."

I breathe in and hold. "Hello?" she says again.

"Hello, Mrs. Alvarez. I was wondering if I could ask you about a patient who you treated about six months ago." I pause. "Her name was, um, is, Miyoko Tanaka. She also went by the nickname Keeper."

The phone line sounds dead, just a light humming rubs at my ears.

"Hmmm. Young girl, right?" Sue asks, seemingly unfazed by the name.

My heart picks up a little, the excitement showing in my voice. "Yes. About ten years old. She came in with a fever, and a really bad ear infection. I just want to know that she's all right."

I hear a fingernail tapping on wood. Click, click, click. "If you care about her welfare, why did you leave her at the hospital all on her own, young man?"

I gulp. The guilt I've felt over the last six months builds in my throat. "I was scared," I admit as I look up and down the deserted street, afraid of prying ears.

A sigh, deep and resigned, wraps its way through the cord and up to the plastic receiver. "You know, you're lucky I didn't send the police after you," she says, though I sense sympathy in her tone. "I do remember her. I remember you as well. There is help, assistance, for people like you."

Oh, I got the $25 dollars they handed out to each of us when we were released, I think bitterly.

"Things are changing. You wouldn't have to go back to one of those places." The lecture brings up a guard like a toothy tire puncture in the road.

I grip the receiver harder and try not to bash it against the phone box walls. "If you could please just tell me what happened to her. I have money. I can pay you for the information," I beg.

I hear papers rustling and her voice sounds a little

more guarded than it did a few moments ago. "Why don't you come here and I'll tell you what I know?" I imagine she's looking for the number to call, the one that summons people who take me somewhere 'for my own protection'.

I glance around again, feeling paranoid, and then I whisper into the phone, "My mother has been gone a long time now, and I have no father. I'm not lost like they're saying in the papers. No family is looking for me. I'm not someone you can save. It's too late for me. But Keeps, I mean, Miyoko, was my friend." Was she more? A little sister? Maybe. "I just want to know that she's okay. Please."

Another loud sigh. "She was in for a while but recovered very well. When she was healthy, she was transferred. They didn't take her back to one of those places, if that's what you're worried about. They don't do that anymore." She talks to me like I'm seven and don't understand that part of our history is over. She doesn't get that for someone like me, the options have always been narrower than the space between two-dollar bills in a miser's pocket. "Miyoko went to a home, a normal orphanage. I think it's called Mason House. She was very sweet. I'm sure she's been adopted by now. If you wanted to see her, I could…"

I hang up the phone. I know where Mason House is and I turn on my heel, heading straight for the subway.

22

OLD FRIEND, ANOTHER LIFE

I almost forgot I had friends before. When I was ripped from school, I was also torn from the hands of girls and boys I'd grown to like. I wouldn't say we were real close. Besides Frankie, I can't be close to anyone. Secrets get in the way of friendship. They're like a swinging knife always ready to sever ties. It's just too hard.

My hand shakes a little as I write the lesson in my notebook. Miss Candace gave us homework this afternoon, which needs to be completed by tomorrow morning. Frankie is supposed to draw a picture of her favorite animal and write a description, but she's distracted by… well… everything.

My fingers are sore from being crushed together in his iron grip. They shake even more when I think about my knuckles grating against each other until I felt sure the skin would break open. He's getting careless. Doing things I can't hide so easily. It's like, now she's gone, he doesn't care anymore. I stretch my fingers and wonder, *Does he want to get caught?* But I dismiss the thought quickly. It's more that he doesn't think he *will* get caught.

"Frankie. Sit down and do your homework," I say, trying to sound stern. Her eyes switch directions every second and then she leans over her chair and hangs upside down, her long, red hair swinging like a flaming curtain.

"What's my favorite animal?" she asks, still hanging over her chair, which is dangerously close to tipping. She coughs once and giggles as she takes her hair in her hands and pulls it into pigtails, clasped by her freckled fists.

My pencil pushes too hard into the paper, and the lead breaks. I roll my eyes, sighing. "I don't know. How about a monkey? They like hanging upside down. Or maybe the orangutan?" I point at her face, drawing circles in the air with my blunt pencil. "You've got the same hair."

Frowning, she flips back up. She drives me mad by sitting on the edge of her chair, just one cheek of her backside touching the seat. "You tink I look like a monkey?" she says, breath whistling through the gaps between her teeth.

I pause, tapping my pencil to my lips, shaking off my irritation and trying to remember that she's only seven. "You *are* a monkey. Didn't they tell you? You were adopted from a jungle nursery when you were a baby."

She stops lurching around in her chair and thinks about what I've just said.

Crossing her arms, she pouts and says, "That's not… I'm not… You're mean."

I laugh. "Monkey's don't think people are mean. They don't have the mental capacity for it."

Frankie stands up on her chair, her lips set crooked in what I think is her attempt to look angry. "I bet they do. I bet if they saw you, they'd have the caper-osity to know how mean you are." She pulls her hair in front of her eyes and sulks, sniffing and sighing dramatically.

I grab her pencil, write one more word, and then grasp her shoulders, pulling her to me. "Oh Frankie, I'm sorry. You don't look like a monkey. You're beautiful. Really."

She frowns for a moment longer and then says, "Deddy thinks I'm beautiful. He says I look just like Mommy, doesn't he?"

I nod, putting my chin on her head. "Mhm. Yes, he does." Little creepy shivers crawl up my arms.

The doorbells rings, and I release Frankie.

"Miss Deere!" Marie shouts from the foyer. "There's someone here to see you... It's a young man," she says, her voice peaking at the end.

I raise my eyebrows and stand up quickly. Straightening my clothes, I turn to leave but Frankie's hand is crumpling a large section of my skirt. "Can I come with you, pleeeeease?"

I shake my head and pull her fist from my clothes like I'm squeezing out the water from the end of a towel. "No, you need to finish your homework."

She theatrically falls to her stomach, burying her face in the rug as I shut the door of the playroom, and I walk downstairs to the rhythm of her thumping the floor with what I suspect is her chair.

I was expecting Mr. Inkham or perhaps a delivery boy, but standing before me is a boy I knew in another life. He ripples like a mirage in my vision as he leans against the doorframe and smirks at me, and I can't help but smile back. "Noraaaa Deere," he says, drawing the 'a' part of my name out.

"Robbie," I say warily. "What are you doing here?" I'm trying hard not to smile too broadly, my hands gripping the back of my skirt tightly to stop myself from throwing my arms around his neck and confessing everything.

"I've missed you," he states simply, taking a few steps into the foyer. "You know I thought you were just taking some time after your mother..." He makes an uncomfortable face. "But then you just disappeared."

I gaze at my sensibly clad feet. "Father pulled me out of school."

At the mention of my father, he grimaces. "Figures."

I'm suddenly very aware that Marie is just in the other room and Frankie is upstairs. Marie will tell my father anything she hears; she's almost as scared of him as I am. I lurch toward Robbie and grab his arm, dragging him out the door. "I need fresh air. Would you like to take a walk with me?" I ask under my breath.

He doesn't get a chance to answer before I've grabbed my coat and pulled him out the door into the common area, shouting out as the door closes, "Marie, I'll be back in half an hour. Frankie's upstairs doing her homework."

A neighbor turns her head just slightly in our direction as she pretends to sift through her mail. I walk quickly, dragging him with me as I push through the glass doors and outside.

Robbie turns his head to me, his brown eyes bright and untarnished. "Is that all I get? You're not going to explain where you've been, what you've been doing all this time?" he asks, teasing.

"That's all you get," I say between my anxious teeth.

I step up onto the stone barrier and turn. "Ready?" I say with a grin.

He steps up onto the barrier on the other side, arms out, pretending to be unsteady for a minute before straightening and winking at me. "Ready."

We both run down the thick, brick walls at the same time. When I get to the bottom, I push up, my face turning from warm to cool as I sail through the air, legs straining. I land heavily but keep my feet, teetering just on the edge of the curb like a bird on a wire. I whip my head to my left to see where Robbie landed and laugh. "Beat you!"

He's standing like a gymnast, arms out in front for balance, a good foot behind my line. He grimaces. "It's not a fair comparison. You're much lighter than me." He flicks a hand in my direction. "You're more aerodynamic or something."

I link my arm in his. "Excuses, excuses."

He tenses his arm like he's showing off his muscles, which makes me quirk an eyebrow at him.

"What?" he asks, not very innocently.

I love this lightness. I wish it would last.

The clouds are thickening overhead. They are lighter than air, yet look like you could grab handfuls and stuff them in your pockets.

He's still staring at me, waiting for an answer. I shrug. "Nothing. C'mon."

We quickly cut across the street and head to the small park on the corner. It's late afternoon and the traffic is building in the streets. Robbie takes my hand as we pass through the iron gate and into the cool, green garden.

I search for a private place and pull him silently into a group of bushy trees that grow in a secretive circle. He curses as a branch scratches his face.

"Nora, you're being awfully strange," he remarks.

I yank him through the trees, and he stumbles into the clearing. He stands before me, kind eyes, roundish face, and cap sitting sideways. He slides the hat from his head and holds it in both hands. I lean back, unable to control myself any longer, and launch at him, wrapping my arms around his neck and holding him close. The cap falls to the ground, and he awkwardly pats me on the back.

His voice breaks a little when he asks, "What's going on with you?"

I release him and a tear at the same time. "Nothing..." *Everything.* "Nothing."

He takes my wrists in his hands and looks down at me. We used to be the same height, but now he's a few inches taller. "Nora, we've been friends for years."

Have we?

"I know when something's up," he goes on.

Do you?

His eyes are pinched with regret. "I'm sorry I didn't come sooner. Honestly, I just kept thinking you'd be back and when you didn't appear in class that day, I'd think, *Tomorrow, tomorrow, she'll be sitting in her chair and I'll poke her in the back with a pencil. It'll all be like it was.*" He slams his hands in his pockets and glares at the ground. "But it's not, is it?"

"No."

We've always skirted around the edge of the truth. Our friendship was only as close as I would allow it. So,

bruises were a barricade, and slow and painful movements were a flag we folded meticulously and placed
in a drawer. I've always felt guilty about lying, but I
was protecting him. My father is not shy of revenge.
He's threatened my friends before. I look at Robbie's
old clothing, the clean but frayed look to them. Robbie
is a scholarship student. My father could easily crush
him and his family.

"Are you going to tell me what's going on?" he
asks, though he knows the answer.

I really want to. I want to throw this burden from
my back. "I'm sorry, but I can't."

His eyes flick to the bushes, shaking with a breeze
and washing out our voices, and then back to me. Pulling out an old-fashioned pocket watch from his coat,
he taps it. "So how much time do we have?"

I bring his palm and the watch closer to my face
and watch the minute hand vibrate, its arm pointed
like the sting of a bee. "Probably about twenty minutes
now."

He pulls my arm down and brings me to sit down
in the slightly damp grass. Above, a neat circle of sky
changes constantly as clouds tumble through and disappear, dragging new ones behind them. I sigh, sending a puff of sadness and loneliness up to join them.

Robbie folds one arm under his head and looks up.
I lie down next to him, and we watch the blue circle.

His finger grazes my hip in a comforting way, just
a small touch to let me know he's here and that he still
cares about me. We talk about nothing. Nothing is exactly what I need. He doesn't push for answers. I think
maybe he's as scared of the truth as I am to tell it.

"I think Donna's glad you're gone." I elbow him in the ribs. "Now she can campaign for worst singing voice unopposed."

I snort and roll onto my side to face him. Parts of my cream skirt are tinged green but since Mother's been gone, no one seems to care about the state of my dress. "I miss her pointy face."

"Oh, she's not that bad..." he says quietly, and I sense the beginnings of a crush growing in his big heart.

"Oh, really?" I tease, "You and Donna? You going to take her to the Summer Fling?" I make a strange face.

He sits up, straightens his shoulders, and says, "Why not? I mean, I might as well."

I blow a stray hair from my eyes and purse my lips. "Well, that's romantic. Make sure you ask her like that. Hey Donna, you might as well go with me to the dance."

He shrugs, ignoring my teasing. "Do you think you'll ever come back? You know, for senior year? What about college?"

Suddenly, the grass looks awfully interesting. I stare down at it and pick at the blades, trying to pull the newer, paler shoots from the middle of tough outer leaves and squishing them between my fingers. It releases a sweet, fresh smell. "It's not up to me. So I doubt it."

"Right." He hangs his head and counts the blades of grass with me. "You know, you could..." He stops midsentence and pulls out his watch, both of us avoiding all the things we know, but don't want to say.

"I can't leave Frankie." I answer the question he didn't even ask.

He points at the watch. I've let too much time pass. "You better get back, before…" Always missing words in our conversations.

We stand together and quickly hug.

"I'll try and see you again soon," he promises, with flurries of doubt in his voice. I fear our friendship will be like the passing clouds overhead. We can't hang on, can't fight the wind that wants to push us apart.

I clap a hand on his shoulder and look into his eyes. Sharp, short little eyelashes blink at me. "It's okay if you can't, Robbie," I carefully say.

Annoyance flashes across his face for a moment, and I know he feels helpless. It's how I feel too. I want to tell him there is hope, that years from now things will change and we might be able to be friends again, but I don't. It's not good to feed him something he may never get to taste. I want him to go live his life.

We walk through the break in the trees, and real life slaps us in the face. Car horns beep and people move, creating noise only masses of material rubbing against material and bodies bumping into bodies can make. The low sunlight spreads over the city in planes of golden light, skating between the buildings and making the craziness kind of beautiful. I blink and wonder what my life would be like if I was in it. A part of it. But I'm not.

So when Robbie asks, "Will you stay in touch?"

All I can say is, "I'll try."

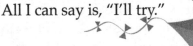

He walks me back to the building door, but I don't ask him in. In these walls are my secrets. I don't want them sinking their claws into him. He tips his hat at me and walks away. If he turns back to look at me one last time, I don't see it because I can't return to that life. I keep my eyes forward and twist the doorknob, pushing my way reluctantly back inside like I'm pressing against the side of a balloon.

A solid lump of heavy fabric and bosoms hits me in the chest as I try to push my way in.

Marie's eyes are wide, her breaths coming fast as she quickly mutters, "I've been dismissed early, Miss Nora." And she shoves me aside and flies down the steps without a backward glance.

Sounds.

I've heard that smell is the stronger sense. The one that can coax memories from a hazy brain. For me, it's sounds. Sounds wrap around my throat and strangle me. Sounds warn like a foghorn in the night. Sounds are all you can sense when your eyes are closed against the fists coming at you and you don't want to see the malevolent expression hovering over your defenseless body.

A cry full of drawn-in breath and tinged with shocked fear mixes with the heavy, purposeful thud of footsteps storming across the ceiling. My eyes follow the noise. My brain has already forced my body into a straight line across the tiles, and I climb the stairs one, two, three at a time.

I'll get there. I'll get there.
I'll get there in time.

23

BETTER OFF

Mason House looks like a grand old mansion. The windows are set in ancient-looking stones that crumble around the edges, yet they still have a neatness to them. The stairs are swept of leaves and a shiny gold plaque reads—*Mason House, Home for Orphan Girls. Est. 1896.*

I pace the sidewalk in front of the brushed steps, not sure whether to knock, to walk away, or just peer in the window. I have no good options, a situation I'm entirely used to. Clenching my fists, I run through the possibilities. If I look in there and see her, what would I do? I can't just snatch her and run away. And if I just peek in, she might make a break for it when she sees me and be punished.

I follow the neat iron fence around the corner and lean my back against the wall of the building. Memories of a place like this swish and sway against my eyes like broken rice paper.

Sneering faces, benches in lines draped with thin blankets. Skinny boys with towels folded over their arms marching toward a hose blasting cold water. The icy stream punches my stomach like a battering ram. "English!" he screams. "You cry, you beg, in English!"

I don't even remember what the place was called. It was a home for boys, but that's all I can recall. And if

I could have given it a name, it would have been hell.

I shake my head to rid myself of the darkness and search for my courage behind the trash cans, in the cracks between the walls. I stare at the ivy stains for too long. The plant is gone but the tattoo, the imprint of where it once lived, is still there.

I don't know what to do.

Girls' laughter peals from the window above, tittering bells clashing against each together. Picking up a trash can, I place it under the window, quieter than fingers tracing shadows, and carefully climb on to the lid to peer in.

Girls sit in a circle, knee to knee, clothed in simply made, simply cut sundresses. One girl is wearing shorts, one sock pulled up to her knee, the other bunched down at her ankle—Keeper. A stern-looking woman strides in and I lower my head, just my eyes above the sill like a toad. She claps her hands together and they jump up, scrabbling for a place at the long table in the center of the clean but sparsely furnished home.

I scan Keeper for signs of abuse, but her eyes are bright. She laughs and elbows the girl next to her as food that looks warm and filling is slopped into their bowls. My nails dig into the sill, conflicted by what I see. She hasn't been adopted, but she's clean, safe, well fed. Part of me wants to hop onto the sill, take her hand, and fly her away from this place. But I don't. I can't. I can't offer her a better life than this.

Sadly, I sink back down, get off the trash can, and place it back where it was, all with a weight in my chest that burrows to my feet. If she gets sick again, she'll get the help she needs. Maybe for kids like us, that's all we can hope for. I wipe my eyes, pissed that there's a tear there. I'll miss her, but that's not why I'm crying. I'm jealous. I'm happy for her, but I'm also mourning a childhood I never had and wondering whether things would have been different if I'd been born on this side of the country, if there hadn't been a war between the races that I'm made of.

There's always been a war inside me. The Japanese side and the American side can't be friends, but not because of their skin color, nor their culture. They just know nothing about each other. I clench my teeth. I don't want to think about this anymore, my kind is a mystery and there's no solving it.

I swear, kick stones across the dribbling alley, and storm out into the street. The sun is high in the sky now, and I know Kin's going to be angry that I didn't show up at the docks.

As I wander the streets, hands shoved in pockets, I look exactly like the angry youth people expect me to be. I stomp to the corner and my feet turn into the well-lit entrance of a department store, the coolness of the air beckoning me inside. Taking off my cap, I stare at the glossy floor. I know my hair is probably sticking up straight like a toilet brush and I try to smooth it as I walk.

Without really thinking, I head straight through the perfume section, women with pinched, powdered noses giving me strange looks as I pass them, and enter the elevator. The attendant doesn't even look at me, just stares at the buttons and murmurs in a detached, bored voice, "Which floor?"

"Four," I mutter, anger and purpose grinding against each other. I fold my cap in half and shove it in my back pocket, watching the lights shine golden and ding like good ideas as we move upwards.

"Fourth Floor, Children's department, toys, clothing, and baby accessories," the old man's words slide out of his mouth slowly. I shuffle from side to side, waiting for him to finish, and then the doors slide open. I want to ask him how you accessorize a baby, since all that comes to mind is earrings and scarves, but I hold my tongue. "Er, thanks," I say, holding out a coin to the man.

His eyebrows rise gradually in surprise, one then the other, and he holds out his gloved hand. "Thank you, sir," he says, staring at the coin like it may disappear. My chest expands for a moment at the fact that he called me sir, but then it shrinks because it's just about money. I roll my eyes. *It's always about money.*

I enter a room packed with colors and sounds that would delight any child. Cymbals clapping, miniature trains tooting their horns, children giggling at the toys and whining to their parents. Head down, I march straight to the doll section.

I'm slightly overwhelmed by the range. The hair colors, eye colors. Frilly skirts clutched in porcelain hands seem so unlike Keeps. I trawl my eyes over them for a long time, groan, and move down the next aisle with the cashier's gaze pinned to me like I'm the most interesting thing in this place. Trucks and building blocks in bright primary colors catch my attention, then, down on the bottom shelf, I see something I've not seen before called a 'Slinky.'

I count the cash in my pocket and grab a handful of Slinkys, several toy cars, and a large box of Meccano. We had one small box of mismatched, donated Meccano at the Home. One box to share between twenty kids.

I dump the toys on the counter to the surprise of the cashier. She gives me doubtful looks as she adds up the price. When the register dings, I proudly, and with a wink, hand over the cash. She doesn't even try to cover her astonishment when she drops my change into my hands, from a height like she doesn't want to touch my skin. I give her a smile. "Thank you, Marla," I say, glancing at her shiny, gold name tag. "Can you direct me to where I can buy toothbrushes and toothpaste, please?" I'm putting on my 'proper' voice, which she seems to find unnerving. Flustered, she nods and replies, "Second floor, near the hair products," as she thrusts the bags of toys at me.

Leaving the store with two paper bags full of toys and toothbrushes for the Kings, I feel like Santa. I snort at the idea of a half-Japanese, half-white Santa delivering presents on Christmas day.

I make my way back to Mason house, my mood lightening. Despite what I was told, threatened, and warned, I've managed to make a life for myself. I don't steal. I go where I please. I can buy gifts for orphan girls. *I* can do that.

I stop at the corner and put the bags down, pulling one of the Slinkys out of the paper bag and putting it in my own satchel. With a pen from my shirt pocket, I scrawl *For the Girls of Mason House* on the outside of the bags. I underline the word 'girls' twice so they don't think the gifts are meant for boy orphans. I run up the stairs, ring the bell, drop the bags, and run down the street with a big grin on my face. I hope she will suspect it was me, but it doesn't matter. She's alive and she's safe. I can release some of the guilt I've felt about leaving her at the hospital. I can try to convince myself that I did the right thing.

I jog to the alley, sometimes skipping, and people don't even try not to stare. The slinky, my 'I'm sorry' gift to Kin, bounces around in its box as I run.

The sun slips between the buildings and then out of sight. It gives little relief from the heat. You can see it rising from the stones in the street, snaking to the sky in plumes like cobras being charmed from a wicker basket. I watch them melt into the air, staring at the atmosphere that's turned murky with pollution and humidity. I slow to a walk when I reach the street Kin and I have been sleeping near. Men in aprons are pulling their fruit and vegetable carts back inside their shops. The noise of packing in and up fills the air, wood on stone, squeaking wheels, over-tired, over-worked voices building in irritation. I stand over a subway grate before crossing the street. Cooler air surges over my skin, making me shiver, making me miss the cool stones of home.

A man knocks into my back, slurring his words as he says, "Scooze me." It's only midweek but some have started celebrating the weekend a little early. I nod and step aside before he knocks me over.

I buy empanadas from a vendor, slip into the alley, and wait for darkness.

It's late but still warm when Kin kicks my leg. The empanadas have gone cold and slimy in my lap. I wipe at my pants, only making the grease stain they've left worse.

He snatches the food and collapses next to me. "What happened to you today?" he asks between mouthfuls. "I fought off five guys waiting for you to fill the space, but you never showed up. I could've used your help today."

I knock his knee with my own. "You stink."

"Yeah. Tends to happen when someone pours fish guts on you," he says indifferently, like it's something that happens to him every day.

"What? What happened?" I say, shuffling a few feet away from him as the smell starts to make its way over to me.

He laughs sourly. "I really don't want to talk about it."

I pause for a few beats. Usually, when he's like this, he just needs a few moments to get his head straight and then he tells me what's bugging him. I wait until he's finished eating, but he still doesn't say a word.

I lean over and elbow him in the ribs, and he winces like I hurt him. In the dark, I can only see movements, shapes, hear his jaw clicking. "Kin…" I start, thinking it's usually the other way round. He's always trying to pry the words from my clamped-shut lips. If *he* won't talk to *me*, it must be bad.

"So you didn't answer my question. Where were you today?" he asks, and then coughs, thumping his chest like something's stuck there.

I turn the slinky box over in my hand, thinking now's not the time to give it to him. I tuck it into my bag. "I went looking for Keeps."

Silence. A wrapper being scrunched in a hand and then tossed across the alley.

"She's okay, Kin, she's in an orphanage downtown. She looked... happy," I blurt.

I see his shadow straighten; his head roll back to the sky. A sigh that pulls his ribs too far apart emits from his mouth. "I'm glad she's okay, but that was a stupid thing to do. If they caught you..."

"They didn't," I cut him off.

"You're not eighteen yet; they'll take you back to *that* place." His worried tone is more familiar than the grumpy one of a few minutes ago.

Together, we gaze up at the sky, our heads leaned way back. There are no stars tonight, just a yellowing light behind a curtain of murky green haze. It moves across the alley like a river. "I'm fine, Kin. Nothing happened."

"Yes, despite your best efforts. You're fine," he snaps.

It goes quiet, well, as quiet as the city can be. There are still traffic noises, sirens, drunken men shouting at each other because apparently, when you're drunk, you lose the ability to hear. But it feels eerily quiet to me because Kin isn't speaking. I know he's awake. He shuffles his feet every now and then, humphs and blows air slowly between his lips with nervousness or frustration or something.

After about half an hour, he speaks. I snort to waking, my eyes shooting open. "Do you think about it?" I can hear him scratching the paint from the dumpster. I can smell him from a mile away.

"Think about what?" I ask, suspecting I know where this is going.

He stops scratching and leans his head against the cool metal. It dimples with the pressure he's putting on it. "I try not to think about it but, sometimes, it just pops into my head. Small things, you know, like finding long, dark hairs on the floor. The smell of the powder she used on her face. Then there are other memories I want to forget but can't." He tenses beside me. "Just can't. I know we ran away, but what about everyone else? Where are they now? I want to and don't want to know what happened to them."

"I do think about it, Kin. I wonder about the others. I wonder where my mother is, if she's even alive... Where they all are. Do they think about us? But you know—we're doing okay—you, me, and the other kids."

He's not really listening to me; I see the shadow of his hand winding round and round in circles as he whispers, "Her hair was so thick and black, like silk thread. You could've sewn clothes with it."

I shake with the tiniest giggle. "That's pretty disgusting Kin."

He slaps at my head, and I duck. "Shut up! I'm having a moment here. Don't you miss our mother?" he asks with a challenge in his voice. He's dangling an idea in front of my face that I can't believe in.

"I miss *your* mother, Kin, really I do, but she was never my mother." *Just the closest thing I'll ever have to a family…*

"Whatever. She loved you…"

I know.

Again, he laughs, and it's bitter and stinging. "And look, I know we're doing all right at the moment, but it can't last. You know that, right? Besides, I don't want to live in a cave for the rest of my life. It's fun for now but at some point, we're gonna have to grow up."

Of course he's right, but I'm not ready just yet. "Not tonight we don't!" I cock my head to the sky and howl.

I get a weak clip over the head but I hear the lighter tone in his voice, a feather balanced on the end of his nose as he tries to sound annoyed. "Shut up! You idiot."

Long after Kin has gone to sleep, I wait for the hand and a treasure to fall from the sky but the air is empty, the dark binding.

24

ONCE AGAIN

I'm super human, made of steel, spider webs, and heart. *So much heart.*

I hit the top stair and clutch my chest, dragging in a panicked breath.

"Deddy, I'm sawry," I hear coming from my mother's bedroom. The door is closed, just a splice of light slamming down on the hallway rug. "I just want—ted to look beautiful like Mommy always did."

His voice is a cool, solid lump of ice. He's furious. "You shouldn't be in here, Frances. You've been told numerous times that this room is off limits." His foot stomp rings out across the second story. Angry waves pulsate through the whole house.

I shouldn't have left her alone. I was selfish. Selfish.

I sprint down the hall, trying to be soundless, but it feels like my heartbeat is causing the walls to thump, the foundations to shake. I grasp the handle of my mother's shrine and shove. There is no hesitation in my actions. I push the door wide open, a brush of air sending shivers up my arms and causing my mother's silk dress, that my sister is drowning in, to flutter around her tiny body. "Nora," she says in a broken voice that's painted with regret.

She's sitting on the bed, lipstick smeared on her small lips, her hair pinched on top of her head with a silver clasp. My mother's pale, blue silk dress hangs off one shoulder, and there are lipstick stains all around the collar. She looks tiny, ridiculous, and so very frightened. Tears are pressing in. My face feels like it may collapse.

My father glances at me sideways and growls, "You have broken the rules. You have violated my trust and damaged your... your... mother's dress. You horrible little devil." He takes an ominous step toward her, and she puts her hand up to her ear.

"Please Deddy, don't shout tat me. It hurts ma ears," she pleads.

I watch his fingers curl into fists at his sides. "Speak properly, child!"

She scrunches both sides of the dress in her fingers and sets her mouth in a hard line. It's such a mistake, but she doesn't know, doesn't remember. "Ahm tryin'. S'not easy with you shoutin' tat me." She shakes her head, tears dripping onto the fabric and staining the dress further.

He takes another step, and I step with him. "Are you saying it's my fault you can't talk like a *normal* girl? I've given you every opportunity, paid for the most expensive and sophisticated equipment. You ungrateful little shit." He rakes a hand through his hair and tugs at it. I feel the wheel turning, the way the very air in the room changes once his mind has settled on hurting someone.

She lurches away from him when he shouts, leaning back into the folds of fabric, in Mother's clothes that have no hope of protecting her. She cries out when he takes another step, her fear getting the better of her, and she starts sobbing.

Father stops for a second. I wonder if maybe he sees himself reflected in her eyes, sees the monster in a nice suit flaring with violence. But then he shouts, "Shut up. Stop crying. Stop it now!"

But she can't stop.

He takes one more step and swings his fist at her perfect, undamaged face.

"No, you stop!" I scream, stepping between his fist and her face. The punch pauses midair, his expression incredulous. He raises his eyebrows at me. "Don't you dare criticize her for something that *you* caused," I say, talking low but strong. *I will not let him hurt her.* I point my finger at his chest, where his heart beats only every other second. "She can't hear because of you. *You. Did. This. To. Her.*"

His lip curls and his eyes retreat. His elbow pulls back, and I scream, "Frankie, get out of here!" as I back up against the front of the bed and brace myself. She slips off the bed and the dress falls to the floor, billowing out with old air like a ghost has left the room. She pauses in the doorway, her eyes round and scared and looking just like our mother's. "Go," I urge just before his fist hits me.

The punch is like a hammer to my temple. It cracks open barrels of pain that spill all over my mother's bedspread. The ones to my stomach I hardly notice and actually, after a while, it all blurs to red. Somehow, I've ended up on the floor, the world flat, spreading endlessly before me in straight lines as if the walls have disappeared. His sharp, black foot comes at me over and over. I grip one hand on the underside of the bed and beg for unconsciousness as I fly up off the floor with every kick until I vomit. That's when it stops.

Disgusted, he shouts down at me, "Clean this up," and leaves, slamming the door behind him.

I kind of laugh at the idea that I'll be able to clean up anything, and then I let out a whimper, the air in my lungs compressed into little balls of pain. I wonder if this time he's actually killed me. I wait for blackness to close over me but nothing comes, just the hard light of the bedroom lamp and the hot air fuming through the window. Sighing, I carefully shuffle back until I'm under the bed, my cheek pressed to the floor, my hand around my stomach. I want to pass out. I want to stay hidden here forever, but everything hurts too much. My lips graze the wood floor as I murmur, "I hate you, I hate you, I hate you," over and over again through a cloud of salt water and blood.

As the world spins wildly, I start to believe that if I stepped out that window, maybe I could fly away. And that maybe Mother is better off where she is.

My hair flops over my eyes, and I let that be my darkness. The door creaks open, and I retreat further under the bed. A small shadow dances across the floor, turns the lamp off, and comes to find me.

Frankie squirms under the bed and forces her way into my unresponsive arms, folding them over her shoulder and burying her face in my chest. I begin to cry, shaking and rattling with tears that feel as hard as ball bearings. She reaches her pearly hand up to my face, strokes my cheek, and whispers, "Shh. Shh. Shh. Thenk you, Nora, you saved me."

I fall asleep with Frankie cradled in my arms. And

I count the one blessing with my shredded pinky finger. She is physically unharmed, thank God.

The morning sluggishly pulls me from sleep, tugging at the blanket beneath me until I am rolled into consciousness. Hot air pours through the window, and I try to drag myself out from under the bed to close it. Frankie still sleeps in my arms, and I carefully pull them out from under her head without waking her. I stand, I sway, the room tilts sideways, and it feels like it's a steep climb to get to the window. I use chairs and furniture to tug myself toward it and manage to slide it shut. The snap opens my stomach and I turn and vomit in the dustbin by her dresser.

I wipe my mouth, sweat beading on my upper lip, the pain in my head turning from splitting to completely cracked open. The smell of vomit wafts up my nose and I hurl again, stumbling toward the door. My view of the world is hazy, like the pollution of the city is hovering in the second story of the house. I blink, blink, blink, trying to clear it, but my vision doesn't improve. Moving slowly to the bathroom, I grip the guardrail for support as if I might slip through the floor if I let go.

I hang over the rail for a second and see my father leaning on the hallstand talking on the phone, the top of his dark hat bobbing up and down like there is an ocean beneath me. "Yes, they are both unwell. I think it best you don't come in until next week; that will give them adequate time to recover. Certainly, I will pass on your well wishes. Goodbye, Miss Candace." He glances up and I duck down, instantly regretting it as the world turns completely upside down. I manage to hold in my stomach contents until I hear the door close, and then I rush to the bathroom. Though by this time, there is nothing but bile left in there.

As I wash, my vision clears enough for me to view my stricken reflection. I am shocked by what I see because I am unrecognizable. I can see why he cancelled the tutor. This cannot be hidden or explained away. The mirror wavers and wobbles like the surface of a disturbed pond and I gag, ripples of nausea rolling through me over and over. I cup my hands to the faucet and take a small sip of water, sinking to the floor.

I can't do this anymore.

I won't do this anymore.

I hammer my thigh with a half-closed fist. My eyes shutter. My head slides against the porcelain sink, and I slip into blackness again. The condensation on the window sparkles like stars as I drift away.

"Miss Nora." Marie's worried voice wakes me, as does her shaking my shoulder. I wince when her dimpled hand touches me. She creeps away from me, clutching her skirt in one hand. "Mister Deere said you were feeling poorly and that I should let you rest in bed today. I've brought you lunch. Do you want to, um, should I bring it in here or to your bedroom?"

The smell of vomit is pungent and hangs on the air in disgusting dribbles. I lick my dry lips and hold my arms out to her. "Help me up, Marie," I manage in a croaky, rinsed-with-acid voice. "Where's Miss Frances?"

"Oh, she's in the playroom," Marie answers as she hoists me up. I still feel a little giddy, but the nausea has subsided. I let Marie help me to my room, testing my feet as I go. They slap down like dollar bills on a bar, but I'm pretty sure I can walk on my own. When we get to my door I say, "That will do. Thank you, Marie. Tell Miss Frances to join me, please."

Marie nods and rushes to get my tray of food, drops it on the bedside table, and hurries out again to fetch Frankie. I shake my head and instantly regret it, reaching out to grab the dresser before I fall.

He nearly killed me. I'm not hanging around to see what happens next. I drag my old ballet bag out from under the bed and empty it of things I will never use again. Satin ribbons twirl to the floor, slippers hitting with a wooden thud. I grab clothing and jewelry to sell, shoving them in the bag.

A knock on the door makes me spin around too fast, and I put my hand to my head. It throbs into my palm as the room spins, up and down, up and down. I'm on a carousel and I can't get off.

Frankie's face peeks inside, a tray of food wobbling in her skinny arms. I hate the way she looks at me now. Whatever innocence she had left has been wiped away with the blood and the bruises. I don't want my world to be her world. I won't allow it. I beckon with my other hand. "Come in. Come in."

"What are you doing?" she asks curiously as she rumbles over to me and puts her tray on the bed.

I try to smile, my face hurting. Pulling her close, I whisper in her good ear. "We're going on a trip."

25

BAIT

A restless night's sleep makes it hard to open my eyes, but the fishy smell creeping through the air runs a rake over my skin and jolts me alert.

"I know," Kin says, watching me shudder and wipe my nose. He shrugs and pulls his cap over his eyes. I eye him suspiciously, wondering why his shirt is buttoned up to his neck.

I stand and stretch, yawning as I speak. "You could clear a subway car with that smell. I think we should go early and take a swim before the gates open."

He stands gingerly, and I narrow my eyes at his stiff movements. His chin touches his chest like he's trying to avoid eye contact. I move under his face and look up. "What's...?"

His lip is split and under his eye is as dark as a scrape of boot polish. He stretches too and I catch the bruise on his left side as his shirt lifts, looking like purple finger paint spotted up to his armpits. My eyes widen, and he bares his flashy teeth at me. "Later."

I don't know what to say. My mouth still hangs open as we walk briskly through the streets to the station. We'll be ahead of most of the workers as it's about 5:30 AM, but some will still get the jump. They're the desperate ones. The ones that'll tear your hair out and stomp on your face.

Coffees and donuts in hand, we ride the subway to the docks. Jittery legs and shoulders bump against each other with the rhythm of the rail. The few men in the car give us a wide berth because of Kin's stench, which fills the space like someone wiped down the windows with day-old fish.

When the doors slide open at the last stop, Kin storms out, his eyes on the horizon as he moves straight through the middle of the deserted street, his long legs making it hard for me to keep up. When our feet hit the sand, I take off my shoes. Kin just walks straight into the ocean fully clothed, and I wonder if he's lost it. Something happened yesterday, and it's got him more aggravated than I've ever seen him. I'm worried about him and selfishly worried about the rest of us. I need him to hold it together. I'm not sure I can handle it all, all of them, on my own.

He stands waist deep in the waves, silently staring past the edge of the water. I take off my shirt and wade in, splashing some water on my face and the back of my neck and wait. The morning heat is already fuming across the sand and the salt water dries almost instantly on my skin. I lick my lips, tasting the sea.

He seems far away in more than one way and I move closer, cupping my hands to my mouth and shouting over the crashing waves. "Kin!" Cold water splashes up to my shoulders. It's refreshing and shocking all at once.

He turns to look at me, his face dark, planed of its usual cheek. He starts undressing, rinsing his clothes of the fish stink and wringing them out.

I glance at my watch. We're going to have a fight

on our hands if he doesn't hurry up. I point to my wrist when he turns around and he nods, wading shirtless toward me.

Usually I'd joke that he's showing off, but something about his expression and the cloud darkening his mood makes me think better of it.

He carries his shoes in one hand, the leather already shrinking and bunching, his shirt slung over his shoulder. "Ready?" he asks.

I nod. "Ready." It feels like he's talking about something other than the cockfight we're about to enter into. I want to ask, but he told me 'later'. I'm supposed to respect that because he would do the same for me.

It's a half-hour walk to the gates and by the time we get there, Kin's clothes are dry, salt running in wavy lines up his pants and shirt like a water color painting I've seen in someone's sitting room window.

"You smell slightly better," I quip as our feet hit the wooden sleepers of the jetty. Two ships sit, one behind the other, in front of us, their paint-dipped tops barnacled and rusty. It'll be a busy day.

I take a deep breath, my heartbeat picking up as I see the masses of men squashed against each other, fighting for life like fish in a net. And just like fish struggling to stay alive as they're lifted from the water, we don't want to fight each other but we each have our own life we're struggling to maintain. At some point, survival instincts take over.

We approach the back of the group, and I already feel like giving up. The crowd surges forward and falls back like the tide. There's no way we can get to the front. But Kin's eyes speak a different idea. He's focused on the rattling wire at the front of the group and he starts pushing men apart, entering the swarm of bodies easily, just like he was wading into the sea again. I try to follow him, but the gap he's made for himself immediately closes up after him.

Wait for me, I think weakly because I know I'm not going to make it through.

Kin's tall figure stands above the crowd like a tree already struck by lightning. Dark and strong. Immovable but damaged. I pull through the crowd just as the gates slide open. I get a moment's breath as space opens up around me before I'm crushed by the mob again and am desperately grappling and scratching at the backs of heads and the points of shoulders, trying to get in.

Kin is in, his back to me. I'm almost there as the gates slide closed. The man in front of me screams out as his fingers nearly get crushed. I hear the bolt slam shut, the padlock clip into place, and I'm shut out.

"Sorry, men." The guard laughs. "Better luck next time, eh?"

A chorus of curses almost sounds musical as the pressure relaxes and men turn away. I'm still gripping the fence. My eyes press through two hexagons of wire like funny glasses, Kin's stalking figure framed by rusty wire as it gets smaller. "Wait. Can't you let in one more?" I beg. *Why won't Kin turn around?*

The guard pulls a pack of gum from his pocket and offers me some through the wire. "Hang around. You can always hope someone gets injured," he says with a wry smile.

Other tired faces, tired bodies, take up positions

on rocks and boxes around the gate to wait. Sadness fills my heart at the fact that we're all sort of hoping for something bad to happen to someone else, someone who's in the same situation as us. But I feel like I need to be in there. I feel like something's wrong with Kin.

I'm melting into the box I'm perched on, sinking in like furniture polish. The sun is high over the docks, blaring down on us with full force. It's almost as if it's vibrating, making a nasty noise like a wrong organ chord. The wind coming off the land is pushing any cool breeze further away. I mop at the sweat on my face with my sleeve, the smell of bird crap, baked seaweed and dead fish is making me want to leave.

I think about going back to the beach when the fence rattles and the same guard that offered me gum parts the gate by a few fingers and shakes a bottle of water at us. I jump up, a little younger and sprightlier than some of the others.

"Thanks, mister," I say with a genuine smile. He grumbles something unintelligible that may have been, *More work moving dead bodies at the end of the day.*

I offer the bottle around. We share the water, germs and all. A drip on the tongue seems to evaporate before it can do anything useful.

The horn blasts within, marking lunch, and I stroke my throat, jealous of the food they're eating right now and the sweet, warmish soda they're drinking. My head hangs between my legs and I wonder if it's safe to sleep here with five other men watching me and more specifically, the bag I have slung across my shoulders. I close my eyes but stay alert.

A few minutes later, the fence rattles again and Kin's voice hits my ears. "Oi! Kettle. Wake up!" I look up to see him waving half a sandwich in the air. "Nice. I'm working my ass off and you're taking a nap," he teases. Maybe whatever I thought was wrong was nothing after all.

I walk up to the fence and he folds the sandwich over, pushing it through the gap into my hand. "Thanks."

He shrugs and arches an eyebrow. "You waiting for someone to get thrown out, huh?"

I don't admit I'm mostly here because I'm worried about him. "Yeah, well, we need the money."

He sinks down to the ground and sits cross-legged, his back perfectly straight as he leans against the fence with one shoulder and looks out toward the sea. "That's very true," he says, wiping crumbs from his lips.

"Hey nip!" a man yells as he walks slowly between two containers, holding something up in his hands. Kin's back becomes impossibly rigid, and he turns very slowly.

I whisper his name. I don't shout out. There's no point.

Everything comes together like wooden beads clicking to the end of a thread. One, two, three. The man approaches, and Kin still hasn't turned all the way around. I don't want him to, because in the man's big, hairy hand is a limp mass of tabby cat fur. Tiger Lily swings lifelessly from the man's clutches, and I can't help but cover my mouth in shock. Kin's eyes rise to mine and I shake my head slightly, my eyes stinging.

I say without saying it. *Don't turn around. Don't turn around.* What's coming is only hurt and pain, but there's nothing I can do to stop this. Or him.

He finally swings around, stands slowly, hardly making any noise except for a sharp push of air through his nostrils. I stand too, my fingers curling around the wire and gripping it tightly. "Kin, don't!" I urge, but he's lost to his anger and grief now.

It's so strange to be looking in on this from the outside. As I rattle the fence and yell again for Kin to stop, to think, memories of guarded boundaries twirled with barbed wire swim over my head like a school of fish. The water from their scaled bodies turns to drips of blood falling to the desert floor, rolling together and becoming coated in ochre dust. I shake my head. The here and now wins my attention as I watch Kin storm toward the man.

I don't know why it matters, but I want to know why. What happened between them that led to this picture I see, where men spit on the ground and glare at each other with eyes of knives? What led to the murder of an innocent creature? A bait that Kin was always going to take. But I'm not going to get any answers. I can only watch the violence grow like an atomic bomb cloud.

Kin's shadow lengthens and his body shrinks as he moves further away. The man stands still, Tiger Lily in one hand, held high over his head, waiting for Kin to come to him. Other men flank him on either side. The idea of a fair fight blows away like dust and leaves.

I rattle the fence again, this time without words. He's going to throw everything away. My eyes dart to the guard, hoping he can intervene, but he puts his hands up like he's surrendering to this group. I do see his fingers wrapping around the gun handle in its holster. I'm hoping he'll only let it go so far.

It's then that I hear a tiny, "meow."

Kin freezes in his tracks. She's still alive. Kin approaches the man more slowly now, his hands outstretched.

The man shakes Tiger Lily hard, her legs flopping uselessly from side to side. "You want her? Come get her," he sneers, cruelty shining in his eyes. The hatred is burning so high it's singeing the clouds.

Kin's voice is calm, falsely serene when he says, "Just put her down. She's done nothing to you, Ernie. Your problem is with me. With my… kind." The words spin deceptively on his tongue. "The cat's got nothing to do with it."

I cringe just like he does when he says "kind".

Ernie smiles, shrugs, and lets his arms fall to his sides, Tiger Lily's hide still clutched in his brutish fingers. "You're right; she ain't got nuthin' to do with this," he says as he hurls the poor creature against the steel container behind him. She makes a horrible sound, it's quick, and then she is nothing more than bones and fur.

"No!" Kin shouts desperately. His hands outspread but empty for something to catch. For one tiny second, he's unsure of whether to run to her crumpled body or to Ernie. My prayers go unanswered as he tips his head down and charges at Ernie, who's braced, ready for the impact.

Men shout and thump their fists on their knees, whooping and laughing as Kin hits Ernie with his shoulder and sends him flying backward into the container. The sound ripples out across the water.

The group moves forward, their toes in the ring. They're ready to step in for their mate as soon as things get dicey. I'm the only one who would help Kin, and I'm stranded on the other side of the fence.

Ernie is winded for a moment and Kin turns his back to him, checking on Tiger Lily's motionless form, her limbs stretched as if she were napping in the sunlight. Ernie scrambles up and lumbers toward Kin. I scream, "Turn around!" and then I start to climb.

Rusted barbed wire, crusted with salt, hovers over my head forebodingly. I look up only once, wanting to keep my eyes on the fight below. Kin hears me and turns just as Ernie, who's much shorter than Kin but very muscular and barrel-like, punches him in the side. Kin's body lurches up, curving around that punch like a 'C' makes a horrible 'ugh' sound like his organs are being shuffled around inside him.

I climb faster.

The men close in, chanting Ernie's name. I hear fleshy thumps and breath being knocked from lungs, but I can no longer see what's happening. They've closed ranks around the pair, and dust and dirt flies up from within the circle as feet scud across the baked asphalt.

I'm about halfway up when I hear the guard shout out, "That's enough, boys. Back to work." He claps his hands once. Some turn around, but most of them continue pumping their arms and shouting obscene things at the scrabbling pair. The guard unclips his pistol and aims it at the sky, firing once. The shouting suddenly stops, and the men turn to the guard. "Do you want to get kicked out or do you want your paycheck at the end of the day? Your choice," he remarks grimly, the gun still poised near his chin.

The circle widens. My eyes squint to see Kin, my feet pushed into the small holes of the fence losing their grip. I stretch my neck and look between the gaps in the bodies. I'm worried Kin really hurt Ernie. The last thing we need is to be labeled troublemakers and not be allowed back in. The men disperse slowly, and it takes me some time to find him. He's lying on his arm, knees to his chest, blood covering his mouth and nose. He rolls over to his stomach and stays there, his face kind of pressed into the ground, just like Tiger Lily.

Ernie walks casually between the containers, shrugging his shoulders as he talks to one of the other workers, who slaps him on the back and congratulates him on winning.

I shake the fence and scream, "Kin! Get up!"

He doesn't move.

I skid down the wire and go to the gate. The guard comes up to me, eyes indifferent. "Looks like a spot just opened up. You want in?" he asks, his eyes going to the other men, who have suddenly got more life in them and are hopping toward me like vultures.

I nod vigorously. "Will you let me check on my friend?" I ask.

The guard sighs. "You'll do better than that. You need to carry him out of here. One for one."

He unlocks the padlock and lets me inside. I

squeeze through the tiny gap and sprint toward Kin, whose chest is rising and falling to my relief.

When I pull up to his knocked-around body, I'm surprised how angry I am with him. My foot is fighting against the urge to kick him in the ribs.

I kneel down and roll him over so I can see his face. "What the hell, Kin? What's wrong with you? Why would you do that?" I say angrily.

He squints up at me, blood covering one eye. "She's dead… isn't she?" he asks with hope in his voice.

"She's gone," I answer, my eyes briefly moving over the animal that's lying against the red container.

He pulls himself up with effort, grimacing when he has to bend his back to get to sitting. "Stupid cat," he says. If he's crying, I wouldn't be able to tell, his whole face is plastered with blood and dirt. I help him to his feet. He only glances Tiger Lily's way once, but I can tell it's painful for him. He shudders as we walk-stumble toward the gate.

Kin's weight is difficult to carry on my own, and he's hardly helping me. One leg seems to be dragging woodenly behind him. "Are you all right?" I whisper into his ear, talking through my teeth.

"Fine," he huffs. "Just sore. Shouldn't have let him win."

I roll my eyes.

The guard gives us a sympathetic look when we reach him. "Look, boys, I'm sorry that happened but you know, with the way you look, particularly, this one," he points at Kin, "well, you can understand why they'd want to punch you."

Kin's chin juts out as he says, "I'm a Nisei. I was

born here. My parents were born here. I'm an American citizen. Same as you."

The guard turns to me like Kin didn't even speak or maybe he's expecting a similar declaration from me. He won't get one. I'm not a Nisei. I don't know what I am. I suspect I am nothing.

The guard's brown eyes are wide, his dark skin is not from too much time in the sun, but he is different to us. "You staying on, kid? I'll see you get a full day's pay. You can collect your friend's wages for the work he did this morning." This is the guard's concession. He's giving us more than most.

I grip the gate with one hand, trying to support Kin's leaning weight. "Err, I dunno," I say, looking to Kin for answers.

"Go," Kin says. "We need the money."

"You sure?" I ask, very unsure myself.

Kin straightens poorly. "I'll be fine. Just put me on that rock over there and I'll wait for you. It's only a few more hours."

The need for money presses down, and I let Kin assure me. I force myself to believe him. "Okay." I nod.

I drag him to a rock and lean him against it and the guard lets me back into the yard, despite the other men elbowing me out of the way. "Don't go anywhere," I warn through the fence.

Kin laughs, holding his hands up. "Where am I going to go?"

I leave him, leaning against a sand-colored, sharp-angled rock. He gives me a twisted smile through bruised lips.

He'll be fine, I tell myself.

26

MEN

It's difficult, but I manage to avoid the men when I return to the workstation. I keep my head down and do what is asked of me. They knock shoulders at the table, ticking their boxes and accepting their next tasks. If they brag, I close my ears to it. Nothing can be gained by starting another fight. I'm not proud like Kin. I've learned through the bars of a cot to the bars of a prison that pride gets you killed.

I swing down from my next container and land steadily on my feet. The five-minute break bell rings and cigarette smoke instantly blooms from the open shed where everyone tends to gather. I make sure no one's watching and sneak back to the front of the yard.

In the shadow of a red container, Tiger Lily lies flat and bony. Her eyes are closed at least. I let out a deep sigh, glancing over to where Kin sits with his arms folded, chin on chest. He doesn't look up when I quickly creep up to her, scoop the feathery body up, and slink through the shadows to the skeleton of the warship that never got built.

The water laps at sludgy gray sand as I tiptoe across the ribs of a rotted jetty with Tiger Lily hanging limp from one hand. I try not to be disgusted by her body. She still feels warm but is most definitely dead. There is no beat inside her chest. I jump from the jetty onto the small beach and lay her down beside me, digging a shallow grave with my hands. I know it'll get washed away, but it's the best I can do.

I don't know what to say so I don't say anything. Placing her gently in the hole, I cover her with lumps of wet sand until she's hidden. I don't cry. I don't really do that anymore. I don't have the attachment Kin had to her. In all honesty, I found her to be an annoying inconvenience and thought Kin wasted his food on her. But I am sorry this happened. I shake my head as I stand, the water smoothing over her grave like it was never there. No one or thing deserves to die like that. The kind of cruelty Ernie showed today scares me, reminds me and warns me not to forget what men are capable of. And not even bad men. Just ordinary men.

The bell sounds again and I run back to the dock to finish my shift.

I wipe the sweat from my brow with the last clean thing I own, a small, square handkerchief. Looking down at the grease-smudged rag, I ache for a clean one. I need to go home. The men around me are similarly sledgehammered, dragging their feet over the hot asphalt, wheezing and coughing.

I pat the cash in my pocket. It was worth it to finish out the day. Shoulder to shoulder, we all drag our sorry bodies to the entrance, the dark clouds overhead keeping the heat in like a plastic bag has been shoved over the city, but it also promises a summer storm. Looking up at the blackened buildings, I think the whole damn city could use a rinse.

The gate opens, and we pour through. Most men continue up the road to the subway. I hold my breath as Ernie and his friends walk through. He sniffs and rubs his nose as he passes Kin but doesn't try anything. When everyone's cleared out, I crouch down to my sleeping friend and nudge him awake. He doesn't react and I shake his arm, his head bobbing around stiffly. He snorts and suddenly, his eyes open. "Shit! You scared me," he shouts, hands going to his face.

I let out my anxiousness with a weird laugh. "Geez. You scared me too." I offer my shoulder and help him to stand. He grips into my skin quite strongly and heaves himself up, leaning into me with almost all his weight. I grunt with exertion.

"Sorry man, my leg's gone to sleep or something." He jerks the offending leg around, jiggling it to wake it up. After a few stretches, he places his weight on both feet and manages to stand. We walk toward the station slowly, dark clouds pulling together over our heads.

By the time we get to the subway stairs, fat blobs of rain have started to plop on the sidewalk. Kin leans against the handrail for a moment, letting the rain cool and cleanse his red face.

"Pool's lucky manhole," he says in a confused tone.

I freeze next to him. "What?" My hand curls around the handrail and squeezes until my knuckles turn yellow.

He shakes his head slowly, and his eyes roll around lazily. "Pool's... I mean... rain's, rain's refreshing." He smiles unconvincingly and then frowns.

I pat his back. "Are you okay? That was pretty weird, Kin." My voice is shaky, and I'm not doing a very good job of hiding my fear.

His eyes clear, and he grins. "I think I'm just tired, Kettle. Stop worrying." But there's something in his expression that tells me he's worried too. "Let's just get home."

I offer him my shoulder again but he waves me off, determined to prove he's fine as he limps down the stairs. He grunts and groans at every step until he gets down to the platform. Thankfully, a train pulls up straight away and we're able to walk right on.

Kin finds a seat and collapses into it, sighing loudly. I sit next him, clasp my hands together, and fumble with my fingers nervously. The air is humid, electric, like it knows something's up.

It's past seven by the time we pull up to our stop. Kin snores next to me. The only other person in the car has moved further and further away from us as Kin's behavior became weirder. He has shouted out, "fishing pole," "razor," and "cheese doodles," so far.

I rattle him when the car stops. He wakes drowsily, glances at me, and wobbles in his seat. "C'mon Kin, we have to get up or we'll miss our stop."

He pushes himself out of his seat, lurches toward the door, and nearly falls onto the platform. I catch his arm, and we both stumble out the doors as they try to close on us.

I drag him from the platform, each step heavier as we rise up and then back down toward *our* tunnel. People stare. He shouts, "Cave, land ho!" really loudly. The stares change to morbid fascination, and people part like the holy sea as we struggle down the last incline. It proves to be too difficult. I can't support him any longer as he has become heavier and heavier in my arms. We skid and tumble down. Kin's motion forces us both to one side of the tunnel where he juts his arms out, touches the stones, and then drags down to the floor. I crash down with him, quickly pulling myself up to kneeling. Kin curls into a ball on his side. He looks up at me and says, "I'm coming to dinner in five minutes." And then his eyes roll back, his face goes slack, and he's unconscious.

"Kin," I whisper, shaking his shoulder really gently because it feels like his head's not attached to them right. "Kin. Kin. Kin."

I run a frustrated hand through my hair and look around for help. A crowd has gathered, but their backs are to me and they're circling around something else.

Kin is breathing, but there's something wrong, I just know there's something seriously wrong. "Help me!" I say hoarsely. When no one turns, I shout, "I need help over here!"

Muttered concern, a woman gasping, a comforting hand goes to someone's shoulder. Sounds and actions that are aimed somewhere else, about someone else. Kin and I lie in the shadows as footsteps thunder down the tunnel and a stretcher carried by two paramedics, flanked by another two policemen, enters the scene.

I lift Kin's head into my lap, a thin trail of blood dripping from one of his nostrils. "I need help!" I scream. "Please!" I beg. But no one is listening. Someone more important is hurting on the other side of that wall of people. We are the street kids, Kings of Nothing, Nowhereland. If we died right here in the subway, no one would notice.

27

THE WAVE

Frankie gives me a distrustful look when I say it. So I say it again, trying to muster up some enthusiasm, "We're going on a trip!" I say, straightening my neck and opening my eyes wide, which makes my head hurt worse. There are two doubtful-looking Frankie's dancing in front of me at the moment, and I'm scared I'm going to vomit again.

The toast in front of me shines with a slick of sickening butter. I pick it up and nibble on the corner, the fat making my saliva glands force a bloody taste into my mouth. I clutch my stomach and threaten it to calm.

Frankie places her delicate hand on my arm and says, "Don't need ta lie to me. I'm eight years old now." She puts her hands on her hips and tilts her chin up to the ceiling. The love I have for this girl wraps around me like a bandage. "I'll run away weth you."

I grasp her neck and pull her to me. She squeezes my middle, and I gasp in pain. "Not so tight, Frankie."

She releases me suddenly. "I'm sawry, Nora. It's my fault Deddy got mad."

Her pink lip quivers a little and her tangled, red hair falls in her eyes as she looks at the floor in shame. I place my finger under her chin and make her look at me. "Daddy may have had a right to be cross at you for wearing Mommy's clothes without asking, but the

186

way he shows his anger is never, *ever* okay. Do you understand, Frankie? He did something wrong, not you."

She nods, but I suspect she doesn't believe me. "He wasn't all—ways like dis. Deddy changed."

I try to think of a time in Frankie's life when he wasn't like this. But I can't. And if I start looking for answers, picking things apart, I'm scared about where it ends, where the finger points the blame. So I agree with her and run a hand through her hair, getting stuck halfway because it's crusted with her breakfast.

"Frankie, can you go pack a small bag? Just clothes, socks, and underwear." She screws up her nose at the mention of underwear, which makes me let out a labored chuckle. "Get your hearing aid and its special bag. I'll get the spare batteries from downstairs."

Frankie grins and bounces around on the rug. Her sudden, jerky movements make me nauseous again, and I clutch my stomach. As she's leaving to pack, I grab her arm and pull her back to me so she can hear me. It sends a wave of pain through my body, followed by hatred, hot and acidic.

"Get your hearing aid and its special bag. I'll… I'll…"

She shakes out of my grip and crosses her arms. "You'll get the batteries. You alreddy said that, Nora."

I close my eyes for a few seconds and open them again. The room shifts, and I find I can focus. Tucking my hair behind my ear, I swallow. "I did? Oh right. Sorry."

She lingers in the doorway, looking at me like my mother used to when I didn't eat enough. "You need a docter," she says sternly.

I can't argue with her. She is as stubborn as me, so I lie. "You're right. I'll go see the doctor after we find a place to stay." This seems to satisfy her and she skips off to pack. I sigh when I think about the bag she'll pack. It will probably contain stuffed toys, hair clips, and no underwear.

I ease myself from the bed and quickly pack the rest of my things. Everything seems to take much longer than I want it to. I have to think really hard about even the smallest movements. It's frustrating and slows me down.

Marie is busy cleaning downstairs. I hear the sound of the vacuum cleaner in the front room, the noise conveniently covering what we're doing. It's after eleven by the time I've managed to dress, wash, and pack. Clipping my belt, I stand on the round rug at the foot of my bed, the swirling circles dragging down through the floor like a porthole. *It's time to go.* I drag the bag into the hall and move toward my mother's bedroom, stalling a little when I reach the door.

Frankie slams into my back as I take the handle in my broken fingers. "Don't go in there," she warns, pulling my waist, and the way I feel right now, she could probably overpower me. The hearing aid is in one of her hands. "You'll get in trouble again."

I turn around and carefully fit it to her ear, tucking the other part in her sash. "It's okay, Frankie. I won't get in trouble because I won't be here when Daddy gets back." I push open the door and walk inside.

My whole body shudders when I see the blood spray over the pretty lace bedspread. The room stinks of the vomit I refused to clean up. I don't dawdle. I rifle through her drawers and pull out the things of most value—watches, pearls, and rings. I stuff them in the bag and move too fast out the room, swaying when I reach the balustrade.

Frankie follows me, patting my back gently as I hang over the rail, staring down at the black-and-white tiles that seem to swirl like a whirlpool beneath me. I take a deep breath to calm myself. It doesn't really work. I'm too angry, too hurt. I don't think about what I'm doing. I don't want to. I just need to get out of here.

Marie calls up from the bottom of the stairs. "Lunch is ready."

Frankie gives me a look, searching for what to do, and I nod. Might as well have one last meal before we leave.

We carefully tread down the stairs. Each decline sends splitting pain through my neck and head. I ignore it.

I should feel fear, shouldn't I? I should be worried about what I'm going to do, how I will manage, but all I can think about is being free of this place.

Frankie tears down the stairs, so fast they barely have time to creak, and waits for me at the bottom. I wave her off. "Just go in, I'll be there in a minute." I reach the bottom and try to pull myself together. This is harder than I would like. My body feels like it's been run over by a tank and my head is fighting with me. I stare down at the tiles, the pattern seeming to jump up in my face and then fall down flat, over and over again. I hold the stair rail and count to three.

One, two, three. *Don't think about what's next, just put one foot in front of the other and move.*

Frankie pokes her head out the kitchen doorway and says, "Hurry up, Nora Snora."

I walk straight through where Mother landed, without looking down. I feel cold air skewer my chest through, but then it's over. I collapse at the hallstand, holding onto it like it's a life raft, and pull out the drawer full of batteries. Picking them up in slippery fingers, I shove them in the bag and kick it under the hallstand. Then I titter to the kitchen, feeling puppet-like and full of determination.

Marie sets a plate before me at the kitchen table, avoiding my eyes. It's a look I've seen before. It's the look in the policeman's eyes, the doctor's eyes. It's the 'I'm sorry I can't do anything for you' look. I try to catch her gaze. She should look. She should take in every bruise and scratch and admit to herself that it's not 'I can't,' it's 'I won't,' and there's a difference.

She turns her back to me and starts cleaning the bench tops with extra vigor. "Marie, what are your plans today?" I ask, poking the food with a fork. Gravy glistens with grease under the dull kitchen light, the muggy day adding no light from the window.

"I've got to go to the market today. Do you need anything?" she asks, spinning around and wiping crumbs from around Frankie's plate as quickly as she's dropping them.

I try to swallow a piece of roast beef. It sticks in my throat, and I grab the glass of orange juice in front of me. Marie's shape stretches in my vision, her big eyes blinking as big as headlights as she waits for me to answer.

"Um sure. Can you pick up some shampoo, a pair of black stockings, and some, some, some...?" I hold out my palm like the answer is hidden in there. The word I'm trying to find doesn't want to come. It's like pulling an anchor from a muddy swamp. I tap the side of my glass, the liquid vibrating from my touch. "Some..."

Marie does make eye contact, her large chest heaving up and down at the sight of my battered face. "Some more orange juice?"

I nod slowly. The words seem alien to me. I scrunch my eyes together and wait for the wave of nausea and confusion to subside. "Yes. Orange juice," I say slowly.

Marie moves to the counter just as Frankie jumps down from it, putting her rough hand over mine. "Miss, are you all right?"

My eyes snap open, anger pushing at me. "What do you care?" I spit. "Don't you dare pretend that you care about us now!" Marie quickly withdraws her hand, and I feel bad for a moment.

Frankie stomps her foot and copies my actions, though it's unconvincing. "Yeah."

"Sorry, Miss Nora," she says, righting herself. She continues to clean as we eat. When she leaves, she announces, "I'm leaving for the market at five o'clock. I won't be back until six. If there's anything else you need, please let me know, Miss."

I don't respond. I don't have the energy.

My fork clatters to my plate as I rest my head in my hands, little splatters of gravy decorating my face.

28
ESCAPE

A t five o'clock, the door slams loudly. I grab my bag, tell Frankie to grab hers, and we creep out the door like burglars. Frankie enjoys the theater of it, and it works for me to have her play along. As long as she's quiet, it's fine. I have to keep telling *myself* that it's going to be fine. Whatever that means. If it's something other than being here, then that's all I want.

Fine. Fine. Fine.

The bag is not meant to carry this much weight, and it digs into my shoulder. I get to the front door and pause, thinking I should feel a pull to turn around. That this place should mean something more to me, and giving it one last look to say goodbye is what I should do, but my head won't turn. I'm happy to say farewell to this place. Within these walls, I've felt nothing except tied down, restricted, and terrified. As I open the door and step outside, it's like every binding just snaps. Pulling the door closed, hearing it lock. That sound. It should be scary but it's triumphant. It's locking him in there. All of it *in* there, away from Frankie and me.

There are no nosy neighbors with their letters fluttering between their fingers as they casually try to assess where I'm going. I stride to the glass doors, the breakable bubble that separates me from the real world, and shove it open. The sounds of the city envelope me, call to me, and I smile.

I hold out my hand and Frankie takes it, her skin sticky in my palm, her hair clumped in ribbons of autumn colors. I strike the match and walk away.

"Where are we going?" Frankie asks as we ease down the steps. Her voice sounds buffered, like she's speaking through wads of cotton wool.

I glance down at her eager face. "Subway station."

I open the purse slung across my shoulders. I have enough for train fare, and a cheap hotel room. Tomorrow, I'll sell what I have and go from there.

I hit the last step and trip a little on the sidewalk. Frankie steadies me. "Thanks, sis," I manage, as I stare down the street that seems to lengthen the longer I look.

We walk slowly to the corner, me gripping fences and steadying myself on walls as we go. The ground is a ship deck and we're in a storm. To outsiders, I probably look drunk, wobbling around, taking small, determined steps so I don't trip over again. I keep my hat pulled down, but I know it does little to hide the swelling of my jaw and the bruises under my eyes.

Frankie sounds smaller and further away when she asks, "Which way?"

I point to the subway station two blocks away and across the street. I take a too-big step and fall forward, crashing down to the pavement like a blown-up building. A man rushes to my side and helps me up. When he sees my face, his brow furrows and he grips me harder. "Thank you, sir," I mutter.

"Do you need me to call your husband, Madam, or… your father?" he asks quietly.

I shake free of his grip, the world spinning, spinning, spinning. Part of me wants to say *yes*. I'm scared I won't be able to do this. The other part tells me I can't go home. That I'm too close to getting away. That I won't last two more years of this. He'll kill me. He might hurt Frankie next time. I can't. I just can't.

"No, thank you. I'm on my way home right now," I say. Reluctantly, he steps away. Thankfully dark is closing in, the light fading in like at the end of a movie. And like the end of a movie, little splotches of black appear in my vision. I keep my head down, my hand tight around Frankie's, and stumble forward.

It becomes easier to hide as more people pour into the streets, clocking off from work. Frankie and I slide into the crowd and follow them to the station. Every now and then, she sneaks a look at me, her expression plastered with concern. I'm making her anxious and I make more of an effort to look normal as the darkness grows in the street and over my eyes. Streetlights blink on one by one, seeming to buzz like fireflies in a bottle. I keep my eyes focused on the one marking the entrance to the subway and doggedly continue.

People gallop down the stairs. I press close to the wall of the tunnel and move sluggishly. I pay for my ticket, the man speaks to me, but all I can hear is the blood rushing through my ears and the sound of the subway tunnels seeming to flood with water. Frankie anchors me and almost leads me through the turnstiles. "Where do you want to go?" she asks, pointing at the various destinations and platform numbers.

I put my hand to my head, trying to think, people bump me, twist me around, and I feel like I'm sinking. "Nora?"

I don't know what I'm doing so I just pick a platform, and Frankie pulls me forward. Everyone's moving faster than me, or I'm in slow motion. I hear Frankie jabbering but it's just noise, not words. I pick out the individual bricks of the tunnel and count them as I run my hand over each one.

The incline down to the platform seems steeper than a high slide and I dig my nails into the wall, inching down carefully, all the while hearing the thump, thump, thumping in my ears as if someone were pounding my brain with a rubber mallet.

When I reach the platform, cool air blasts through the tunnel and sends my hair flying around my face.

The doors slide open and we step onto the train, pushed along by other commuters. As the train starts to move, I feel my stomach protesting. I watch the stations zoom by, light hitting my eyes like new punches. If people stare, I can't see them. I'm focused on the closing circle of light in my vision.

As I grip the underside of the chair, nausea rolls through me. I push up and out of my chair. "I need to get out," I whisper, touching the back of my hand to my mouth. The doors open at the next station and I stumble out desperately, my sister's trembling hand in mine.

I pull up as the doors close and the train moves on, feeling like I'm trapped between two plates of glass. I can't move for fear of being ill. I can't think. Everything is dim, dark. Frankie tugs on my arm, her little lips moving, her eyes tearing up with worry. I wonder if I've made the right decision and how much I've scared her.

The tunnel lights flicker, or my eyelids flutter, and the bulbs in the lamps all black out. Fabric tears, my shoes slip out from under me, and I fall. I don't feel the landing.

My last thought is a bad one. *He's going to find us.*

29

THE KING

"Kin. Kin. Kin. Kin..." His name loses its meaning as it turns into a mantra, a prayer. I stroke the side of his face, his sweaty sideburns, and his greenish skin. He looks wrong. Too peaceful. His face should be angry, contorted with the fight I hope is still in him. His chest rises and falls, but his body is so slack it's like his nerves are gone.

I look up to see the paramedics carrying a woman from the platform on a stretcher. I can only see little cuts of the view through the splits in the fabric of curious onlookers. One pale, limp hand swings back and forth as it hangs over the stretcher. It's clad in silk buttoned to the wrist. A smaller, paler hand reaches out and grabs it, squashing the fingers together in what would be uncomfortable if the woman was awake or alive. I'm not sure. I don't care.

The paramedic talks into his radio, "Incoming. Female appears to have lost consciousness on the platform. We're bringing her in now."

I yell out again, too scared to be careful. "Hey! What about my brother? Are you going to help him?"

People swing around and finally notice me now that the rich woman has been helped. The paramedics stop for a moment, and one of them has the decency to look upset. "We'll be right back. We have to get Miss

Deere to the hospital, and then…" His words are swallowed by the crowd as things return to normal. Men and women hop off the train and others hop on. They give me sad looks, but no one offers to help. Someone throws a dollar bill at me. I want to gnash my teeth and launch at him like the animal they think I am, but I daren't move.

They said they'd come back. They'll come back. They have to come back.

The nighttime rush settles down, and the platform empties. I cradle Kin's head like it does some good. *I don't know what to do, and I'm doing it wrong.*

I glance at my watch. It's been an hour. He breathes, but shallowly. There's a weight on his chest I can't move.

I smooth his hair and speak to him. "Remember when we first met? I woke up face to face with this wise-ass boy who smirked at me and tried to act like he was tough despite the fact that he was curled up next to his mama on an army bed. You made faces at me until your mother woke up and scolded you." I sigh. "I was so scared. I'm sure you were too, but you always made the best of it. Even when she got sick, you did. Kin, you saved me. Your mother too. Without your family, I would have died out there in the desert and there would be no one to mourn me." I'm trying really hard not to cry, but one tear hits his face.

He blinks and opens his eyes. They roll around for a while, and then he coughs. "Take me home, Kettle," he manages. He lifts his arm up to me. When I don't move, he says, "Please. I want to go home."

"But the paramedics will be here soon… We need

to wait, Kin," I say desperately.

"No one's going to help me," he says without bitterness or an edge to his voice. It's just simple fact in his mind.

"But…"

He gives me a tired look, and I don't finish.

I help him up, but his legs are like jelly. Worse, only one seems to be working and it's incredibly hard to move him at all. Luckily, it's not far to get home and the platform is deserted.

I drag him inside and close the door.

By the time I reach the second door, Kin's unconscious again. I bang on it and hear the scurrying. They're waiting for the secret knock, but I can only thump the wood with my elbow. "Let me in. It's me, Kettle."

The door slides open, and I'm greeted with hungry eyes and shocked faces. "What's wrong with Kin?" Krow asks.

"He's hurt," I splutter. "Help me lift him onto his bed."

The boys help me lie him down. We cover his unresponsive body with a blanket and just stare at him for several minutes. I pull the curtain around his bed and tell the boys to clean up the room, walking over to my area and throwing my bag down.

The slinky I bought tumbles out and lands at my feet. I never got the chance to give it to him. Picking it up, I pull it out of the box and let it hang from my fingers. I watch it, detached, as it bounces up and down until it stills. Each time it plunges down, my heart strangles itself a little more. I feel cramped, caged in for the first time since I left *that* place. *The place where we were expected to look after ourselves or die.* But at least there were adults there. I feel so out of my depth that I'm sitting on the ocean floor. Just sitting there, looking up at the black sky and wondering how the hell I'm going to get out of this. How will I manage on my own?

I gather up the slinky, tangling it together until it looks more like a ball of barbed wire than a toy. I try to untangle it but make it worse, until my frustration, my helplessness, reaches its peak and I scream, hurling the toy at the wall.

Burying my head in my hands, I allow myself one moment of panic and tears. One. That's all I get.

The boys are all frozen, staring at me with frightened eyes. I gather myself up, take a few deep breaths, and face them.

The boys sleep restlessly. They're worried. I am too. Whatever is wrong with Kin is not going to mend itself. He needs medical attention. I find Krow and shake him awake, whispering in his ear, "I need you to help me."

He nods, sits up, and pushes back his sleeves. He's only fourteen but he understands.

"I'm going back outside. I'm going to make a phone call, and then I need you to help me carry Kin to ground level as quick as you can. Okay?"

He grimaces. "Okay… but he's pretty heavy."

I pat him on the back. "You're my second. I need your help."

He nods seriously.

I sneak out, ignoring the loud splats and splashes my feet make as I run through the tunnel. The nearest phone box is located near the ticket station before the tunnels branch out. I think about what I'm going to do and it makes me sick, but it's the only way. I think about the rich, white arm hanging off the stretcher, her perfect clothes, peachy and unblemished, and hatred blooms in my chest. Kin might die because the priority went to Miss Deere, some woman who fainted.

I gulp. He might die. Slamming into the phone box, I dial 911, panting as the phone rings and rings.

"Hello, please state your emergency."

I swallow dryly. I have to do this right or they won't come. "Hello. Yes. I need to report a mugging."

The nasal voice on the other end of the phone says, "Connecting you to the police department…"

"Wait! No! The man they mugged is badly injured. They took his cash but left his wallet. His name is James Washington-Kellar. Wait… isn't that Senator Washington-Kellar's son?" I spew out in one breath.

There's a click on the other end and the woman's voice, which had sounded bored up until now, suddenly kicks up an octave. "I'm connecting with the paramedics. Where are you?"

I give the station details.

"Is he conscious?"

I stall for a second, pretending I'm checking the man's condition. "No. He's unconscious and beat up pretty bad."

"The ambulance is on its way," she assures me. "The police will be there soon."

I drop the receiver and run back to get Kin. The man in the ticket office leans back in his chair, snoring loudly, his arms slack at his sides, his chin on his chest. The sick feeling creeps closer to my mouth. There are so many things that could go wrong. My hope is once they get down here, even though they'll know it's not the senator's son, they'll treat him anyway. *They have to, don't they?*

I bite my lip as I run. I don't want to do this.

The platform is dead quiet, and I easily slip into the tunnel without anyone seeing me. When I get to our door, I stop. I breathe. Try to anyway.

This is goodbye. Goodnight. A tear slides down my cheek, and I wipe it away. There's no time.

I take Kin's arms and Krow takes his legs. We pick our way over the sleeping bodies. Kelpie stirs and sits up, glancing around in confusion.

"Kelpie, can you open the door for us?" I whisper.

He nods and pads over to the heavy wooden door, holding it open for us to pass through. "Bye Kin," he says, waving one hand. He says it casually, like he'll see him again one day.

Damn it! I'm losing a battle with my emotions as I awkwardly stagger back toward the second door. Krow's ruddy face turns to mine for a moment, but he has the decency to ignore my sniffling. When we reach the platform, I speed up, hoping I can reach the ticket office before the paramedics. We walk as fast as we can, our legs and arms burning under Kin's weight. His face, paler than I would have thought possible, bumps up and down with our less-than-delicate movements.

Kin, I'm sorry.

The reflection of red, flashing lights bounces off the glass and metal, coloring the walls of the subway station. Krow's getting anxious, dancing from foot to foot. "Where?" he asks, swinging Kin's legs out like he's going to dump him and run.

I jerk my head to the phone, and we quickly lay him down. I get less than a second to look at him, to understand that I have no choice, before I hear footsteps and have to run away from Kin's resting body. Doubt blares in my ears like the sirens that have started to wail outside. Krow and I press ourselves to the wall around the corner and listen.

"Pulse?"

"Steady. Pupils unresponsive."

"Wait, this isn't…?"

"Let's worry about that when we get back to Mount View."

There's a small heave, the men grunt, and when I chance a look around the corner, they're carrying Kin away on a stretcher.

Relief and fear collide in my crowded head, fighting each other with fists dipped in doubt. If he lives, he'll never forgive me.

Kin is seventeen. I may have just given him a chance to survive, but I've also sentenced him to months in a home and several chances of being abused until he turns eighteen.

The train rattles loosely, the cars shaking over the tracks like they're just as scared as the rest of us. Packed into three carriages, separated from the rest, families sit shoulder to shoulder.

Possessions are balled up in sheets, women grasping them in their laps. Giant cloth balloons filled with memories most of us would like to forget.

I look down at my own small bag and pat the $25 in my pocket. It's harder for most of them. They had a home they are not allowed to go back to. I don't have that. I'm heading toward something, not away.

He slings an arm over my shoulder and pulls me close, whispering in my ear. "Let's run away. You and me, brother."

I don't answer. My small legs swing from the train seat. I miss her. I miss the four walls and blankets strung between bedrooms. Is it wrong that I miss the camp?

I frown. It is. She is gone, and now he is the closest thing I have to family. I think of the bloodstained handkerchief, her dainty cough, and blood-splattered dress.

"I don't know," I reply doubtfully.

He grips my shoulder tighter. He is only a few months older than I am, but he thinks he's much more. "We're both orphans now," he says, staring at the ground. The woman opposite us looks up for a moment, her dark brows pulled together in sadness. The emotion sits over the whole train, pushing on and upwards to an unknown destination. "They're gonna put us in a home. They might put you back where they got you." He shakes his head, and I believe him. "With fifty dollars between us, we can live like kings. I say at the next station, we make a break for it."

"Okay," I say, shuddering at the thought of going back to the Home.

He grins. "And a new start means new names." He

holds out his hand and says, "I'm Kin."

I quirk an eyebrow at him. "Kin?"

He shrugs. "What about you?"

I gaze down at my hands, nervously clasping and unclasping. Waiting for something to come. The memory of steam curling from the small stove, the hot tea that seemed to soothe her coughing, wafts in front of my eyes. It was always my job to boil the water, to pour the tea. I would offer it to her wilting hands and receive the rare smile and nod. Her face like a heart framed in black. The deep sadness I felt at her illness was eased by that simple gesture. I knew it was not going to cure her, but it made me feel useful in a hopeless situation.

"Kettle," I mutter.

He doesn't make fun of me. He just says, "Okay, Kettle it is."

"Kin is perfect," I barely whisper.

Kin is loyal, accepting. Kin is my brother.

30

THE DEVIL

I don't want to open my eyes. It's impossible to shut out the noises of metal trays shaking, fluid dripping, and leather shoes scuffing on a linoleum floor, but if I keep my eyes closed, reality will stay on the other side of my eyelids. I can pretend I'm still lying on the platform, Frankie's hand in mine.

Frankie.

I blink awake, my eyes moving around the small, white room. A view of the sky to my right and a hunched figure folded over the end of my bed to my left. A messy head of dirty-blond hair buried in strong arms lies across my legs. Arms that struck me until I thought I would die.

I freeze, but it's too late. My small movement has stirred him, and he rolls up to sitting. His eyes are crinkled, his face imprinted with the sheets he was lying on. He turns to me, relief washing over his expression. "Thank God. You're awake."

I try to pull my legs back, try to disappear into the wall, because I don't understand his face. *I'm afraid this is a dream. I'm afraid this isn't a dream.*

"Fr-Frankie…" I say hoarsely. He stands suddenly and I cower, bringing my arm up to my face as a shield. When the blow fails to connect, I let my arm drop a little and peer out from under it. My father is standing there with a cup of water in his hand, his eyebrows drooping in sadness and confusion. I warily take the cup and drink.

As I swallow, he says, "Frances is fine. She's safe."

Safe. *Safe?* I want to cry, but I don't. I stare up at his mask of a face and wait.

"I'm so glad you're all right. I was very worried about you. Nora, you could have died." A nurse walks in and starts checking the bottle of fluid that runs into my arm, sending a cool shot under my skin. "I just wish you'd talked to me. Hurting yourself was not the answer." He puts his hand to his forehead and looks down at the floor. "Oh, I blame myself. I'm not home enough, but I need to work. And now with your mother gone... Oh God! I can't believe I nearly lost you too."

The nurse sighs and puts a comforting hand on my father's shoulder.

I stare in astonishment at the performance before me. "Hurt myself? What are you talking about?" I feel my heart picking up. "I don't understand. You...*you* did this," I stammer, pointing a weak finger at him.

He pats his chest like I've just shot him and calmly says, "You're confused. And yes, I know you blame me for not catching your mother when she fell. Believe me, I think about that every day. I know you want to punish me, and I guess I deserve it for not saving her. But Nora, don't you remember what happened, what you tried to do?" The emotion in his voice is sickening and obviously convincing by the way the nurse is tearing up and shaking her head.

I play along, pulling this cart of lies behind me, collecting up what little dignity I have left and adding it to the pile of crumpled-up hopes and stabbing injuries. "No. I don't remember," I say hatefully and as flat as my will.

His voice is hard, coated in a warning only I can hear. "We had an argument and you threw yourself from the stairs. Telling me that it was all my fault. And when I went to you and tried to help you, you ran from me in shame. I'm sorry I let you leave, I didn't realize how badly you were hurt until it was too late," he says, trying to add a little croak of sadness to the end of the sentence.

A smile teases at my lips. His honeyed eyes are on mine, piercing, on fire with a threat so big it fills the room. But I don't care. The smile turns to a grin and I throw my head back, pain shooting up my neck, and laugh, hard like a cough. "Oh yeah, that's right. I threw myself off the stairs. I hurt *myself*. It's all my fault." I snort and raise my hands to the sky. "I was so angry at you that I thought, I want to teach my father a lesson. I'll kill myself. That'll teach him!"

He takes a step back, and there's a silent exchange between him and the nurse. The laughing stings, slices through my lungs like knives. My control is gone. I failed. I failed to escape. I failed Frankie in so many ways.

My hands shake, but not from fear. Fear is gone. I'm just letting the hysteria win because whatever he does to me now, it just doesn't matter anymore. I've lost.

And he knows it.

My giggling peters out into a long, windy sigh and my body relaxes. My arms feel heavy, as do my eyes.

I press my lips together and feel the power leaching from my body like she's drawing it out with a needle.

The solid thing my mind wraps around is hate.

Hate as a fact.

I hate him.

Leather restraints dig into my wrists and ankles. I'm unsurprised but can't help but tug on them just the same.

A hand goes over mine, and I can't pull away. The room is dark. The metal window frames a starless sky. A small and steady flash of light pushes up from beneath the sill—a neon sign. I stare at it until my eyes start to water.

"Nora, I'm sorry," he says.

No, you're not. I refuse to look at him. I don't want to see the wounded look on his face. Not because I'll believe it but because I want to believe it so much and looking into his lying face is like another kick to the stomach. I'm pathetic, and I start to hate myself just as much as I hate him. I don't understand why I can't let him go.

"I didn't mean to hurt you as much as I did."

Yes, you did.

"Look at me."

No.

"Please look at me."

I turn my head just slightly, still mostly looking out the window, wondering what the sign says. Soda ad, or bar, or one of those *Girls! Girls! Girls!* signs? I snort.

"It will never happen again," he promises. But I

catch the twitch.

Of course it will.

I ignore his promise, his sad face and sad eyes. It's a lie I've got memorized. "I don't care what you promise or threaten to hold over my head. If you ever touch Frankie again, I'll make you pay." He turns from me—not in shame, he doesn't harbor that emotion. He's just trying to keep his anger in check. "Look at *me*," I demand, slamming my other hand on the bed, my arms straining against the restraints. I want him to see my swollen, determined face. "I'll find a way. I'll find a way to ruin you." My fingers have wrapped into a fist under his.

He opens his mouth to say something, and then claps it shut.

"Get the hell out of my room," I say between gritted teeth.

He stands and leaves slowly. Once his shadow has disappeared from the doorway, I slump into my pillow. I honestly can't tell between mistake and good judgment at this point. Sadly, I realize that it probably doesn't matter what I do. I'm trapped.

A nurse comes in half an hour later to check on me. As she pulls the blanket up, I ask her, "When can I go home?"

She shakes her head and rolls her Rs as she speaks. "Well, your father has gone against the doctor's orders. It was recommended that you be admitted for at least a week so you could receive psychiatric treatment. But he is signing you out against medical advice," she says as she gently unties my wrists and ankles. "You're going home tonight."

There's something sickeningly comforting about it. The *knowing*. I'm not scared because I know, without a doubt, that something horrible awaits me. Maybe it's true—better the devil you know.

I fall back into the squeaky bed and let the quiet hum of the hospital lull me to what little slither of peace there is left inside.

My wheelchair squeals as it grinds across the surface of the gritty, ground level of the hospital, sounding like I'm rolling over broken glass. I shakily grip a bottle of pain pills in one hand and it rattles, showing my nerves. The other hand is firmly grasping the arm of the chair. My mind wants to leave, to see Frankie, but my body is turning inward, protecting itself against future harm. I shield my eyes as we move under the bright lights that worsen my headache.

The doctor came to see me before I was discharged. He told me I had a bad concussion and a very bruised body but really, for the fall I had, I was lucky. It was hard for me not to scoff at that. He didn't ask me why I did it. People don't lean toward peculiarity, especially doctors. The idea that a famous civil rights' lawyer could hurt his own children simply can't be possible.

I remember Robbie telling me once that doctors are taught to look for the most ordinary, most plausible diagnosis. "Horses, not zebras," he said.

"Huh?"

He'd shaken his head and tapped his chin like he wasn't really sure what it meant either but said, "It means the most likely cause is usually the correct one. Sometimes people just have unusual symptoms to a usual disease." Then he'd cupped his hand to his ear and started galloping, puffing as he continued, "So if you hear hooves clopping, you think horses, not zebras."

I think I might be a zebra, but no one's going to hear me. My hand shakes so hard that I drop the bottle.

The nurse scoops them up and places them in my lap, speaking to me like I am a child, "Don't worry, dear. Your father has sent a fancy car to pick you up and take you home."

My ears prick from the closeness of her mouth and the prospect that I won't have to face him just yet. "You mean he's not taking me home? He's not here?" I ask hopefully.

"He was called away to Washington. He does very important work, your father. He told me to tell you that Marie will stay at the house until he returns. He also told me to tell you that a police car will be parked out the front at all times, in case you need anything."

I roll my eyes. In case I try to run away again, more likely.

The doors roll open to a humid night, the air wraps around me, closing in like a heap of smelly blankets. I feel suffocated, trapped in this chair, in this life. I sigh heavily when I see the sleek black car pull up. Sally rolls down the window and tries to smile at me, but it's a sad mixture of pity and denial that crosses her face instead.

"Do you need help, Miss?" she asks, false cheeriness to her voice.

I shake my head and stand, opening the car door and sliding into the back. The nurse closes it, and

I thank her as she does. The dark interior of the car swallows me whole, shrouds me in the blackness that reflects my mood.

I couldn't do it.

I lasted about an hour. One miserable hour. The failure presses me from both sides, flattening me like I'm in a vice.

I. Couldn't. Get. Away.

Me, only me.

I am responsible for what happens next and what could happen to Frankie.

I draw in a broken breath and try not to cry. My mind is clouded with how angry I am with *him*. How he's ruined my life over and over again. How it will never stop.

I wring my hands in my lap, wanting to throw something, break something. Sally eyes me in the rear-view mirror. "I'm sorry, Miss," is all she says.

I can't respond because all the words I have are tangled around hatred and anger, and I will sting her with what I say. I stare at my lap, rolling the bottle of pills between my fingers. My head still throbs, but it's hard to tell if it's the concussion or the feeling of being squeezed dry that's doing it.

We pull up to the house, behind a police car. Sally runs around to my door and opens it. She offers her hand, and although I don't want to take it, I do. Her skin feels soft, squishy, as I dig my fingers in to pull myself up. I get a little dizzy as I stand. Putting my hand to my head, I check it's all still there.

It's late, maybe ten o'clock. I stare up at the second story devoid of light and my heart turns icy as I start to worry what has happened to Frankie in the two days I've been gone.

I linger on the bottom step. "Okay," I whisper under my breath. I take a step up, releasing Sally's arm. I never wanted to set foot in this house again. I climb the steps painfully slow, my whole body unwilling to come with me. It knows the horror inside, the shadows that fill every corner of every room. "You're going to be okay," I whisper, tapping my heart, but it drops down and away from me. I'm so lost. My only companions are anger and distrust.

The door flies open and Marie stands there, eyes wide and fearful. She beckons me inside and gives Sally a knowing look.

"Come inside, come inside," she says, eyes darting quickly to the police car. I slowly follow her, placing my pills on the hallstand by the door and swaying into the foyer. The stairs pulse in front of me, long, dark, winding, lit up in spots with the golden glow of the hall lamp.

"Where's Frankie?" I ask in a slightly robotic voice.

Marie tries to take my coat, but I snatch it around my body, shivering suddenly.

"Where's Frankie?" I ask again, taking a few steps into the center of the room, standing right where *she* fell. Anger pounds from that one spot like a giant heart is buried under the floor.

Marie seems dumbfounded for a moment, but she finally manages to say, "Didn't Mister Deere tell you?"

To this, I snort loudly, take a few more steps, and sit down on the bottom stair, my knees knocking together, my head collapsing into my hands. "Tell me what?" My heart is batting against my ribs.

"Miss Frances has gone to stay with Mister Deere's cousin. She's probably sleepin' safe'n'sound right now," she answers, trying to placate me, or reassure me, I'm not really sure.

I stand again, the room whirling suddenly. A rush and then it stops still. "What cousin?" I take a step closer. "Where?" My eyes feel aflame; my hands are fisted at my sides. "And you know as well as I do, we're never safe. Never."

I buckle as the mist clears, and I understand. He's taken her away from me.

She gives me a weird look like she doesn't get what I'm saying, although I know she does, and says, "I don't know any more than that, Miss. I'm sorry." She backs away and mutters, "I've got some cleanin' to do. Excuse me."

We don't speak of these things. We never have. But I've lost the will to keep up the game any longer.

"When is Mister Deere returning?" I shout across the foyer, gripping my skirt and wishing, wishing, wishing for days and maybe weeks without him.

"Tomorrow, Miss," Marie manages, her face wrinkled with stress.

He took her away. My head pulses with pain and fear. He's punishing me more than I ever thought possible.

"At least he can't hurt her if she's not here," I say, doubting it even as I say it.

Her eyes expand at my candor and she stalls, moving uncomfortably from foot to foot while I glare at her plump, worried face for a moment too long. But then my expression softens. I don't blame her for keeping quiet. She has a family of her own, and I'm sure my father would have threatened her and them for her silence.

What's worse than a violent man? A smart, violent man. He has notes filed away on everybody, money in pockets, and daggers ever poised for use. It must be exhausting for him, keeping track of it all. It makes me let out a weird little laugh. Poor Father. So many secrets to keep track of, people to pay off and threaten. Poor, poor man.

Hysteria teases me. Invites me to let it in, to stop caring, because he's taken the last thing that would have held me down. Now I'm a balloon floating desperately to the sky.

I gaze around this vast space. The giant window over the landing casts eerie light over the stairs. That window has seen too many things. Too many horrible, undoable things. If only he could look through that window and see himself. If he could watch it from a distance, I wonder if he would change his behavior? Would he be ashamed? My head drops as I realize it doesn't matter. Nothing matters. My anger at him and myself forces me upright, and I storm up the stairs. The feelings twist into something else—a desperate sadness I can't contain. Tears fly from my eyes as I reach the top, my hand gripping the banister hard as I pause on the top step. *Why couldn't you hold on? You left us. You left me.*

I creep to Frankie's partially open door and peek in. I'm hoping Marie's mistaken and that she's sleeping soundly, her face to the window, her breath rattling. The room is empty. I gently close the door with a wobbly hand. It stings when I breathe out. It hurts in every part of me, my skin itchy with rage.

He was going to hurt her. And now he's hiding her. My sister. My small, hurricane of a sister...

I turn and walk down the hall, my feet spurring me on independently of my brain because I am empty and adrift. I am no hope and no thought.

The mania builds, my hands wanting to smash, burn, and tear, anything to not feel like this anymore. Because it's too much. Losing her is too much. My body shakes with out-of-control emotion. I can't hold it inside.

I place my hand on my mother's bedroom door and shove it open. My headache is forgotten. My body is in line with me now.

Everything she owned glows with what I can't have, what I've lost... am going to lose. I hate her for leaving, and I hate him for staying.

A barbed cry escapes my throat and I grab the first thing in reach, a silk scarf smelling of her perfume wrapped around a felt, brimmed hat on the end of the bed post. I rush to the window, fling it open, and throw the hat like a Frisbee out into the night air. The scarf and the hat separate, and I watch as the hat spins into the black and then sinks beyond sight and the scarf twirls down like smoke being sucked back into a pipe.

Self-control has abandoned me and I start gathering up other possessions, whatever I can find, and hurl them out the window, making sure they clear the fire escape. But it's not enough. It's not satisfying the roaring beast within because I want to hurt him. I want to take something important, something close to his heart, and destroy it. Rummaging through drawers, I throw the fancy clothes she'll never wear again on the floor. I suddenly stop, panting like a crazed animal because there's nothing in here that means enough.

I dash out the door and sprint to his den. I should, but I don't hesitate as I open the door and stomp inside. On his desk is a heavy, silver frame with a photograph of my mother and father, taken before I was born. Neither looks at the camera. They gaze at each other, looking happy and in love. It's not something I can really comprehend. I stare at it for a long time, trying to identify them, but these people are strangers to me. The love captured here is dead. I grip the photo to my chest and take it back to her room, thinking I might hide it. Because infuriatingly, he still has a hold over me and I'm scared if I throw it out the window, it will be the end. But then I look around at the chaos I've created, torn dresses, smashed ornaments, and jewelry strewn all over the floor and laugh hysterically. There is no saving me now. I walk slowly to the window and lean out, my hand stretching past the fire escape.

I release the frame and listen for the glass to smash. The still, night air answers with silence.

Putting both hands on the sill, I poke my head out to see where it landed. As soon as I do, something clamps down on my arm and yanks me from the window.

32

KETTLE

THANK YOU

Words clash in my head. *Paralysis. Brain injury. Internal bleeding. Swelling.* Those words echoed off the tunnel walls as they took Kin from his home, his almost-lifeless body bouncing up and down with their hurried movements. These words hurt me in a strangling, tighter and tighter way, like someone's turning a crank key at my side, winding and winding until my ribs part and I explode. I lift my hand to my throat. The lump there doesn't want to move. It's buttoned under my skin. It grates every time I swallow. I can't let him go. I'm stuck in a narrow place between grief and not knowing. Neither is appealing.

I gaze up at the burned apartment in front of me. Windows are being replaced. Timber lies in promising piles in the alley. Soon, I won't be able to come back here. It's probably a good thing. Sitting here with my back against the cool wall, I wait to hear Kin's steady breath. Or hear him chuckle. But there's nothing. Just the humid air causing metal to creak and wood to crackle. The city does sleep, despite what some might say, but it sleeps like an old, arthritic man, coughing, wheezing, and creaking its way to rest.

I left Krow with the boys, needing time on my own. When they asked me when Kin was coming back, I said, "soon," which was a lie.

I should visit him, make sure he's alive, but I'm too much of a coward. What if he's not there? What if he is there and he won't forgive me? What if they catch me? The boys can't be left with no one. There are too many obstacles that I easily let get in the way. So I've waited four days in hell.

I curse and bang the back of my head on the wall, feeling the pain bite into my skull, almost enjoying it because it's a distraction from the anger I feel toward this faceless woman who took Kin's place. Miss Deere. There is hatred brewing and then boiling inside. It's aimless yet growing too big for me to contain. *Her* and that goddamn cat. I hate them both.

I stand up. It was a bad idea coming here, because I feel like I might scream, howl into the night, and get myself reported in the process. Lifting my head, I search for just one star, but all that hovers over me is murky green clouds heavy with moisture.

I slam my hands in my pockets and step out from the wall, out of tears but not out of curse words. I'm turning to leave when something flutters in my peripheral vision, and then I'm blind.

Sweet-smelling silk covers my face and I yank it off. Things are flying from the window. A hat sails past and hits the opposite building before landing into a dirty puddle, then other clothes and jewelry follow. It's like some grotesque rich person's rain, and it only fuels my anger. I see the arm. A perfect pale arm just like the one I saw hanging from the stretcher days ago, and I see red. What is it this woman wants? Does she feel sorry for us lowlife's living in the street, or is she just lazy, throwing her garbage into the alley for others to clean up? I can't stand the idea of pity or indifference.

Blood rushes in my ears and I breathe hard, all my anger propelling me up the dumpster and then onto the fire escape quietly, my hands crackling and pulsing with unspent energy.

I climb onto the railing of the escape and wait for her to come out again. I want to see her face. Frighten her. Tell her what a selfish, rich bitch she is.

I rock back and forth on the railing, finding my balance, and then perching like a bird of prey. A few minutes later, the curtains flutter and the arm stretches out, a framed photograph in its hand. It lingers in the air, shaking, and I cock my head to the side, wondering what this is all about. When she releases the frame, I catch it, tucking it into my waistband. The hand withdraws and I look at the picture by the light of the window, hiding in the shadows like a peeping Tom. I trace the image. A perfect couple gazing at each other with love, and I want to smash their faces in. I want to ask them, demand from them, *Why? Why did my life work out like this? Why have I lost everyone?* It feels like it's their fault, them and everyone else who looks down on people like me. Like Kin.

Kin. I wipe the last tear I have in me from my eye with a dirty hand. *Damn it.*

Pale fingers grip the windowsill, and then the shadow of a head pokes out into the night.

I'll make her pay. I'll teach this rich woman a lesson.

I grab her hand and pull her from the window, her small body coming at me with my own force. She lands on my chest and knocks the air from my lungs, simultaneously knocking the anger from my heart when she looks down at me with a face bruised, cut, and vulnerable. Her eyes are lit up in gold and honey from the light of the room within. They widen with surprise... and then droop with sadness.

"Thank you," she whispers.

33
RUNNING

Thank you? The words make no sense, yet the relief in her eyes is so solid, it's as if I could reach in and take it, squeeze it out in my hands. My emotions slide around, bouncing off each other, anger to confusion and very quickly to panic as I realize I've made a huge mistake.

My hand is clamped around her cool wrist and *her* breath is easing into *my* chest as it goes from short, sharp bursts to a steadier yet still fast rhythm. She's still lying on top of me and makes no effort to move, her neck pulled back so she can see my face clear as day under the light of the window. This is more than a mistake. She's seen my face, my very distinct, blue-eyed, Japanese face. *Damn it!*

I grunt and push her back from my chest by her shoulder, holding onto one of her arms. In a dark tone that scares me, I say, "Get up."

She shuffles back onto her knees, her arm hanging limply from mine like she's not connected to it. Her honey eyes look up at me with something of a plea in them, but she doesn't say another word so 'thank you' just floats between us with no explanation.

Between us sits the framed photo, glass smashed, two faces staring past us and into nothing. We both look down at it for one small moment and then back up.

A red light streaks across her face, its source a police car that's reversing, closing the gap between the buildings. One escape route blocked.

I run a shaky hand through my hair and swear. She makes a strange, shocked sound at my curse words, and I remember she's a society girl unused to uncouth youths such as myself. I pull her to her feet more gently and mutter, "You're coming with me, princess," and tug her toward the edge. She sniffs but doesn't argue with me.

With more precision than I would have expected, she jumps onto the dumpster, landing well. Spreading her bodyweight so evenly, she barely makes a sound.

Above, I can hear someone shuffling across floorboards and panic rising as the person, perhaps her mother, realizes she's gone. A loud woman's voice sails over our heads, and the girl looks up at the window, her face twisted with regret. "I'm sorry," she whispers, looking like she might climb back up. I jump down to stop her. I'm not going to jail for this girl. And I know I'm too easily recognizable. No, I need to get her somewhere quiet and convince her not to report me. I nod to myself, thinking it's a dumb plan but it's the only one my sleep-deprived brain can come up with.

This silent dance we're doing is strange. She seems too willing, and yet tied to the lid of the dumpster. Crouched facing each other, I get ready to grab her and pull her down to the other end of alley. I stare directly into her shadowed face and say, "Look lady, I don't want to hurt you, I didn't mean to..." I sigh, exasperated by her gaping silence. "I just want to talk to you somewhere safe, okay?"

Her head falls and she gazes at her fingers, spread wide over the dimply blue metal. "Okay," she says

I'm hopping from foot to foot in a frog squat, the surprising permission, the *okay*, taking a second to register. But voices are louder now, and I can hear car doors opening and closing, boots sloshing through puddles. I've got to move.

"Okay?" I say like a question as I jump from the dumpster and pull her down, mud splattering her clean clothes and shoes. And even though she said okay, I don't let go of her hand. I clutch it tightly and press close to the wall, moving as fast as I can to reach the other end.

She runs with me, not fighting, not lagging, and with every drop of filthy alley water that splashes up our clothes, a new question pops up in my head about why she's willingly coming with me and what the hell have I gotten myself into?

The police sirens begin just as we round the corner.

At this time of night, a few drunks, cabbies, and people like me shuffle through the wet streets. They pay me no mind as I dart across the road, avoiding the pools of golden light under each street lamp and straight into the next alley.

Stop. Think.

My head swivels this way and that, like maybe there's a glaring solution in front of me I've neglected. My chest tightens when I remember there's a girl on my arm. A girl I just ripped from a window. A girl they'll be looking for.

"Sh! They're looking for us," Kin warns, his skinny arm

pressed across my chest. I gulp and wheeze like a squeezing accordion.

The bricks dig into my spine, or my spine digs into the bricks, I'm not sure, all I know is, it's uncomfortable and I'm scared. I'm scared they'll find me. I'm scared they won't find me because then we'll be alone again.

Kin's intense, dark eyes fall on my face and his tight expression relaxes. He elbows me and smiles. "Don't worry, little brother," he says. "You and me, we're gonna conquer this city."

I nod. Redness in my cheeks and cold air freezing my nose.

"The count is out by two," a soldier mutters, pausing in the archway, two long shadows reaching our feet.

We slide further away, the brambles of a bush growing up against the wall welcomes us into its arms. Stick fingers scratch my face sluggishly.

He says our names loudly, mispronouncing every part of them.

The train is shushing and anxious to leave the station. "What do we do, sir? Do we just forget about it?"

The other soldier's voice is angry. "Would you forget our friends who died at Pearl Harbor? Hell, why do you think most of them can't go back there? People haven't forgotten and they don't want them returning to the West Coast."

These words are not new. These words were drilled into our heads from the day we arrived.

"Sir...?" The soldier awaits an answer, and Kin and I hold our breath.

A loud sigh. An impatient tone. "We'll notify the local authorities. These boys were supposed to go to an orphanage up state. They'll find 'em. Two nip kids won't get far in this *city. They'll stick out like mouse turds in a bowl of rice."*

I crouch down, press as close to the wall as I can.

Kin and me, we're on our own now.

She tugs on my hand. A growing concerto of sirens, voices, footsteps shake me from the memory. The sounds bloom from the front of her house and will soon stretch to where we are. I turn to her pale face. Her mouth is open and puffs of mist come out with her breath. She doesn't look scared. She looks… sick.

I tilt my head and try to really see her. I arch an eyebrow at her bruises and she straightens, a cold mask slipping over what I thought were excited features a minute ago… until I say, "Can you climb?" and even in this thinly spread light, I can see spots of color in her cheeks and a touch of life returning to her eyes.

Her lip twitches up at one corner, and she replies, "I can climb."

We run between two more buildings and take a few corners, winding our way through the city maze while I try to think of the best hideout. It must be past midnight now and my thoughts turn to the boys waiting for me and to Kin. I can see him slapping his forehead right now at my stupidity. He would kill me. He will…

I come to a halt beneath an older, more crumbly building but it's an important one filled with important people. The girl looks up and then dubiously back to me. "Here?"

"Yep," I pant, releasing her wrist and linking my fingers together to give her a boost. I'm squatting down, waiting to bear her weight, when the metallic twang of the platform above me makes me jump. She's standing on the platform, swaying a little, having swung herself up on her own. I shake my head in disbelief and follow.

Quietly, we creep up the fire escape, just the sounds of our breath filling the closed night. About halfway up, she pauses, one foot on a rung and the other on the platform. "What's your name?" she whispers.

I hesitate, but realizing my name will mean nothing to the authorities, I give it to her. "Kettle."

She lifts her foot and hangs from the ladder, leaning toward me, her thick hair dangling near my nose. "That's odd."

I grimace. "What's your name then?"

"Nora." She sighs, continuing up the ladder.

I like it, but I don't want to say I do. "That's just boring."

I think she laughs. I grip the rungs beneath her. *I don't care if she laughs.*

We reach the top, and she quite easily rolls over the edge and lands on the dirty roof.

I point to the thick brick wall with several chimneys sticking out of it. "Over there."

She nods and crawls over the apex of the roof until she reaches the small space between the two walls, a five-foot-wide, maybe only six-or-seven-feet-long rectangle of concrete between two banks of chimneys. She steps in, and I follow.

She moves to the far end to give me room, dusts off her skirt, and pulls her legs under it, wrapping her arms around her knees. Although she's only a couple of inches shorter than me, she looks tiny in here. Defeated.

I want to ask her what happened to her. I don't know why. Shaking my head, I lean my back against the warm chimney, my legs pushing into the opposite wall.

Up here I can see some of the stars and I tilt up, counting them and almost forgetting that she's next to me until she speaks.

"Is this where you sleep?" she asks. I turn, noticing she's staring at the sky too. "It's beautiful up here."

I laugh in a shocked kind of way. "No. Look, Nora, I'm really sorry I pulled you out the window. I shouldn't have done it. It's just, well, I was angry about some... stuff and you throwing your garbage on me was the last straw, you know? But I was never going to hurt you. I just wanted to give you a scare." My words are not my friends right now. "If you could just please promise not to report me, well, I could take you home and we could forget this ever happened."

A rustle of skirts.

A tightening of her brown pea coat across her chest.

"No," she says, her voice carved yet soft, ribbons tied to rocks.

"No?"

Her words slide from her mouth like a cloud just begging for the sky. "I don't want to go home."

34

AN AGREEMENT

*I WONDER IF I'M DAMAGED BEYOND REPAIR. I HEAR HIS VOICE
AND I THREAD PAST THE ANGER, THE DISTRUST. I SQUIRM
BETWEEN THE BANDS OF DISDAIN AND THINK I FIND KINDNESS. I
CAN'T TELL IF IT'S REAL OR IMAGINED, BUT I'M CLINGING TO IT
NEVERTHELESS.
ALL I KNOW IS THAT I DON'T WANT TO GO HOME YET.*

He crosses his arms over his chest and frowns at me through the dark. The murky clouds are clearing and stars and a crust of moon light up his dark features, his eyes looking black although I know they're an unusual shade of blue.

"What do you mean, no, you don't want to go home? You know I could, I could…" He clenches his fists and rests them on his knees, but they are disarmed bombs. I know what the beginning of a punch looks and feels like. This is not it. I dare to move closer to him. I'm not sure whether to be honest. Too much truth and he definitely won't help me. Especially not someone like him.

"I know this may sound strange to someone like you, but I want to see where you live. How you live. I'm… curious," I say, leaning in as he leans away.

"No. No way," he answers through mumbling lips,

his hands coasting flat like he's sanding a bench.

I rise to kneeling, his folded-in form seems so tense, everything looking like it's about to snap and splinter like dry bamboo. "Then I'll report you," I state.

He groans and swears, then kicks the wall in front of him. He's staring at the bricks when he says, "Or I could throw you from this roof." It lacks any type of conviction. He doesn't understand that I am well acquainted with violence. I know threats and murderous eyes. He is not that person. The feeling wraps around my bones like frayed cotton thread. I'm loose from my tethers of sister and shield and I'm placing too much trust in my 'feelings'. But what I have lost is already lost. My hands are empty.

"Let me spend a few days in your world," I plead. "My father, he's so strict, I feel like I can't breathe." I sigh dramatically. "I just need a break from all the rules." I'm lying, throwing my hair back awkwardly, trying to pretend I'm someone else whose life is some picture of normal. He doesn't answer straight away, which means I might have a shot. The moon reads *running out of time*. The stars are seconds fading. "Please. I promise I won't be any trouble." I clasp my hands together and smile. It turns to irritation on his face.

He shrugs. "How do I know you won't report me anyway once you've had your fun slumming it?" I wince at the words 'slumming it' and watch him shake his head as he talks himself out of it. "No. It's too risky. My home, it's… special, er, secret. People can't know about it. I don't know you, and I definitely don't trust you. It's not a good idea."

I feel like this might be an opportunity or at least

the beginnings of one, but like the slippery tail of a fish, I'm losing my grip on it. "Kettle." His eyebrows rise when I say his name. "Unless you *are* going to throw me off the roof, you'll have to trust me. I give you my word. If you let me stay with you for a few days, I won't report you. I promise." I hold out my hand for him to shake. "Deal?"

He eyes me suspiciously for a long moment, his capacity for silence impressive. My hand starts to quiver from hanging in the air too long but he finally grasps it strongly and shakes. "Don't mess with me," Kettle warns quietly and in a voice which makes me think he's been hurt before.

The sharp parts of oxygen slice their way out of my throat. I miss Frankie. But something pushes me forward, a need to escape, to look for a way out. Kettle and I are still holding hands, the up and down motion continuing as we both retreat into our own thoughts. "I wouldn't dream of it," I manage, pressing my other hand to my heart.

Our hands slowly break apart. It doesn't feel as uncomfortable as it should. "Fine. Good," Kettle concedes. "We'll rest here for another couple of hours, and then make a break for it just before sunrise."

My heart stammers a little at this agreement. It pushes unwanted blood to my brain, which still aches. I tell myself Frankie will be okay. She's not with him, and that's a good thing.

I wonder if he'll even tell her that I'm missing. And then I wonder if I'm convincing myself of things just so I can keep my eyes forward, keep *moving* forward. I start tapping the bricks in front with my feet in agitation. Tap, tap, tap, like the tick of a clock counting down to nothing.

I need to find her.

The sun lashes the edge of the city, spreading warmth and shadows over our contained bodies. I haven't slept and my arms are stiff from being crossed over my chest for two hours. Kettle slept for minutes at a time, quickly startling awake at every pigeon coo or car horn. It's like he's constantly on alert, waiting for the next threat.

I unfold myself like a rusted card table, clicking and clacking.

We haven't spoken since we made the deal. In fact, his eyes have barely looked my way since then.

The sun slants over him scrunched in the corner, his knees up but spread apart, his cap pulled over his brow. As he lifts his head and squints into the light, I see his face is smooth and unblemished, and his arms and legs are at odds with it, covered in scratches, cuts, and scars. I want to ask him *how… why…?* But if I do, he may ask me the same questions and I don't know how to answer those.

"Take a Polaroid, it'll last longer," he sneers beneath the shadow of his once-white baseball cap. He eases from the wall and rolls his shoulders, crackling like sappy leaves in a fire.

I startle and heat floods my cheeks. "Sorry," I mumble, timidly putting my hand to my own bruised face. *How can I hide a secret that lies on my skin?* "You know what a Polaroid is?"

He stands, swinging his head past the chimneys, smiling when his eyes reach the horizon. "You think just because I'm not rich that I don't know what a Polaroid is? Geez. I'm poor. Not stupid."

I wonder if you can even see the blush underneath the purple of my bruises or if it just makes them darker. I stand with him and stretch my arms. "I didn't mean it like that."

He shrugs. "I know." He stretches his toned arms and swings his head downward to the wakening streets. "Do you think you can climb back down?" he asks, a tiny hint of concern in his rich, melted-chocolate voice.

I crack my neck, and he flinches at the pebbly sound. "Of course, why wouldn't I?"

"No offence, but you look like someone took a baseball bat to your face and now that the thrill has worn off, you may be feeling a little less... brave," he says, his hands stapled to his sides, fingers tapping, tapping, tapping.

"I'm fine," I say unconvincingly. My stomach gurgles and blends with the morning tweets of birds and the sound of a garbage truck ambling down the street. "Just a bit hungry."

We climb down the fire escape, more slowly now, hiding when the inhabitants stir in their beds. He's right, though I wouldn't tell him so. I feel woozy as I descend, the ground tilting and seeming out of focus every time I look down. Every now and then, he throws careful glances in my direction, an arm shooting out to stabilize me when I get to the last platform and sway a little. I step back from his touch.

We land on the ground just as day truly breaks,

although it's still dark in the alley, and I look to both ends, wondering what to do next. Suddenly, he grabs me by both shoulders. I step backward and hit the wall. I think I should scream, but I'm silent. It's a habit ingrained and scratched against my voice box—*don't scream.*

He's just staring at me, tilting his head from side to side, his grip firm but not too tight. "What are you doing?" I stammer.

"Your face," he says, suddenly releasing me as he registers my fear. "If you're going to come with me, we need to disguise you better. Will you stay here for a few minutes?"

My lips feel dry. I am toasted, nothing left but charcoal. "How do I know you'll come back?"

He straightens, his brows lowered. I've offended him. "I made a deal," he states, then he points a finger at me like I'm a naughty child and says, "Wait here."

I have no way to fight him on this, so I let him go. He jogs down the alley and disappears around the corner.

Standing alone in this cold, damp alley, I start to wonder if my brain has been permanently injured. Because I should be worried about this boy. I shouldn't be going anywhere with him. But I can't seem to stop myself. My curiosity, my need to see if there is a life outside of the brownstone walls, is so strong that it overrides every logical thought. The thought slips from my unconscious to my conscious subtly but strongly. *I have to try.*

Twenty minutes later, Kettle returns with a scarf and a pair of sunglasses with lenses the size of saucers in his clenched fists. "Here," he pants, thrusting them at me. He helps me tie my unruly hair down with the scarf and I put the glasses on.

I put my arms out in front of me and wave them around. "I can barely see," I say, giggling when he jumps away from my swiping hands.

"Whoa. Watch it," he says, bending away. I catch the slight amusement in his tone. He offers his elbow, and I thread my arm through.

"This feels strange," I say, still batting at the air.

He laughs short and slicing. "No kidding."

I meant wearing sunglasses when the light is still dim. I have a feeling he meant something else.

35

BLINDED

Kin's disapproving voice is in my head, so real it's like he's standing next to me, shaking my shoulder. *"What are you doing, man? Are you nuts?"*

"I know what I'm doing, I think." I'm torn, a hair splitting. *"She looks like she needs help, and I think I could use hers."*

"What makes you think she needs your help? You're nothing but street trash to someone like her. Besides, you can't save everyone."

"You didn't see her face." The built-up tower of sadness in her eyes.

I lead Nora into the street. Lights flicker off as the sun starts to warm the edges of the buildings. But it's still a colder morning and puffs of steam run from every mouth of the hardworking people who are up at this time. She keeps up with me though I can hear her wheezing and groaning in pain.

I wish I didn't feel bad for her, but I do.

People don't look up from their work yet but if she keeps swinging her head around so anxiously, someone will. "Keep your head down…" I say, pulling my cap just over my eyes. She tips her chin to her chest for a moment, but then she's looking up again.

"Nora," I whisper through my teeth. "Get a grip."

She huffs out a breath and shakes her head, pulling her coat across her middle with one hand. "I'm sorry. It's just… there's so much to see."

I pause and try to understand what she's talking about. People are waking, opening up, whistling, humming or yelling at their wives. Garbage cans glint with early morning light. Leaves twirl between them and the rhythmic crunch of the first wave of commuters' rumbles across the pavement.

I shrug and pull her into the crowd of people heading toward the station. Strange girl. It's like she's rarely been outside before.

Just before we go down the stairs, I stop and buy some food for both of us. She seems surprised when I pay, but she manages to say thank you.

She takes one step down and pauses, nearly getting us barreled over by the other people who know you can't stop on the subway stairs. "Where are we going?" She goes to lift her sunglasses, and I stop her.

"I can't tell you that. It's a secret," I reply, sounding way too sinister.

"Oh." She sighs.

She seems disappointed, but she lets me lead her down the stairs and through the subway station to the platform. I can see it's hard for her not to put her arms out in front like she's feeling her way in the dark, and I have to keep reminding her to act normal.

Down here, she's almost blind and the way I'm leading her around, I think people think she *is* blind. It works brilliantly. She won't be able to find her way back here if she tried.

When we get on the car, people make way for her. An elderly man offers her his seat, which she refuses.

She holds onto my arm nervously, her eyes down now, suddenly shy and unsure of herself.

I lean down and whisper close to her ear, "Have you ever been on the subway before?"

Nora shakes her head and replies in a dreamy voice, "Once. And it was wonderful." She sips her drink and gazes at the racing lights out the window, a sad smile on her lips.

I don't know what to say, so I don't say anything. Just glare at the people who stare at the two of us, their minds collapsing over the idea of someone like me, and someone like her, standing together. She seems oblivious, but then she can't see much.

She is completely blind once she's in our tunnel, tripping and falling, her hands out in front of her.

"This reminds me of…" she loudly starts.

"Shh!" I snap.

She starts whispering. "…a trust exercise we did at school. You know where you fall backward with your eyes closed and someone has to catch you?"

She's waiting for me to respond, to say, 'oh yes, I remember that'. But of course I don't. My schooling was limited and directed toward patriotism and how not to snare the sewing machines. "Um yeah, my school didn't do that…"

The light from the door ahead warms her face, her bottom lip folded under her top teeth.

We stop and her hands touch the beat-up wood, her fingers running down the length of the plank in front of her. "Oh."

Yeah, *oh.*

"You can take off your glasses now if you like," I say as I knock, smiling as I realize she probably could have taken them off as soon as we entered the tunnel. She startles and removes them just as Krow opens the door. His eyes grow round and dark as seven-inch records when he sees her and he just stands in the doorway gawking, his lanky arm blocking our path.

She blinks, the glasses poised at her chest, and then Kelpie slams into my legs and squeezes them together so tightly I nearly lose my balance.

"You're back." He gazes around my legs, peering into the dark tunnel. "Where's Kin?" he asks softly.

I pat his blond head and say, "He's not with me, Kelpie." My eyes connect with Krow's and he nods solemnly.

Nora is a statue, a porcelain doll in a window except I can almost hear her heart beating. She smiles at Krow, says, "Excuse me," and tries to walk forward.

"Scuse yerself," he growls and looks to me for reassurance.

"Let her in, Krow. She's err, staying with us for a few days."

He drops his hand but not his angry stare as she passes through the doorway.

She takes strong, un-timid steps into my home. My head tilts, curious, as I find myself wanting to know why and wanting to know more.

36

THE LOST BOYS AND ME

The scent of soap mixed with the dirt it cleans dominates the air. It's earthy water slipping between chunks of gravel. Cool, heavy air flows past my face in waves.

It's not dirty in here. It's some sort of organized chaos with clothes, shoes, and bedding grouped together in small piles.

No, it's not dirty. I raise an eyebrow… It's not exactly clean either.

"What's her name?" a young boy shouts, looking at me with his head flipped back like I'm a beanstalk climbing to the sky.

Kettle strides past me toward the back of this beautiful hollow, his boots barely making a sound on the solid stone floor, and throws his satchel to the ground. My ears are tuned to floorboard creaks, soft, threatening footsteps. Everything about this place is different to my home. Rich, golden light bounces off Kettle's back, his dark head turns just slightly, and he throws my name over his shoulder in a regrettable tone. "Her name is Nora."

The little boy frowns at me, hands on hips. "That's not right. What's her King name?"

Kettle sits down on a pillowy bed, made on two pallets, and glances sideways at us both. "She's not a

King, Kelpie." It seems like an insult.

The little boy seems unsatisfied with this answer and he grabs my hand, dragging me further into the vast room. My feet trip over golden bricks, framing tiny beds, each hedged in with a small box or case, sweet personal belongings waterfalling over the edges. Each bed is different in color and shape, and I understand that each space is someone's bedroom. I carefully tread between these private spaces until I'm facing Kettle. He looks up at me with tired eyes and I try unsuccessfully not to gasp at the beauty of them, the unusualness of dark blue eyes in a Japanese face.

"Why isn't she a King? Is it coz she's a girl? Keeper was a girl. Girls can be Kings," Kelpie says in one strained breath, blowing his blond curls from his eyes.

The lanky one that wouldn't let me pass lurks near the door, talking to three other teenage boys in low whispers.

"She's not a King because she's not staying. She's a visitor… a guest." He's starting to untie his shoes, unbutton his collar, and I'm still staring at him.

I avert my eyes, sweeping over the grand arches and the green tiles instead. This place is a lot to take in.

Kelpie accepts this answer, although he pulls me down to his level and whispers, his voice scratchy and tinny, "If you stay, you get a new name. You should stay."

I smile and then my face rearranges to a frown. *I miss Frankie.* Kettle stands suddenly and pulls a curtain between us with a swish. "Kelpie, why don't you show her around while I get cleaned up?"

Kelpie tugs on my arm and begins to lead me away.

A rustle and a clatter behind the curtain makes us stop, and Kettle laughs strangely. "I forgot about these. Um... wait," he says, parting the curtain just a little. I catch a glimpse of his shirtless torso, and it makes me very uncomfortable. I'm so embarrassed that I gulp. He thrusts a handful of boxes into my hands, and I think he's smirking a little at my awkwardness. "Here. Can you hand these out to the boys for me?"

I look down at my palms to see five toothbrushes of various colors and two boxes of toothpaste. I raise an eyebrow and my eyes to catch his face, but he's already pulled the curtain closed again.

I feel like I've stumbled into a play, a commercial where five ratty-looking boys get educated on dental hygiene. I tighten my hold on the toothbrushes and on Kelpie and let him lead me around Kettle's home.

"And this is where I sleep," Kelpie announces, pointing down at a large crate with one side cut out. It's filled with blankets and about four small, flowery pillows. They look familiar. I lean down and pick one up, examining it.

Kettle's voice startles me as he comes from behind and says, "Found them in the dumpster outside the toy store. Doll's bedding..." He studies my expression for a moment, his lips pressed together like he's trying to read me. "We scavenge but we don't steal."

I start to say, "I never thought..." but then I decide not to finish, turning to Kelpie. "Well that's very resourceful." Truth is, I assumed he stole. I shouldn't have... but I did.

Kelpie beams up at me and then runs off to join the other boys, clutching the toothbrushes. They lift their heads and accept him into their circle, one ruffling his hair as they snatch up the brushes. A larger boy chomps his teeth loudly and says, "Thanks Kettle. Gotta keep my breath minty fresh for the ladies."

The others chuckle.

I stand right in the center of this arched home, my hands behind my back, just admiring the beauty of it. I don't want to move lest it dissolves into a pile of sand like a mirage. I gaze up at the black, iron lights, and they fill me with an unfamiliar feeling. Hope. I bite back a grin.

This place is amazing.

Kettle breaks the silence. "So this is it. Home sweet home." He shifts awkwardly and scratches the back of his head.

I want to say a lot of things and with too much enthusiasm. I rein my thoughts in and manage to say, "It's incredible."

He tips his chin, and I think I catch a smile. Under the light, I can finally see him clearly, especially now that his face is wiped of dirt and his cap isn't pulled over his eyes. He's very different. He doesn't look like anyone I've ever met before. If he's handsome, I'm not sure I can tell, having little to compare him to, but I know I like seeing him. I feel my lips curving like a half moon, and I quickly stare at the ground.

"They're not swords. Make sure you brush twice a day, boys!" he shouts, looking over my shoulder at the boys who are jabbing each other with their freshly unwrapped toothbrushes. Then he stares at me. "They need to be reminded about things like washing and brushing their teeth, you know?"

I nod. I'm pretty lost. I don't know where to stand, how to stand, what to do. My hands scrunch and un-scrunch at my sides. This is all so very strange to the point where it doesn't feel real. "Kettle, what is this place?" I ask, looking up at him with eyes that could swallow the world... that want to.

He grins at me and something hurts inside my chest. My fingers creep up and touch my heart to check if it's still there. "This is where the Kings live!"

Kettle leaves again within an hour of bringing me to this place. Before he goes, he turns to the lanky kid. "Krow, show her the ropes. I'm going to the grocery store."

It all seems so domestic and completely wrong at the same time.

Krow stalks toward me when the door closes. I tuck my hair behind my ear and try to not look ter-rified. He stops about two feet from me and sweeps his arm around the abandoned tunnel. He points to the beds. "We keep our beds clean 'n' neat. We eat over there." He points to some upturned boxes and a card table that's had half the vinyl peeled from the top. "Toi-let's over there." He points to a dark part of the wall near the back that on closer inspection looks like an entrance. "Toilet bowl's long gone, but the hole in the ground is still hooked into the plumbing. Ya just need to take a bucket of water with ya when you go..." He points to an open maintenance closet on the opposite side of the disused railway tracks, and I suck in a panicked breath, making him smile. "Um… I dunno where you'll be sleepin'." He scratches his chin, eyes darting around the room. He does remind me of a crow with his black, intelligent, and suspicious eyes and his jerky movements. He seems ready to take flight at a moment's notice. "Last of all, we keep outta trouble. No stealin', and we get food and a place to stay." He takes another step forward. He's shorter than me, much thinner too. He runs a hand through his unkempt, greasy hair and snarls at me. "Number one rule is—we keep this place a secret."

"I promise," I say, trying to reassure this ferocious little urchin. I've made a lot of promises in the last twenty-four hours. "I will keep your secret." I hold my hand up, doing scout's honor. He tilts his head and stares at my gesture with curiosity and no understanding.

Some of the other boys begin creeping up inch by inch, trusting me one small breath of air at a time. "Do you want to hear my secret?" I say, whispering and crouching down to Kelpie, who's already wrapped his sticky hands around my leg.

Krow leans in despite himself. "I s'pose." He shrugs but I can tell he's intrigued.

I take a deep breath in, stalling and building suspense, and my voice grows quieter. I'm planning on saying something funny, like I'm the Queen of England or I'm a mermaid, but what slips out in a hushed tone is, "I ran away from home… and I don't want to go back." I clasp my hands and look down. They're scratched and bruised. They're the reason I can't lie. "I ran away from a bad man. A bad place."

A boy with sandy hair like mine but straight as a ruler pats me on the back. "Kettle'll look after you. Kin too, when he gets back." Krow elbows him in the ribs.

A tear slips from my eye and lands on the stones. It's absorbed instantly. Krow stares down at it and then back up at me. A wary smile grows, one cheek lifts, and he seems to accept what I have said. Begrudgingly, he asks, "Wanna play cards til' Kettle gets back?"

I smile, stand, and straighten my clothes, wiping the moisture from my eyes. "Sure."

We sit around for an hour or so, and I learn the boy's names. Krow, Kelpie, Klam, Keg (due to his barrel like shape), and Krop. "So those aren't your real names, I assume. Why did you change them?" I ask as I flick the cards out to each scratched and smudged hand. They pull up the cards and we all match. It's sad and comforting.

"New start, new name," Krow answers.

"Did Kettle and… K…"

"Kin," Keg finishes.

I nod staring down at my pair of sevens. "Yes, did Kettle and Kin name you?"

This makes them frown, five pairs of narrowed eyes. "No, we named ourselves," Krop replies.

Krow throws out two of his cards, and I deal him two new ones. "When you join the Kings, you choose a new name, coz down here, no one can own you but you."

I want to be a King. I want to be a King. I want to not be a Deere.

"So who is this Kin anyway?" I ask casually, pushing a button marked five into the center of the table.

"Kin is Kettle's brother," Kelpie answers, cheating as he pops up behind me and looks at my cards.

My eyes flip from my cards to the boys, shuttered, trying to play it cool. "Where is he?"

Krow calls me and then says, "Kin got sick. He don't live here no more. Least not for now," as we lay our cards down on the table.

The look he gives me tells me I shouldn't ask any more questions about Kin. But I have so many others. I want to know how they all came to be here. How on earth does Kettle care for them? It seems impossible, but I'm starting to learn I know nothing of what is possible.

Kettle pushes through the door, arms full of overflowing grocery bags. The boys attack him like hungry seagulls, and I watch him gleefully and responsibly hand out an equal portion of food to each one. When he gets to me, he hands me a sandwich and a drink.

"You should eat," he grunts, a lick of concern flapping across his eyes.

I take it, realizing I haven't eaten very much at all in the last twenty-four hours, having only nibbled at the Danish Kettle bought me earlier. "Thank you."

I devour the food like it's trying to escape my hands and it hits my empty stomach like a rock, churning and grating against the sides until I feel like I might vomit.

I put both hands out to steady myself, feeling the color draining from my face and collecting in my copper-tasting mouth. I dig my fingers into the stone floor as the world slopes and I feel like I need to hang on or fall out. Kettle's face appears in my vision, distorted and stretching, and I release my hold on the world. His words cut through to my ears in pieces like they're being passed through a cheese grater. But I think he says, "You... don't look... so good," before I feel myself falling. My head anticipates the cold, hard stones because there's never been anyone to catch me before, but I land against arms. Arms that scoop me up and pull me away from the others, whose noise sounds like lapping waves and seagulls squawking.

I'm laid down on lumpy pillows and a blanket is pulled over my legs. He leans down and touches my forehead with the back of his hand, sighing with relief.

My blinking gets heavier and longer. I fight it for a short second, until all goes black.

Rest.

You're safe, I think. *For once, you might be safe.*

I wake to hear the snoring and sleeping sounds of five boys squished together. I shiver in the coolness, the sense that it is night reinforced by the lower temperature. I feel better. My headache has gone and my eyes don't feel glued to my eyelids. I finally slept. For the first time in years, I slept undisturbed by fear, real or imagined. It has done wonders. My mind is fresh and sprinkled with dewdrops.

My fingers search for the blanket and knock two small cardboard boxes at my side. When I lift them up, I see a bright red toothbrush and a small tube of toothpaste.

I close my eyes again and smile. Falling back into glorious unconsciousness.

37

UNLOCKED

She's not what I expected. Not at all. Safe to say, I don't like that. I wanted to hate her. Blame her, but there's something in her eyes, in the way she moves and reacts, that makes me think life has given her a raw deal too. As impossible as it may seem, she is... *maybe*... like me.

Lighting the candle by my bed, I check my wallet. I poke at the handful of coins I have left in my palm and sigh. I haven't worked in days. I have to go back to the docks.

The clock on the wall reads four in the morning.

I rustle through the bags and find a bagel with seeds on it. I take a large bite, regretting it as it's so hard to chew. The curtain around my bed sways and I roll my eyes, expecting Kelpie to come slinking in. Instead, it's the purple fingers of a girl grasping the curtain.

Nora peeks her head in and sort of smiles when she sees me. My mouth is stuffed full of bagel, and I try to chew quickly as she squats down and starts to speak. "I just wanted to say thank you," she whispers. She sweeps a hand across her forehead and drops her chin, mumbling to the floor. "Honestly, I don't know what happened back there. I'm usually... I mean... I'm better at..." She blows her hair from her eyes, frustrated by herself. It's like she's battling with her conscience, trying to decide what to tell me. Anyone can tell she's been hurt. But how she was hurt is something I don't feel I can ask her. "Sorry."

I shake my head and swallow the large lump of bagel, coughing a bit when it gets stuck.

She's still squatting uncomfortably on the stones and I stand up, ushering her to sit on the bed, while I pull my chest over and sit on that.

"You hungry?" I ask, offering her another bagel from the bottom of the bag. She nods and takes it shakily, picking small pieces from it like a bird.

We sit in silence for a while, eating and avoiding eye contact until she says, "Am I sleeping in your brother's bed?" she asks, her eyes wandering all over my face. She tucks her feet in, keeps them pressed neatly together.

I nod. "He got sick. So he can't stay here anymore." I clasp my hands in front of me and talk to the floor. "Truth is, I don't know where he is. After the paramedics took him away, I don't know what happened to him." I close my eyes, scrunch them against the dark that's closing in, the fear. "He could be dead for all I know." I don't tell Nora about the lady who fainted at the platform and the reason why I pulled her from the window. She wasn't there, and it's not her fault. "Please don't tell Kelpie," I plead.

She reaches out and pats my shoulder, real quick, and withdraws. "My…" she starts and then bites her lip. "I'm sure he's not dead. Why don't you go to the hospital and find out?" she asks innocently. Not understanding that I can't. I made a false report, I'm a runaway, and I'm in the system. If they let me in the door, it would only be to arrest me.

"Yeah maybe," I mutter. "I can't today, though. With Kin gone, there's not as much money to go around. I've got to make up for his income. I've got to work today."

She raises her eyebrows. "You work?"

"Last time I checked, money wasn't falling from the sky," I say sarcastically, then add, "just hats, stockings, and necklaces."

I stand and pull my work clothes from my old suitcase, casting my eyes over the large bag of dirty clothes that's sitting like a lump at the end of the bed. I need to go to the laundromat. I sigh again. It's a lot. I'm going to have get Krow to take on more responsibilities, starting with this. I kick the bag and put my hands in the small of my back, stretching. When I straighten, Nora is glaring at me, eyes aflame.

She stands suddenly, our bodies too close in this small space. She's breathing hard, her lips pursed. And I don't know how we went from quite civilized to this so fast. "P-please," she stutters. "It's not a joke."

Her arms are jangling like ribbons in the wind and I want to reach out and still them, but I get the sense that I shouldn't touch her, not unless I want a black eye to match hers.

Usually this kind of thing would make me want to press for details, usually I'd be defensive, but she seems so earnest and affronted, I feel like I need to just apologize.

"Sorry," I say quietly. "I didn't mean to upset you." *But why? Why are you upset? Why were you throwing your stuff, your expensive stuff, out the window in the first place?*

She calms, ceases shaking, and I can see her mood

unwinding before me, her eyes opening wider, her mouth relaxing into a neutral expression. I need to change the subject.

She does it before I get a chance. "Where do you work?" she asks, forcing lightness into her tone. It doesn't work that well. Her voice is layered, thick as a bank vault buried in concrete. There are secrets and truths I feel are just below the surface and then more of them, buried even deeper.

"Down at the docks," I reply. Reaching out to lean on the wall, I miss, my hand scraping down the bricks and making me stumble. "I, um, actually, I need to get ready now if I'm going to make it on time."

She's sits back down on the bed and rests her chin in her hands. The clock ticks over for a few awkward seconds before she says, "I should come with you." I shake my head, but she ignores me. "No really, I should. You've lost a worker, I can work," she says, knotting her brow like she's not even sure that's true.

Her eyes tell me I'm not going to convince her otherwise, and I figure why not? She wanted to live in my world and this is it. Besides, there's no way she'll make it through the gates. I won't let her get hurt. My guess is she'll see how brutal it is and she'll give up and go home. Which is what I want… right?

I cast a disapproving look her way. "You can't work at the docks in a skirt and twin set."

She snorts and daintily covers her mouth, and I'm reminded that she's not from here. She's from the sky, and I'm a blade of grass searching for the sun that's always getting trodden on. "You know what a twin set is?" she asks, glancing down at her chest and playing with the button on her cardigan. The way she plays with it between her fingertips teases a memory from my brain. A little girl plucking Kin's braces like a guitar string. A button falling to the ground. We stare at each other for a moment, but if she remembers me, she doesn't say. I laugh to myself. She's not going to remember someone like me.

Her lashes fall, and heat creeps into my cheeks. Thankfully, in this small light, she won't be able to see it. "I can see into shop displays," I say defensively. "I can read a sign."

She huffs. "Okay, well, if I can't wear this," she says, holding her skirts in her balled-up fists, "do you have something more appropriate?"

I think for a moment. "I'll see what I can find," I say, ushering her out of my space. "Just let me get changed."

She backs up and stands there, looking a little lost. A little determined. Again, her feet seem stuck together, her legs bowing so her knees don't touch.

"Um. I'll be a minute. You can go back to your bed." I wave her away.

Closing the curtains, I wait to hear her footsteps padding away from me. I crouch down and drag my lockbox to my feet, grabbing the key from my pocket.

I lift up a few things, scarves, long beads, and pull out a pair of riding pants that Nora threw from her window months ago. They're classy and kind of grown up for a teenage girl. The navy-blue fabric has a slight shine to it, but they feel thick and strong. Good enough for the docks anyway.

I'm not good at keeping secrets. I don't have any. I

have memories I'd rather forget, songs and faces that are painful to remember. But this girl has secrets.

I'll be honest with her. I don't expect her to return the favor.

38

CAN'T HIDE

I twiddle my thumbs, anxiously waiting. I want to prove myself. Prove that I'm not weak. Not to him. To me. I need to prove to *myself* that I can survive out here, in this vast city and this small tunnel, on my own. If I can do that, I can find Frankie and there will be no reason to ever go back there. To him. To hands that hold me down and drag me under.

Kettle approaches me with clothes bunched in his hands like a bouquet. His expression is unsure... wary. He runs one hand down the length of his simple clothes, dark pants and a white-collared shirt that's gone beige from lack of proper cleaning. My eyes follow his hands and avoid his face, stopping at a missing button on his jacket. He's taking his time, which is an achievement considering it's only about ten steps to get to me, and I find myself holding my breath as I wait. When he finally reaches the bed, he shifts from foot to foot and mutters, "Here," thrusting the clothes toward me, the other hand resting behind his back.

"Thanks," I say, taking the clothes from his outstretched hand as he takes a step back from me. I angle the bundle toward the light. One thick shirt similar to Kettle's but cream-colored. It will be too big, but I'll roll the sleeves up. The pants shine slightly in the light, a slither of metallic thread running through them. It gleams at me in dark colors of distrust and bad memories, and I take a sharp breath in.

"Thought you might like them back," he says quietly, his voice hinged on nervousness, his legs bending awkwardly away from me.

"Where did you get these?" I whisper, running my hand over my mother's riding pants, the ones she bought and never wore, saying she would take us riding in the country one day, but it never happened. Flashes of her smile, mashed with Frankie's, slap me in the face. And then the reason I threw them pummels me and I'm reliving the beating. I never wanted to see these again, be reminded…

Kettle looks down and mumbles, "I got them from you. You threw away a perfectly good pair of pants." He blusters air through his lips. "They don't even look like they've been worn."

I lay them gently across my lap and look up at the stones arching over my head, each perfectly balanced against another. If you took one out, the whole thing would come crashing down, burying us.

I'm gripping them rather tightly when I say, "They haven't. But… I threw them out the window months ago. How have they come into your possession now?" My fingers tighten around the clothes.

I hate the way I sound like my father right now. My voice sounds angry, but I'm not. I'm just sad and confused and I didn't want to go through this. I thought, I thought, I thought that he was new, unconnected to my old life. That I wouldn't have any reason or need to tell him.

I'm breathing too fast. My chest constricting, my

fingers and nose tingling from the lack of oxygen. It's something more than panic. It's secrets spilling out from holes I can't patch fast enough. Pouring in all directions like ants fleeing the rain. *I can't breathe.* One of my hands cramps and freezes into a claw like an old crone. I hold it up shakily, stare at it, and keep breathing in too quickly.

"Nora, breathe. It's okay."

He holds out his hand to me. *Should I take it?* I take it.

"Breathe," he says in his warm, poured-coffee voice. *Breathe.*

He pulls me up, the pants fall to the floor, and I step on them as he leads me back to the other side of the room to his bed. On the floor is every item I threw from the window over the last six months. Every punch, every slap, every lash of the belt is there, strewn across an abandoned subway platform in a swirl, the colors mixing together until they become a murky, oily brown.

KETTLE

She stares down at the floor in horror. And I'm afraid of what I've done. Though I shouldn't be. I don't know this girl. I shouldn't care how she feels. But each little part of her she lets slip past the mask is handing me a puzzle piece I have to fit.

Caring about her... I think it's carving out a bit of old hurt, yet I'm scared of the possibility that it's just making room for new pain to nestle in there.

She kneels down and scoops up the string of pearls,

holding them out from her body like they're something disgusting. Rolling one pearl between her fingertips, she drops it back on the pile, returning to standing, her palm coming to rest across her stomach like she's worried it may fall out.

I stand next to her, our hips not quite touching, staring down at her pile of belongings too, trying to decipher the mystery. My eyes go to her stomach. "Are you feeling sick?"

She shakes her head and sadly laughs, a sound like leaves being blown across the sidewalk. "No, I'm not sick."

I run a hand through my hair and sigh, waiting for her to say something, to explain her reaction to a simple pair of pants.

She breathes in deeply and seems to steady, although there's a slight tremor to her voice when she speaks. "I… I don't understand. Why do you have all of these things?"

My explanation first, I guess. "I've been sleeping in the alley for a while now, ever since the fire. It's a good spot. Cleaner and less looked on since that apartment building is vacant. When you threw that brooch from the window, I was there. I caught it. And I guess I kept it because, at first, I thought it meant something." She won't look at me, her eyes firmly tethered to the items on the floor. "After a while, I think I just held onto them because I liked having something that was just mine. A small secret. A treasure." Her eyes flick to me so briefly, harboring a withered expression. "Why does it matter anyway? If you threw these things away, you clearly didn't care about them or want them." I feel defensive, mostly because she won't look at me.

In a cracked to almost broken in half voice, she whispers, "They're not *my* things. But they do mean something to me..." She holds her hand across her chest like a sling, like she's trying to stop herself from falling apart. "But I never wanted to see these things again." Her head shakes slowly back and forth.

I feel like I'm in the dark, clawing at the sides of a well and searching for a foothold. I want to know. I don't know why, but I do. *Tell me.*

I pick up a pair of stockings and hold them up to her, coming around so that we're facing each other. "What's so important about a pair of stockings?" I challenge, careful not to sound angry, but she's not giving me anything.

She flinches, her hand going to her cheek, her finger crawling into her hairline. Her amber eyes are bleeding pain, and I suddenly feel very sorry I asked. She looks down at her feet, seems to count to three, and then looks up, a truly honest expression on her face. "That time it was a book." She presses her hand into her head a little harder until it tips to the side. "It was one of his law books, real thick, heavy." Her fingers drum lightly over the side of her head. "Leather bound, gold writing..."

I think I've stopped breathing now. The pair of stockings drops, with my hand, to my side, and the cardboard bends under the pressure of my grip. Sorry is all over my face. I expect tears to be all over hers, but they're not.

Between our feet is a mess of memories. Ones she probably wanted to forget... and I've just opened the box to her nightmares.

She bends down and grabs the scarf. "She used to wear this in the fall. Lightweight," she says, weighing it in her hand. "Not too hot or too cold." She runs it through her fingers like a magician and says flatly, "That time, it was the belt." She shudders. "I'm used to the belt."

Oh, Jesus.

She drops the scarf and goes to pick up another item. I gently take her wrist to stop her. "Nora. Stop," I say. "Shit. I'm so sorry. I didn't know."

My heart aches for this girl. Aches and understands.

We are more similar than I could have ever imagined.

I kneel down and start packing the things away as she stands there, woodenly watching me. Once I've closed the box and locked it, she seems to wake from her dreamy state. "They're my mother's things. I guess when I threw them away, I was trying to get my own back, just a little."

"So every one of these things is…"

She nods. "Everything in that box represents a time when he hurt me."

I kick the box behind my bed with the back of my heel. I want to burn it. Or set it on the tracks and let a train smash it into tiny pieces.

She shifts nervously. Her eyes downcast like she's ashamed. She shouldn't be ashamed. "So when you said your dad was strict, you weren't kidding, huh?" I say, snapping my mouth shut straight after. *I am the biggest idiot.*

She rolls her eyes. "Um. Yeah."

"Your mom must be pretty angry that you threw her stuff out the window."

"My mother's dead," she emphatically replies. The mask is coming back down. Unrolling like a blind.

"Oh." Things are starting to make a little more sense to me.

Blankets shift, someone yawns. The boys are stirring.

I wonder what I should say. She looks real uncomfortable, and I don't want to push it any further than I already have. "So are you coming to the docks with me?"

She lifts her heels from the ground and seems to shake off the heaviness of before. "Just let me change," she says brightly, turning on her heel and walking away from me. But I don't miss the stumble, the tremble in her legs as she reaches Kin's bed and pulls the curtain closed.

I feel like I've just walked into a swamp. There's a light across the water that I have to reach, but my legs are being swallowed by mud, deeper and deeper. It's still a long way off.

This changes everything.

If she wants to, I have to let her stay.

39

WORK

WHAT SHOULD I BE FEELING RIGHT NOW? ONE SECRET IS PINNED TO THE WALL LIKE A BUTTERFLY WING. THE OTHERS LAY BENEATH, PULSING WITH THE TIME I'M GOING TO RUN OUT OF.

I think of his eyes. Where I expected to see pity, I saw… solidarity, understanding. There was anger there too. A small fire I shouldn't feed. I see it in my own reflection sometimes, and it can only destroy me. And it won't touch *him*.

Kettle doesn't make me wear sunglasses now, and this tells me something has shifted in the way he sees me. That maybe he trusts me. I'm well disguised as a boy wearing Kettle's shirt, some beat-up sneakers and my mother's pants, which we roughed up so they wouldn't look so 'girly' as he put it.

We stand on the platform, and I'm reminded of the last time I stood somewhere like this with Frankie's hand in mine. I was so ready to leave my father and that life behind. I stifle a gasp as I remember the world slanting and then turning black so fast, all my hopes dripping into a puddle that everyone would walk through. It seems like that was years ago.

My feet slip as I step back from the memory and Kettle throws me a concerned glance, but he doesn't say anything. He is focused, cap low, eyes narrowed.

The train rattles the few occupants in unison like there's a string running through all of them. The men look up briefly with their darting, suspicious eyes. They yawn and stretch their legs, flex their muscles. Thankfully, their eyes pass quickly over me.

A hand brushes my neck, and I swing around. Kettle's cheeks flush dark under his eyes as he tucks a loose curl back into my cap. "Sorry," he whispers. "Your hair fell out."

I check the back of my neck for any other loose strands and tighten my bun. "Thanks," I mutter, and he gestures for us to sit down.

We slide onto a bench, our bodies vibrating with the subway car, our shoulders accidentally touching and then drawing away. The scuffed, white linoleum floor is covered in black rubber streaks like someone's crossed it out and started again, over and over. "So what do the boys do while you're away working?" I ask quietly, very aware of the men sitting across from us.

Kettle sits up straight, hiding under his hat, hands on knees. "They do their own thing. Run the streets, sneak home to sleep if they can manage it until I get back."

My voice goes up an octave. "What?" I think of Frankie, roaming the streets, playing with stray dogs and sleeping in the alley, and my heart crushes to dust and clippings in my chest. "Even little Kelpie?"

Kettle laughs, deep and rich. "They're street kids, Nora. Most of them have been living like this for a long time. They know how to take care of themselves." He shakes his head and smirks. "For the most part anyway."

I don't know anything anymore. "But you help them out?"

He stares through the window at the whooshing lights, his eyes hidden to everyone but me. "I guess so. I try anyway. At least if I feed them, give them clothes, I know they're not going to get busted for shoplifting."

"Wouldn't they be better off in a Home, you know, where they can be properly cared for?" I say, stupidly regurgitating someone else's opinions.

He snorts. "It doesn't work like that for everyone. Do you think you would be better off in a home?" he challenges.

I don't have an answer. Maybe I would. But if I couldn't be with Frankie, then no. "I don't really know."

Kettle shrugs his strong shoulders. "Besides, they make their own choices. Some of them ran away from *Homes*." He says Home like it's a nonsense word, made up by Tinkerbell and Peter Pan. "I can't... no, I *won't* force them to do anything they don't want to do."

I turn to him, our knees knocking. He's a mystery. What he's doing is truly admirable. Incredible. And I don't really understand why he's doing it. If he kept the money he earned for himself, he could live in a small apartment. Make a life for himself. He's so young to have so much responsibility. But then I understand that kind of weight.

I tap my finger to my chin. "Kettle, how old are you?"

He doesn't answer for a while. "Seventeen. Why?"

I gently nudge his shoulder. I want to say, *You're*

pretty impressive for a seventeen-year-old. More than that...

I smirk. "I'm older than you."

He raises an eyebrow. "Really?"

"I'm eighteen," I say in a teasing tone.

The train slows and he stands, indicating for me to go first. "An older woman," he whispers with a smile. Then more loudly, "This is our stop."

The men push past me, and I'm affronted by their rudeness.

"Excuse me!" I say, breaking from character and using my own voice. A man grunts and turns to stare at me, but thankfully, he is pushed out the exit by the pressure of several bodies behind him.

I step back from the door until Kettle's hand is on my shoulder, moving me forward. "Remember what I said?" He guides me through the door. "You can't let them push you around. If you want to get through the gates, you have to be fast and you have to be aggressive." There's a mountain of doubt hidden under his tongue.

I nod, and we start running to the turnstiles.

I start by brushing men's shoulders and not letting them shove me out the way. As we approach the top of the stairs, it turns to elbows jabbing and swear words uttered. I'm swallowing apprehension by the gallon. I try to reassure myself with the fact that Kettle is right behind me, talking me through the next move.

The men slow when we all have to go through the turnstiles one at a time. I push through, my head swinging back and forth, and search for an opening, a space in the stream of people. Just ahead, I spot a newsstand and a break in the traffic like a bubble. I take quick strides toward it, my elbows out at right angles, and my heart pumping fast.

Until it stops. My heart stops.

It's my face. My face and my father's face printed side by side on the front page of the paper. The headline reads: 'Daughter of JA rights attorney, C. Deere, MISSING.' In smaller letters beneath, it says, 'East Coast compensation case on hold until family reunited—Christopher Deere.' I gasp and turn around. *Kettle can't see this. He can't.* I don't know whether he was put in one of those camps, but it's definitely a strong possibility.

Kettle slams into my chest, his eyes wide and confused. "What the hell?" he remarks. He gets shoved against me repeatedly as people try to move past us, his chest squashed against mine.

I grab his shoulders and steer him back into the crowd, away from the stand. "I think I know the man at the newsstand," I lie. "He might recognize me."

He frowns and I think he might ignore me. I'm sure he doesn't believe me, but he grabs my arm and pulls me away from the stand. "Come on," he says through gritted teeth as we move to the opposite side of the road. I sigh in relief with what little breath I have left in me.

Once the street widens, we start jogging to the docks.

I move as fast as I can, praying there will be no papers left when I return in the evening.

This is some medieval contest. Teeth gnash, men

who smell much too much like men and… fish… grab at each other's heads and hair, pull each other down and claw at each other's necks. They are a desperate, scrabbling entity. I stand back from the jostling crowd, wondering whether I can do this. I bite my lip, lock my limbs, and decide it can't be worse than anything else I've experienced. So I take a deep breath and await instruction.

"You don't have to do this," Kettle says as he edges into the throng from the western side.

Yes I do.

"I want to," I say, trying to keep my voice low this time. Kettle chuckles at my attempt to sound like a boy, his blue eyes flashing with excitement.

Over the noise, he yells, ducking when a fist comes flying at his shoulder, "You're small, fast, try to squeeze your way in." He shoulders his way in and disappears. I hear him shouting underneath a tangle of arms, "If you don't make it through, wait for me outside."

He doesn't think I'll make it. It makes me more determined to prove him wrong. I test a foot on the edge. It instantly gets stepped on. I grimace.

Think.

I think about a slap coming toward me, my father's palm aching to mark my cheek red. If I could have avoided it, ducked out of the way, what would I have done? How would I have done it?

Each man in this throe of clashing bodies becomes my father. And I'm surprised that instead of wanting to hurt them, all I want to do is get through, stand on the inside of the fence where he/they can't get to me anymore.

There are small shadows of space opening up before my eyes, and I hurl toward them, I stop thinking, stop worrying, and just react. Under elbows, between bodies, over large legs trying to stomp on me. There are no walls to be thrown against. No one to protect. There is an escape, a way through for me to find.

The freedom tastes delicious, salty and hard earned on my tongue.

I'm nearly there. The fence vibrates, ringing for me. Calling—*You're close, so close.* My hand stretches to the wire and I grab at it, missing as my head suddenly jerks back. Someone's fingers dig into my collar and pull me backward. The top button on my shirt presses into my neck and I can't breathe, a strange cacking, gurgling noise coming from the back of my throat. I turn around to meet the owner of the hand. A small, twisted man, a skeleton almost. My cap tips back and he sees my face clearly, suddenly releasing me. "Sorry, ma'am," he says. Then he's scattered behind me like a spilled bag of bones, and I'm thrust forward.

The gate slides open and my feet don't feel like they're connected to the ground. I'm carried along, through the gap by a sea of muscled, grunting flesh and thrown into the clear, sea air.

The guard at the gate claps it shut and shouts at me, "Lucky last, eh?"

I made it. Me.

40

KETTLE

MEMORIES

I get through easily. The men seem tired and lacking the will today. When I've cleared the gate, I turn around to check for Nora's defeated face on the other side of the fence. I scan disappointed, exhausted expressions, a heat haze already warping the view. Shielding my eyes from the morning sun, I curse when I can't find her. My heartbeat picks up a little at the thought that maybe she was hurt.

Or worse? Ran away in fear.

I take a few steps closer to the fence and suddenly, I'm walking in Kin's footsteps. My skin prickles, and I'm burning beneath what's left of his shadow. I look to the water, the sun bouncing off in diamonds of white light.

Where are you? The break inside me teases open... *Are you?*

Someone tugs at my sleeve, softly pulling my arm down. And for one moment, I think, *maybe it's...* But I know it can't be.

I stare at the cracked concrete, and an all-too-feminine shadow joins me. "I did it! Did you see me? I got through!" she says, all breathless and excited. I almost pat her on the head, but stop myself.

"Calm down," I say, trying to contain my surprise. *I can't believe she got through.*

She wipes sweat from her forehead and smiles at me, a little unsure. "It smells like the sea," she exclaims. "So refreshing and... fishy!"

"Your voice," I mutter, turning and heading into the sign-in station.

She skips to catch up with me, saying, "Oh right, sorry," in a low voice.

I smile despite myself. "This is going to be more difficult than I thought," I say, wondering what the hell I'm going to do with her now. "Stop skipping," I warn under my breath, this unwanted grin inserting itself on my face.

She stops and tries to walk in a more manly fashion, swinging her arms and parting her legs. I just sigh and let her. It's better than skipping and rocking her hips. No one's watching her anyway. At least not yet.

I scan the area and am relieved to find that the men who beat up Kin are not here today. I crunch down on those feelings. Of anger and worry. I need to focus today.

Black stands impatiently at the station, arms crossed, foot slapping against the concrete like a paddle bat. "Mornin' Kettle. Who's yer friend?" he asks, eyeing Nora appraisingly as she stands there, clueless. I know what he's thinking, but she's not ready. I curse myself for not planning out what I would do if she got through. I just didn't think it was possible.

I shift awkwardly, realizing we haven't come up with a boy's name for her. "Um..."

Nora steps forward and offers her hand. "Kite, sir,"

she says quietly but confidently.

Kite.

Kite.

God, it suits her so well that I have to stop myself from puffing out my chest with pride.

Black takes a step closer, his eyes running from her feet to her oversized shirt, which is hiding things I shouldn't be thinking about, and up to her bruised face. I snap out of my moment of pride and step in front of Nora, bumping her backward and out from under his intense gaze.

"This is his first time, so I was thinking shoveling scrap and cleaning containers might be best," I say quickly and with too much anxiety in my voice.

Black leans up on his one good foot and peers over my shoulder. "A cherry, huh? Yes, that would be best but, well, sorry Kettle, the easy jobs have all bin signed for," he says with a devil's smile and then throws at Nora, "Kite!" She glances up at him, eyes popped full of innocence. "You look light on yer feet. You look like one of them…" He musses his hands in the air. "Err… acrobats or somethin'. You'll go up like Kettle."

My heart sinks.

Her golden eyes follow his pointed finger, aglow as she watches a container sailing through the sky, eclipsing the sun.

Black turns away from us, his dark, curly hair pulled into a loose ponytail that trails down his back like bunch of rotten grapes. "Show Kite what to do and then get on with yer work," he snaps, toddling away like a lame penguin.

Nora's eyes are still pinned to the sky when I grab

her arm and take her to the loading area.

She's nodding like she understands me as I talk her through the safety procedures, of which there are few, but I'm unsure. Her eyes keep wandering to the clouds in this dreamy kind of way, and it worries me. I gently put my hand to her face and steer her gaze back to me. Her skin doesn't feel as soft as I would have expected, maybe because it's pulled so tight over her bones. "Nora," I whisper, trying to catch her eyes. "You don't have to do this."

She straightens, takes a step back, and steel works its way over her features. "I want to." And I know she's made up her mind.

I make her watch me first. Her eyes shadow me up the side and onto the roof, and as I lift off from the ground, I feel uneasy, strange. The sense of freedom doesn't come. It's replaced with fear and a stretching feeling as she becomes smaller and I rise higher. This seems like a bad idea and I regret bringing her here. But right now, there's nothing I can do. She's down there and I'm in the sky, unable to reach her.

My eyes are on Nora instead of the horizon and I watch Black slap a hard hat on her head and push her toward the next container. She looks up at me, but I can't make out her expression. From here, she is thin, pale, and dwarfed by the giant container she is climbing.

I track her fast movements, the way she agilely scales the side and then presses flat to the roof like I told her. My fingers grip tightly around the rusty chains as I lean dangerously close to the edge to see her more clearly. She lifts off the ground and her body startles.

She looks like a spider clinging to the side of a spoon, unsure of whether to make a jump for it or stay put.

My container starts to sink below the others on the ship, but I manage to see that she's decided to stay put before she completely disappears from view.

When my container sets down, I climb off and wait for her in a narrow gap underneath. Hers crashes down soon after, a wavering "oh!" pours down the side and hits my ears and I find myself scrambling up to meet her.

I climb up and come around the side just as she's scaling down. She turns around, swipes the stray hairs from her face, and tucks them under her hat, exclaiming, "Goodness! That was fun." Her teeth break her face into two halves of an openmouthed smile. It's infectious and I smile back, though it feels a little like a grimace.

"Just be careful," I say, shaking a finger at her.

She touches her chest with her palm, pats it once, and nods. "Always." It sounds like a lie. Then she stands on her tiptoes and whispers, "Race you to the bottom?" as the shadow of the next container bears down on us from above.

Before I can answer, she's darting down the giant steps toward the deck and I'm struggling to keep up.

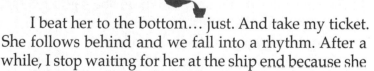

I beat her to the bottom... just. And take my ticket. She follows behind and we fall into a rhythm. After a while, I stop waiting for her at the ship end because she seems like she's got it covered.

As I'm stepping off my container, I hear the siren

blare for break time. Nora is riding the container right behind me, so I wait, climbing up and to the side so I can see her flight over.

She's doing the right thing, staying flat, giant smile reflecting the sunlight, white as the foam cresting the surf. I blink. I'm blinded. But then she looks up, sees me, and stands. She waves and my stomach becomes my feet and my feet become the seafloor. She holds onto the chain with only one hand, her face fronting the sea in some defiant, lungs-full-of-fresh-air moment. I wonder if this is what she's been doing this whole time or if it's just for me. Either way, I'm going to kill her. Then she starts walking across the moving container and I realize I won't have to.

I cup my hands around my mouth and shout, "Get down!" to which she just grins and waves again, sheer delight plastered all over her pretty, stupid face. My heart rams my chest in a punch made of stone. *She's going to fall.*

I dance from foot to foot, helpless. The shadow of the container reaches me before she does and I hold my hands out like I could catch her, let them fall just as quickly and run to where I know they'll set it down.

She's still standing, swinging from the chain like she's dancing around a maypole. She's so reckless. A giddy giggle showers my panicked ears. I climb up to the container that's next to where she's going to set down and crouch low, bracing for the impact.

"Nora," I try again. "Get down low!"

She's not even looking at the ship and the ground approaching fast. She's still looking out to sea when the container drops down suddenly with a loud clang.

I watch her hand part with the chain, her pale freckled fingers releasing their grasp. She doesn't have time to scream, if she was even going to. She stumbles forward, her legs slipping out from under her, and falls forward. Her chin makes a teeth-gritting clunk as it connects with the corner of the container. Her legs spin over the edge and I jump, catching the top of her torso before she slides off the edge and into the dark water.

Panting breath mixed together, our heads hang down as we stare at the narrow gap between the ship and the dock, the beaded, green seaweed slapping the sleepers of the pier, the rusted pillars that would have torn her body to pieces.

I swing her back onto the roof and check that there are no other containers coming. A puff of smoke billowing from the crane cab tells me the driver is on break.

I roll her onto her back and pull her head into my lap, staring at her upside-down face and her chest rising and falling fast. I want to scream at her for being so goddamn stupid! And I will, when she opens her eyes.

I pat her cheek gently. It's hot and crusted with salt. "Nora, open your eyes. We have to get off the ship."

Her eyes flutter open, showing me honey and light. I frown.

She sits up suddenly, turns to face me, and coughs.

Blood sprays from her mouth, painting my shirt, her shirt, and the metal space between us. And from beneath the memory I'm slowly getting buried under, I think I hear her say, "I think I bit my tongue."

I press my small, needle-pricked fingers to my cotton shirt. They come back printed with bloodstains, thin, black-

ened like cherry juice. I show her my hand and she slowly shakes her head. It's too hard for her. This isn't fair.

Maybe I should touch her, but I don't want to. She doesn't look the same anymore. Her face is too pale for the desert now. She's the creamy clay that lies deep below the red surface.

Her dark, silken hair hangs over her shoulders like a shawl, but it won't warm her. I want her to be warm. Warmer.

"I'm sorry, little one," she whispers, reaching out to my face with a cool, damp rag. I lean away, and she tsks. "Don't be scared." Her coal-colored eyes flick to my big brother, standing beside me like a statue, his arm around my shoulders. He eases me forward, and I let her clean my face of her blood.

My chest hurts. It's like something's stuck in there. I don't like this feeling. I don't like what's happening to his mother.

Her touch is so light as she gently wipes away what's left of her. She is good. This shouldn't happen to a good person.

She gazes at me with what he tells me is love. But her eyes seem smaller, like they're resting back in her head. She smiles at me and says, "Chisana ichi..." then starts coughing, pressing the rag to her mouth.

Pink.

The men in khaki clothes lean in, masks over their mouths. A muffled word from the one holding a stethoscope to her chest, presses deep into my heart and stays there. "Soon."

Soon.

My tears are hot and messy, and I wipe my nose with my

sleeve. My brother's hand grips tighter around my shoulder.

"It says here she has one son, husband is serving in the 522nd. Who is this little one?" A pen taps on a clipboard.

Little one. I want to kick him in the shins. I don't want to be called that by anyone but her and… soon… no one.

Another voice, all high over my head. "Orphan, sir."

Another cough pulls their attention away from my brother and me. This one doesn't stop. It doesn't ever stop. Wet, rasping coughing over and over and over with no break to breathe in.

We are pushed into the night, canvas flaps hitting our backs on the way out. A kinder voice that doesn't understand says, "Why don't you go kick a ball around for a while, boys? You don't need to see this." His hand shoos us away like we're stray cats begging for food.

We don't want to go anywhere. We sit on the edge of the rough wood floor that sticks out from beneath the tar-paper walls and listen. The tower lights scan the desert, sweeping dust into piles that will only be carried by the wind back under the door. We sigh in unison. The dust entering our lungs.

Coughing, men muttering, coughing, a flutter, a sharp bang, a glass knocks over and water splashes on the floor.

Silence.

The door flaps open. A man approaches. He doesn't lean down; I don't think he wants to look us in the eyes. I watch the man's chest move as he talks. He is a greenish shadow beneath the moonlight, his medals jingle and shine as he says, "I'm sorry."

My brother jumps up and pushes past the man. The man steps aside and lets him back into his mother's room.

I clasp my hands, look down. Blood patterns my shirt in sprinkles of red that will turn brown. Then they'll make *me wash it.*

Now we are alone.

"Kettle?" Nora shakes my shoulder. I look up from my shirt to her concerned eyes blinking at me, blood running from both corners of her mouth like she's in a cheesy vampire movie. "Kettle!" she says, louder this time.

I can't speak. She unhooks the container and takes my arm, pulling me to the ladder. Mechanically, I climb down, take my ticket, and walk the plank to land.

Blood. Blood seeping into our clothes. Blood the color of the desert and the lines running across the giant rocks that stood sentinel over our camp. Blood is all I can think about.

I reach the station and take my lunch. Nora copies me and follows as I make my way to the water, to the ship bones, in heavy silence. We ignore the teasing that trails after us as the men laugh at Nora's accident.

She is quiet, although I know she has questions. Sitting down, I take a bite of my sandwich. I watch as she takes off her shoes and dips them in the water.

She glances at me. "You should take off your shirt and wash it," she says.

I stare at the waves. "You should wash your shirt too. And clean your face."

She narrows her eyes for a moment and then says, "Fine. Turn around." I turn around and listen to splashing and wringing for several minutes. "Ugh!"

I spin around suddenly. "What?" My eyes skip to her wet shirt before quickly looking away. I don't need an answer because her shirt is completely see-through.

"Oh."

She crosses her arms over her chest to cover herself.

"Don't worry. It will dry soon enough," I say, pulling my shirt over my head and dipping it in the water. She spins around so fast she nearly tips into the water.

I laugh. "You don't need to turn around."

"I want to," she says haughtily, and I snort. Small silence grows between us, just the seagulls squawking, and then, with her back still turned, she asks the question. "So what happened up there, Kettle? You sort of disappeared for a few minutes."

I sigh. *Today, you get truths I've never uttered. Memories I've tried to suppress.*

"How did your mother die?" I ask to her wet back, her peachy skin showing through. Her shoulders rise up to almost touch her ears. "Kin's mother's death was messy and long. She was dying for almost the whole time I knew her. She had TB. It happened often in the camps. Mostly to the elderly. But well, I guess she was just lucky. When you coughed on me like that, it pulled me back there. Happens sometimes," I say, shrugging. *Happens more than I'd like.*

On her knees, she slowly shuffles around to face me, her eyes struggling not to look at my inappropriate lack of clothing. It makes me smile. I pull on the wet shirt and it sticks to my skin like glue.

"What about your own mother? What happened to her?" she asks, blinking.

"Kin's mother was my mother for the four years I spent in the camp. Before that, I had no mother. At least not one who wanted me," I say.

"You mean, you're an..." It's just a word. Not a word that means much to me these days anyway.

"An orphan," I finish.

"Sorry."

"Don't be."

Her eyes search sideways. Something building inside her that she wants to say. I can sense it. A bubble of air rising in her throat.

She spreads her arms wide and says, "My mother had a beautiful death." It's the oddest and most honest thing I've heard her say so far. She uses her hands to show me as she declares, "She flew through the air like an angel. The part after though, was like you said, messy." The water laps loudly at our feet, slowly eroding what we thought we knew of each other and crusting our toes with salt.

"I'm sorry."

She dips her head and watches the waves. "Thank you."

Then I spend the next ten minutes telling her in many different and colorful ways how reckless and downright stupid she was for standing up on a moving container.

41

INDEPENDENCE

YOU SHOULD HAVE SEEN ME, FRANKIE. I WAS FLYING.
YOU SHOULD HAVE...
YOU WILL SEE ME.
SOON.

I've lost my breath. My heart. It's all coming fast and hard, and it's exhilarating. Kettle, this strange boy, this strange mix of responsible and courageous, he's shoved me from the nest. And I can fly.

"Nora, did you hear me?" He slaps water at me, and I flinch. "You need to promise me you will be more careful this time. Please." The concern in his eyes is sweet and foreign. I'm used to disgust and rage flaming in a man's irises.

I nod. My arms locked over my wet chest. He waits, eyebrows raised, for me to actually say the words. "Okay, okay. I promise."

I chew on my bottom lip and glance at him sideways. I have so many questions to ask him. Where did he come from? How did he get here all the way from the Arizona desert? What happened to his real parents? Does he even know who they are? I also now know for sure that he is one of those Lost Children. He was in the camps.

He sits with his elbows resting on his knees, turns his head slowly. "What?"

"So Kin, your adop—ted bro—ther…" I span the words over several seconds, waiting for an eyebrow arch, a response to tell me that's the right or wrong word. He doesn't say anything, nor stop me. "Why can't you inquire about him at the hospital? Is it because of your circumstance, you know, being…"

"…a street kid?"

I nod and bring a blush with it.

Kettle's eyes are serious, narrowed as he talks. "No, not exactly. It's because Kin and I are runaways. We're meant to be in Homes. The cops have been looking for us for a long time."

I purse my lips. "Really? Even after all this time?" I sigh. "Don't they have anything better to do?"

He stares down at his lap, an answer or a story there. "Just coz the war is over doesn't mean people forget. At least, they don't forget about people like me. They like to know where *we* are and what *we're* doing at all times. If I showed my face at the hospital, they'd detain me and then what would happen to the boys, to our home?"

I see the fear in his eyes, feel that he really believes his words, and I understand. I know it's difficult to shed years of abuse. Like a plant trained over a frame, my body has grown rigid and able to take a punch. Kettle's has grown to seek the ground and learned to hide. After a while, you don't know how to do anything else. But I'm not so sure he needs to keep running. Things have changed. "Are you sure that's what would happen?" I ask warily.

He crosses his arms and his expression darkens. "I can't take the risk."

And maybe he's right. I understand losing so much you can't stand the idea of losing more.

I am resolute. My branches lean down, offering him some sunlight. "Okay then. I want to help you find him." These words—*I want to.* They are like raspberry cordial dripped on my tongue. They are words I've barely spoken until a few days ago and I owe him big because he gave me the chance to use them.

His head drops down and he laughs softly as he shakes his head.

"That's funny?" I ask, confused.

He looks up, eyes full of stories, rolls and rolls of script written in dark blue ink. "No. I just thought I would have to work really hard to convince you to help me and here you are, just offering it to me."

The horn blows and we jump up and walk back to the loading area. I tuck my hair in and glance down at my shirt. He was right. It's already dry, a little stiff but at least it's not transparent. "I'm going to need some different clothes if I'm going to be convincing at the hospital."

"We'll go in a few days, when the docks are closed," he mutters as we approach the group of men waiting to be assigned.

A larger man shoves Kettle as he passes, grumbling the words, "Go home, Nip."

Kettle keeps walking like he wasn't touched and I just stand there, eyes wide until he has to circle around and take me by the arm to pull me away from the horrible man.

285

"How can you…?" I start.

"It's not worth it," he replies with hard-edged sadness in his tone. Softly, fists clenched, words calm but driven with anger, he mutters, "It's never worth it."

We start the second part of the shift, and I abide his wishes and am more careful.

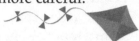

"Kite! Kite!" Heavy, uneven footsteps approach from behind. I'm slumped forward, barely able to lift my legs. I am so happy and exhausted, my muscles burning, but it's a good pain. It's not about bruises, bones cracking, or organs being squashed to make room for a fist. This is my *own* pain, something I earned for hard work. "Kite!"

Kettle carefully nudges me. "Black is calling you."

I slowly turn around, and Mister Black is waddling toward me with an envelope. "Good first day, son," he says, smacking the envelope of cash into my palm. I hold it up to my eyes and grin. My first paycheck.

"Thanks!" I say in a low voice. Kettle snickers at my side as Black hands him another envelope and limps away.

"Feels good, right?" he asks.

I nod as we walk toward the gate, stinking of sweat, squinting into the sun, and aching for a bed. "Feels good," I agree.

He slaps me on the back and I cough, startled. "Sorry," he mumbles, looking down at the ground that's leaking heat back into our sunburned faces.

"It's ok," I say, wishing that it really was and that the slap he just gave me didn't send my whole body into a shock of shuddering, shivering fear.

I have a long way to go, I can tell. But that's life. That's my life. One foot in front of the other. Courage. Toes testing first. Even if what's beneath is unsteady, a bridge made of brittle bones and broken shoelaces, I can do this. Eyes forward and keep on walking.

"You did well today," he says with a wary smile. The words beat one, two, three, four like the knock of a door inside my heart. This is my acceptance.

"Where are we going?" I ask when Kettle steers us away from the subway station and toward a group of buildings blanched black as coal. The sun attempts to sweep the walls clean with rays of pink and gold but fails, a murky yellow wash dripping down the walls instead. I blink up at the washing lines strung between them, flapping in the cooling breeze like wedding bunting. Faint smells of soap and linen rush over my skin, mixing with the salt and sweat of the docks.

Kettle looks up and down as we cross the street and shakes his head, leading me around the corner. "We don't sleep in the tunnel every night. It's too conspicuous."

My wooden legs struggle to catch up with him. He peeks his head in the alley between the next two buildings where it's dark, dirty and lined with large metal bins on wheels that stink of garbage. There is no clean laundry hanging from the sky here, just a rectangle of graying air lined by broken windows. "You have a second home?" I gasp, my eyes wide with surprise.

Kettle snorts and sweeps his arm out grandly.

"Sure. Welcome to my fall home. It's a little draughty, but the views, as you can tell, are spectacular! The cardboard mattresses are real good for your back too."

Shut your mouth. I'm gaping. *I can't sleep here. I... I...* "We sleep here?" I ask, pointing at the slimy, stained stones that slope into a drain in the center of the alley.

Kettle nods, his face serious. "We sleep here."

Stepping into the shadowed space, I try not to look as afraid as I am. I lift one arm and grip my elbow, biting my lip as I mumble, "Okay."

Kettle seems surprised. "Okay?"

I'm not saying it again, so I just nod.

"All right, well, how about you find some clean-ish cardboard for us to sleep on and I'll get us some dinner?" He motions to a dumpster that appears to growl at us with cardboard hanging from its metal jaws and slings his bag over my shoulder, removing his wallet. "Look after this."

I want to say *wait, don't leave me here,* but I don't. I clamp my mouth shut and let him go, while I stand in the middle of a slow dripping stream of foul-smelling water and try to work up the courage to touch one of the bins.

I think I let myself forget, pushed it out of my mind somehow, that Kettle, the boys, they're really homeless. And this is how they live every day. It's how they survive, and I shouldn't complain.

I hold my breath and stomp over to a bin that looks slightly less wet and slimy, and start pulling old boxes out for us to sit on. A screen door slams and I duck down behind the bin, listening to a slopping, squishy sound as food scraps are dumped right by my head. The smell of rotting lettuce, off milk, and cigarette smoke makes me gag. I press a fist to my mouth and try to stay still. A man yells to another man at the door in an Asian language I don't recognize, finishes his smoke, and goes back inside.

I gather up my cardboard and move further away from the where he came out, which was clearly the back door to a restaurant or café of some sort.

I dump it all in the small space between another dumpster and a large stack of wooden pallets and sigh shakily. Once I've run several pieces up the wall and along the floor, I stand back and admire my work, pushing my hair from my face and shivering. It's getting darker by the second. *Where is he?*

I sit down, pull my knees to my chest, and a feeling of lonely sadness surrounds me like the cold. Sadness for Kettle, for his brother, and for the other boys. People shouldn't have to live like this. I try to think and feel this now before Kettle returns. When I try to put it aside, I find I can't. I deliberately try to turn my thoughts to Frankie and how I'm going to find her. I fish around in Kettle's bag and find a pen. Tearing off a small square of cardboard, I quickly scribble down a list.

The list is too short. I have three names here. Three addresses. These are the only relatives we have in the city. The only homes I can think of where he may have hidden her. Three places that may be crossed out very soon. It makes me afraid to even look.

I hear a splash and press myself closer to the wall. Fearful, small, the confidence I had earlier pouring off me like beads of rain from an umbrella.

I let out a rattling, relieved sigh when I realize it's Kettle. "What's that?" he asks, handing me something wrapped in paper. It's warm and smells tart and sweet.

I fold the cardboard over and tuck it into my palm. "It's a list."

He can't know who I am. Not yet.

"A list of what?" he asks, crouching down in front of me and taking a large bite of his food.

Lie. "Um. Of what I'll need to get before we go to the hospital to inquire about your brother," I say very ineffectually.

"Oh right, let me see," he says, expectantly holding out his hand. The sun has pushed a line of light right through the alley and it strikes my face. It will only last a few minutes and then all will be black.

I tip my head and think, shuffling my backside on the cardboard. "I'll definitely require a nice blouse and a skirt. Some makeup… Oh and…" I glance down at my chest.

Kettle is staring at me, a serious expression on his face. His eyes keep going to the paper in my hand. "Yes?"

"I'm going to need some personal items," I whisper.

"Huh, like what?" he asks.

I lean closer and whisper, "Undergarments. I only have the ones I'm wearing and…"

He jumps up suddenly, his dinner scrunched in his hand. "Oh right. Yes, of course. Um…" He rakes his fingers through his dark hair, his cheeks flushed. He looks down at his half-eaten food. "I'm just going to put this in the trash." He takes a few steps backward, nearly trips over, and then walks away quickly, with me covering my mouth to stop from giggling. When he returns, the paper bag is still in his hand. He laughs awkwardly. "Huh, I hadn't actually finished eating." He stares down at his own hands, his earlier curiosity about my list forgotten.

That worked well. And guilt worms its way into my thoughts.

42

SLEEP

"A re you tired?" I ask to Nora's open, yawning mouth. She pats her pink lips and nods. I am sad when the sun sets because she becomes a gray shadow and I can only just make out her features.

"I can't believe we're going to do it all again tomorrow," she says through another yawn. She lifts one leg and then the other, dropping them down with a thump. "I can barely move."

"You get used to it," I say, squinting through the grainy light and trying to catch an expression before it becomes too dark to see her. I think a thin but satisfied smile crosses her face.

She shifts awkwardly and sighs. "How do you sleep?" she asks, her voice gravelly with exhaustion. Her clothes rake the cardboard, making small scuffing noises.

"Close my eyes and just..." I start.

She shoves me gently. "No, I mean. Where...? How do you lie down?"

I can tell by her unsure movements, her shaky voice, that she's very uncomfortable here. I shuffle closer and our shoulders bump. She doesn't move away, and I feel her skin shivering against mine in the cooling night air. "I don't lie down," I reply, very aware of how close we are.

I show her how I arrange myself so I can sleep sitting up, and she copies me.

We are hip to hip, shoulder to shoulder. I close my eyes as silence settles between us.

She exhales loudly, rearranging and shifting for about half an hour. Then I hear her sniff and I think she may be crying.

"I don't wanna do this, Kin," I sniff, wiping my nose with my sleeve. It's cold and my belly hurts. A man threw us some coins, which we used to buy a roll of Lifesavers. We only ate two each. Kin says we have to save the rest. I shudder and cross my arms across my chest, but I can't stop shivering.

The shadows look like tall men in coats ready to grab us and take us back, and I'm scared to close my eyes.

"Shh! It's gonna be okay, little brother," Kin whispers, opening his arms and pulling me closer. "We'll look after each other. Just close your eyes and try to get some sleep."

The wind howls like a coyote, and I start to miss the desert. A bottle breaks and a man swears. The noise of traffic rises and then disappears as nighttime arrives. I'm scared. I feel small. Smaller than Kin. Smaller than the shadows growing around me. I miss her warm arms, blankets tucked in tight around my body.

"It's gonna be okay," Kin whispers again, his arms shaking with cold and hitting the back of my neck. This time, I think he's talking to himself as well as me.

Something white, like shreds of down from a pillow, start to fall from the sky. It's my first snow.

"Nora," I whisper. She flinches, sniffs again. Her arm moves and I know she's wiping her nose. "What's wrong?"

She takes a while to find her voice. I sense she's trying to be brave, but I do understand this is really hard. I remember.

"I just don't think I can sleep sitting up like this," she says. "It's terribly uncomfortable." I hear the words between what she actually says. She's scared. She misses her own bed. She doesn't want to sleep in a cold, filthy alley. *No one does.*

I take off my jacket, shove it in my bag, and put it next to me. "Here, lie on this." She lays her head down, her hair fanning across my leg.

"Thank you," she whispers, her body shuddering from the cold. The fall weather has been kind to us so far, though. Winter is always the hardest.

I carefully shift her hair from my leg with one finger and watch her legs pull into her chest. Folding the cardboard over her torso, I put a hand on her shoulder, gently stroking her arm. "It's going to be okay. Just try to sleep."

She yawns, covering her mouth. "I'm sorry."

I pause. "Sorry for what?"

"I'm sorry your life turned out like this. I'm sorry you have to sleep on the streets."

I laugh sadly. "You're sleeping on the streets with me."

She sighs, long and airy. "That is true."

What am I going to do?

It's late. And I can't sleep. All I can do is watch the small, curled shape of her body, folded under my arm and under cardboard. I want to rattle her awake. Hear her voice

again.

I shake my head, trying to rid myself of these thoughts. Because they are no good to me. No good to her either. My mind is unfocused and focused on the same thing — this star out of reach.

43

BUILDING

SHE'S IMPRESSIVE. SHE DOESN'T KNOW IT, BUT SHE IS. HER BRUISES HAVE FADED, HER SKIN IS BRUSHED BY THE SUN, AND SHE IS STRONGER.

It's early. The street sweepers have been by and the pavement smells less like trash and urine than usual, which is nice. After three days at the docks, Nora smelled as bad as any of the men, so I took her to the YMCA to have a shower and clean up. She 'borrowed' a pair of sunglasses, a scarf, and a jacket in the lost and found.

Nora links her arm in mine so I can lead her to the store. This works well for us. Me, being the servant leading the rich, blind woman around.

A man in an apron sweeps the sidewalk in front of us, the thick brushes scraping across the wet concrete. I halt Nora's stride while he sweeps cigarette butts and gum wrappers into the gutter.

We stand there for a moment, and I close my eyes, imagining what it would be like to walk arm in arm with a girl and not be stared at. To not be stared at period. I laugh hollowly as we start walking again. It's not an idea I should entertain.

"What are you laughing about?" Nora whispers,

clinging a little closer as a cop strolls toward us.

"Nothing really. I was just thinking it would be funny if people thought we were a couple." She doesn't make a sound. Her lips purse in what looks like irritation. The cop walks past us, tipping his hat at Nora when he passes. When he's gone, I say, "You know, you and me, together, people would find that funny." *What am I saying?*

Finally, she speaks, "Yes. I suppose it would be pretty strange."

There. That shouldn't hurt, but it does.

We walk in silence after that.

When we reach the store, she stops and turns to me. "I can manage from here. I'll meet you out front in about half an hour?" The tone of her voice is very clean, businesslike.

I scratch my cheek and pause, thinking separating might be a bad idea. "Shouldn't I go with you?"

She lowers her glasses and stares at me with those amber eyes. "You want to come into the underwear department with me?"

I take a step back, put my hands in my pockets, and feel all this heat creeping into my cheeks. "No. I'll wait for you here." I point to the ground in front of one of the window displays like I'm going to stand right on this spot until she comes back. She plays with her coat button and then fastens it.

"I won't be long." And she's gone, blasted with warm air conditioning and into her world. She walks with purpose and comfort like she's at home in there. It adds another brick to the wall that was already standing between us.

I've checked my watch about a hundred times. The security guard came and told me to vacate the entrance, so I've been strolling up and down the window displays. Each one shows a season. Mannequins in fur coats standing in front of a Christmas tree to women in shorts holding tennis racquets. They are wooden, sad, frozen in some typical scenario that's nothing like anyone's real life.

I snort and kick a stray pebble. Pigeons squabble and flutter around it, shooting me beady, hateful glances when they realize it's just a rock.

I think I'm losing it.

She should be out by now.

Someone taps me on the shoulder and I spin around, apologizing as I turn, "Sorry. I know... move on," I say, expecting the security guard again.

A lithe woman, pinched in at the waist and wearing a polka dot blouse and red lipstick, faces me. She smiles and then she sniffs.

"Oh. It's just you," I say, scared she can hear my heart bounding about in my chest.

"It's just me," Nora replies. She sounds so sad, her shoulders hunched, her fingers messed together.

"Are you okay?" I ask.

She nods and walks away from the store. "Where's the hospital?" she asks, looking left and right.

I run to catch up with her as she wipes her eyes under her glasses. "It's not far." Even though she's standing tall, she seems crumpled like someone scrunched her up and tried to straighten her out again.

I want to ask what's wrong.
I know she won't tell me.

I can't believe she's not with any of them. *Any of them.* Each phone call was like an icepick to the heart, turning, turning, turning. I shouldn't be surprised, but I am. Every time, I am. *Frankie, what has he done with you?* I'm going to fall apart. Someone's pulled the pin, and I'm going to disintegrate right here in the street.
Kettle takes my hand.

KETTLE

I pat her hand. She feels cold, the freckled skin of her hand threaded with tiny veins. "We can walk there." Her pulse beats under my fingers. Fast. Frenetic.

The hospital casts the large shadow of an H across the lawns in front, stretching to the sidewalk. As we start to cross the road, Nora's feet dig into the ground and I find I'm half having to drag her to the entrance. "Are you sure you can do this?" I ask, holding onto her trembling arm.
She squeaks a trembling, "Yes. I want to," and straightens a little.
She fumbles around in the pocket of her skirt and

pulls out a lipstick. Pursing her lips, she applies it, sucks her lips into her mouth, and tries to smile.

"How does that look?" she asks, lifting her sunglasses and blinking at me innocently.

I frown. Tilt my head. "I don't like it," I blurt.

She looks down. "Oh," and goes to wipe it from her mouth with the back of her hand.

"Wait." I grab her hand and she stares at me, amber eyes melting. I lift my thumb to the corner of her mouth and rub away the red smudge. She blushes, lowers her eyes and again… *My heart.* "You look nicer without it, but it makes you look older. So leave it on."

I drop my hand from her face. She almost says something, but it's stuck behind her teeth and her waxy red lips.

I take a step back and usher her forward with my hands. "I'll wait around the corner," I whisper. "Leave the glasses on, so no one recognizes you."

Waiting. Always waiting.

Looking through windows never walking through doors.

Nora's shadow appears before her body, shrinking as she catches up to it. She takes off her sunglasses, her face carved from sorrow, and I brace myself for the bad news.

Kin is dead. He's dead.

My neck feels like it will snap from the weight of my thoughts. I bow my head, wanting to cover my ears to block out what she's going to say, but I don't have the strength.

That voice—stars and dark blue sky. "He's alive

and I know where he's staying," she says.

I link my hands behind my head and sink down the cool, brick wall I'm leaning against until I'm crouching close to the ground.

He's alive.

"Where...? How is...?" My hand runs down my face, an imitation of tears. I stop. Turn up to where she sways in her red leather shoes. "Did you get away with it? I mean, they didn't recognize you?"

She softly shakes her head, the angles of her face softening too. "I'm fine," she says, hitching her skirt up so she can crouch on the ground at my level. "How are *you*?" She reaches for my cheek, hovers halfway, caressing the air instead of my skin, and then her hand plants on the sidewalk for balance.

"I don't know." *I'm scared.* "Nora," I say, staring at the grooves in the slabs of concrete, neatly lined up, dropped into place. I want to follow them home. I tell her the truth of what's inside me right now. I don't know why, but it isn't hard. "I'm scared."

She laughs and stands up, extending a hand. "He's your brother. You don't need to be scared. You need to go see him."

I take her hand and she pulls me up, releasing me quickly.

"Shit. You're right," I say, watching her eyes widen at my cursing. A smile gathers in the corner of my mouth. "So where is he?"

She smiles and taps her finger on her jaw. "Out of the city. Where there are lawns and picket fences..."

301

A house that used to be white sits gray on the end of a noodling driveway. Rusty tricycles sprout from the ground, their wheels frozen in place. A blur of dirty clothing streaks across the shoulder-height grass.

Three steps from the top. 'Creak'

Quick! Everyone hide.

She stares at my clenched fists, and I try to relax them. "Ever caught a bus?" I ask her. Though I know the answer.

44
KIN

Kettle is quiet, something playing behind his eyes that I can't see. His fists are clenched, each finger, each muscle wound up tighter than a jack in the box ready to pop open. I don't understand his mood. I thought he'd be happy. But then there are a lot of things I don't understand about Kettle. *Though I'd like to.*

We sit side by side on the silver bus, a crevice in the seats separating us. I stare out the window, lean my head on the glass and let the vibrations chase my thoughts out of my ears as the land lowers gradually. Easing down like giant steps until the spaces between buildings become larger and their height lessens.

Front lawns shimmer with moisture, green carpets leading to the white-boarded homes and bright red doors with large brass knockers.

I roll my face toward Kettle. He seems to tense more and more as we leave the city behind. So much for the relaxing 'country life'. I snort quietly and he snaps out of his trance, showing me the deep, dark blue of his eyes that seem rimmed with fear. "Thanks for coming with me. I don't..." he starts, looking at his lap.

"You're welcome. Besides, I want to meet the boy whose bed I'm sleeping in," I say with a smirk.

Kettle's eyes stay on his hands, his lip curling

slightly. "I wouldn't tell him about that."

My eyes fall to the floor, which looks like a tin roof about to lift off. "Oh. Will he be upset?"

The bus shrieks to a stop and we stand and wobble. "No. It's nothing like that. It's just... he'll tease you." He wraps his hand around the metal bar just above my own. We are so different. I look away. "That's just Kin," he says with a more relaxed smile on his face. "He teases everyone."

He steps behind me as we exit, and I hear him unevenly exhale. This is the street. We cross over and check the numbers. It can only be a couple of blocks down the road.

Kettle walks painfully slow. Stopping every now and then, glancing down the empty driveways. Scaling the walls of every home with his eyes. He's acting like a wary, wild animal, like there's a man with a net tiptoeing toward him and he's counting the exit routes.

We reach number two hundred and two and he stops, his feet lining up neatly against the crack in the footpath, an invisible wall preventing him from walking further. Orange and brown leaves scuttle over his scuffed sneakers and a sign hung from metal chains on a messily painted, white post swings reluctantly in the breeze. It reads in neat, black writing: *Craftman House, Rehabilitation for Returned Serviceman!* I arch an eyebrow at the exclamation point.

Kettle shoves his hands in his pockets. "You said it was a Home."

I don't know why it matters. "That's what the

nurse told me."

"How the hell did you swing this one, Kin?" he mutters to himself, nudging the signpost lightly with his foot.

He stalks up the garden path, ducking under hanging planters, which seem to be dripping from every horizontal beam or branch.

Wind chimes and pinwheels are planted in every garden bed of the overgrown yard. They clatter together, making an ungodly noise with every breeze. Kettle gives me a sideways glance as if to say *be careful* as he starts climbing the stairs, pausing on the last step, which creaks under his feet. He mutters something I can't quite make out and steps up to the porch.

I join him on the welcome mat that just reads we… me, the middle letters scrubbed away from so many polite boots. He lifts his fist to knock and I grab his hand, startled at how hard it is. Shakily, I let go.

"It says ring the bell," I murmur, my eyes going to the large brass bell screwed to the doorframe on our left. He rings the bell. It makes an odd, dull clunking sound, which I doubt anyone would hear, and we step back and wait.

There's something stirring inside him. A bad memory. Guilt. Anger. I'm not sure, but the way his eyes wander over every inch of the porch, the way his finger picks at the peeling paint around the door, makes me worry. It makes me want to know what he's thinking.

KETTLE

Loose change jingles in his overall pockets. It's our warning bell.

From beneath the porch stairs, all I can see are two large boots. Two untied shoelaces.

I touch my heart and remember how those boots felt pressed down on my chest. His sneering face, the flour that rained down on my face, in my eyes, up my nose.

"There," he'd said and then he spat on me. "It's no good. You're no good. Ain't nothing we can do about yer yellow skin. Yer useless."

I rolled away, tears turning to glue.

He hates me. They all hate me.

Nora

Kettle rings the bell again just as the porch vibrates from footsteps within. "All right! All right!" The door swings open and a large woman wearing a circus tent fills the entrance. She narrows her eyes, squishes her lips together, and scrutinizes us through the screen door. "Yeah?"

Kettle coughs, pulls his cap over his eyes, and says, "Scuse me, ma'am. We're looking for…"

A tall woman swans up behind the larger lady, peering over her shoulder. She is beautiful, with kind, crinkled eyes. She smiles at us both and leans over the larger woman. They both laugh and clap their hands. "Visitors!" the larger woman exclaims.

"Splendid! Visitors!" the tall lady shouts. "Come, come. Come in." She extends a long arm around both our shoulders like a lasso and pulls us inside.

Our hesitant feet skid across the dark wood floors. The scents of vanilla and burnt butter hang in the air, and I lick my lips.

"I'm Miss Anna and this is Miss Lake," the taller one says. "Now who did you say you were looking for?" She sweeps us into the kitchen like two dust bunnies. Kettle seems lost for words, his face flushed, his eyes unsure of where to look.

"We're looking for Katsutoshi..." I say slowly, trying to remember Kin's last name. Somehow, we're already sitting at a yellow kitchen table, hot tea being poured into pretty flowered cups and steam pluming in front of our eyes.

They both throw their arms up in the air, and then Miss Lake turns around so Miss Anna can tie her apron strings. "Oh, he'll be glad to have some visitors. He's outside with the physical therapist right now. Determined young man, he is." She points out the high kitchen windows, the paint wanting to feather and fly away just from staring at it too long. We both stand in unison to look.

Kettle whispers, "Kin," pushing his chair back and making his way to the back door. I stand more slowly, giving him some space and giving myself a second to breathe, for my heart not to strangle itself by taking on his pain, his hope, his love. It is so clear that he loves his brother very much, and it hurts me. It makes me think of Frankie. It makes me like him even more, which seems like a bad idea.

I pause in the doorway, my toes hanging from the back step as the door hits them, bang, bang, bang. I watch from behind the screen, my vision blurred by a thousand tiny holes. The scene darker. Greener.

KETTLE

For a moment, I forget everything. Everything. My feet hit the wet grass and I walk fast toward the back of my friend, my brother. He sits in a wicker chair, cane stalks spraying from the back like a peacock's tail. There are men on my left and right, dressed in pajamas, robes loosely open. A puff of cigarette smoke sails into my eyes and I stifle a cough. Someone laughs.

My eyes are on the back of Kin's head, his dark hair combed and oiled, his shoulders looking strong beneath a khaki shirt. He looks okay. *How can he look okay?*

A man in uniform with close-cropped hair is kneeling down, talking to him, his expression open and encouraging. Kin mutters something and the man in uniform chuckles, holds out his arms, and goes to hug Kin.

I slow. Stop. Don't know what's going on.

Kin leans into the embrace, and then the man pulls him to his feet. My throat crackles and dries out. I put my hand to it, rub my skin, and swallow. They're not hugging.

Kin leans all his weight on the man and wobbles to his feet. A crutch is handed to him. He relies on it and the man's shoulder heavily.

He is not okay.

They inch toward parallel, wooden bars with blue mats beneath them. One of Kin's legs seems to move fine, but the other is dead weight, dragging behind him like the bat in a man's hand as he's about to beat you. My own feet are leaden in my sneakers. I tell them to move, but they won't. They dig deeper into the grass until I'm sure I'm only two feet tall. I am so close to Kin, and I can't move.

He hasn't seen me yet. Kin's eyes are on his own feet as he holds the bars and moves from one end to the other. Turning is difficult and he kicks one leg out with the other to shuffle one-hundred-and-eighty degrees. When the man offers to help, Kin shakes his head. A small smile creeps up my arm and lands on my face. That's my brother. Always so proud.

Once he's arranged his feet, he glances up and that's when I realize I'm just standing there, staring at him. He takes one look at me, looks down at his legs, back up, and frowns.

Move your feet, I tell myself, and Kin as well. It's selfish. But I don't want to be responsible for this. I don't want to be the reason he's here.

I lift one foot and then the other, two things I've always taken for granted, and move.

Kin shuffles through the bars to meet me, lifting his eyes to mine every now and then. I wait at the other end, my eyes stretching over the large tree shading the yard. Then they rise to the city, to the sky, to a place where I don't feel so ashamed of what I've done.

When he reaches me, his face is red and sweaty from exertion, his arms wobbling under his weight.

To me, he says casually, "Hey Kettle." To the man in uniform, he says, "Kevin, let's go again."

Kevin nods and helps him turn around.

Through bursts of breath and curse words, he turns his head to me and says, "Walk with me." Impossible humor in his voice. I move next to him and creep forward at his pace. My mouth is holding in all these sad, scary things. I want to tell him I didn't think I had a choice. I didn't want him to die. *I'm sorry. I'm so, so sorry.* Before I can say any of these things, he grunts, "It's not your fault," as his hands jump forward on the bar.

"Huh?" I manage.

"Stop looking at me like that. I know you already have the weight of the world on your shoulders..." He pauses, breathes in and out, and slips his hand further along the bar. "But I'm not on that scale, brother."

I shake my head and stare at the ground, my hand going to the bar to steady myself. "I'm so sorry, Kin. I really am. I wish I'd made it through the gates that day. I wish I'd gotten you help sooner. I wish..." *I just wish things were different.*

Kin sighs loudly and stops. "Look at me. Stop looking at the ground or the clouds. Kettle, I'm okay. I'm going to be okay. And that's *because* of you. You did what you had to, to protect me and to protect our home and the boys." This is a new voice, not big brother, not best friend. It is independent of those things.

"But..." *Look at you, Kin. Your leg, your body...*

He reaches the end of the bars, and Kevin hands him two crutches. "I think that'll do for today, Mister Ikeda." Kin nods and then winks at me, throwing one crutch on the ground.

"I'm Mister Ikeda here, not nip, not street kid, can you believe it?" he asks.

I laugh, throttling some of my anxiousness. "I really can't."

At this, Kin holds the bar with one hand and takes a swipe at me with his crutch. I jump back, but he connects with my shins. "I might be slower these days, but I can still beat your ass."

A door slamming shut and a rush across the grass.

Nora's panting breath hits my ears. I watch as Kin's eyes widen with surprise and then settle into a smug smile.

"Kettle," she says breathlessly, her hand going to my shoulder, hovering and then clamping over the wooden bar instead. "What's going on? Are you two fighting?" Her eyes dart frantically back and forth between us.

Kin laughs loudly, dramatically. "Even in my sorry condition, there would be no fight. Little brother wouldn't dare!"

I grumble. Nora blushes and turns her eyes to the grass. "Oh, sorry. I was mistaken." She glances up at me, warm honey eyes sort of smoldering. "Kettle, would you like me to leave?"

Kin hops toward the chair. He collapses and the wicker squeaks. Smiling widely, he says, "Please don't," in his best charming voice. "Thanks, Kevin. See you tomorrow."

Kevin tips his chin and leaves. I roll my eyes.

"May I have the pleasure of your name?" Kin drawls as we approach him. He holds out his hand for her to take, and I'm way too happy when she doesn't take it.

She whispers shyly, "Kite."

Kin arches an eyebrow. "Kite. Well Kite, Kettle, have a seat." He gestures to the grass. We both sit down at his feet, moisture seeping into our clothes. I watch Nora tuck her legs to the side, the skirt making it difficult to sit on the ground.

Enjoying his captive audience, Kin says with great drama and flair, "Let me tell you both a story."

He starts at the docks for Nora's sake, retelling the story in classic Kin fashion, with lots of comic-book style 'bams' and 'whammos'. She listens quietly, her eyes wide, her mouth open, making shocked noises and touching her fingertips lightly to her mouth at the right times.

It's not a story to me, and hearing it again makes my stomach turn.

"...and then I fell asleep in the sun, waiting for Kettle to finish his shift. The rest is a blank until I woke up at Mount View to a pretty nurse holding a clipboard."

My arms straighten and I lean forward in disbelief. "You don't remember getting back home... All the weird things you were saying?" I'm talking too loudly, and Kin puts his fingers to his lips to shush me. I start to whisper. "I guess it's a good thing. If you did, you would remember how we got back to our station and you collapsed on the platform." I shake my head as I remember. "I screamed and screamed for help, but no one would even look at me because some rich girl had fainted on the platform just a few feet away from us." My head falls into my hands as I remember the hopelessness of it. The fear that he would die in my arms and no one would even care. "I'm sorry, Kin, I tried to get help, but no one would listen. They gave that woman priority and stretchered her away, telling me they would come back for you... but they didn't come back."

Kin's back is pressed into his chair, his head nodding knowingly. "The doctors told me they wished I'd got to them sooner, that I would have had a chance at a full recovery if they'd caught the swelling early. But listen, you can't blame yourself. Blame the rich chick who'd probably had one too many glasses of champagne with her fancy lunch. Don't blame yourself. You did everything you could."

I wish I believed him.

I glance at Nora and she's as white as a sheet, her hands pulling clumps of grass from the ground. This is a lot to take in, I guess. Her hands are covered in dirt. The smell of crushed, fresh leaves should be calming, but I feel like I'm barely holding onto the surface of the planet right now.

"After the paramedics left with the woman, you woke up, but only for a few minutes. You begged me to take you home, and I did, but I couldn't look after you there. I knew your only chance was to get to a hospital. Even if it meant ending up in a Home, it was better than you being dead. You didn't seem to think so, but I had to make the call, Kin."

Kin leans into me and slaps the top of my head before I have a chance to duck. "You should know better than to listen to me." He laughs. His eyes go to Nora's lap, where she's piled grass clippings and shredded roots onto her skirt without noticing, and I wonder whether he recognizes her.

She speaks, her voice a breath of barely audible air. "When did this happen?"

Kin taps his chin and says, "Oh, it'd have to be about ten days ago, right Kettle?"

I nod. "Sounds about right."

45
BLAME

N*o.*
There should be sinister music playing. A finger pressed down on this line in the play, this moment in time. *Here's the big twist! Everyone gasp.*

It was me. It was me. Me. I'm the reason Kettle's brother is partially paralyzed. I am the 'rich chick' who received priority over Kin. I try to think back to that day, but I can't remember seeing him. I can't remember anyone shouting out for help, which makes me feel even guiltier.

So many things had to fall into place for this to happen, for our paths to cross in such a way. *If.* If I hadn't left the house at that time. *If.* If I hadn't made the decision to go down that tunnel, to that platform...

Green juice runs through the cracks between my fingers as I squeeze grass in my fist.

"Anyway, I ended up here with tenpin and bowling ball," he jerks his head toward the kitchen, "all because my father died serving *our* country," Kin says with a large amount of sarcasm and I can't say I blame him. "It's not so bad here, really... I..."

"Tenpin and bowling ball? That's pretty rude, Kin," Kettle mutters. But Kin's not listening, he's staring at me, and then Kettle turns too. I'm under a spotlight of their gazes—one concerned, the other curious.

I squirm as their study of me intensifies. *Guilt.* Guilt is reaching up from the earth and trying to pull me under the earth's crust. This polyester blouse is tightening across my chest. I need to take a breath, but the air feels poisonous. My lies, my life is poisonous.

I like being a part of his world. It has possibility. I feel safe. But if Kettle realizes who I am, that I'm the reason his friend is like this, he'll throw me out and I'll lose my place. The board will be turned up like a sore loser. The pieces will slide to the ground. I'm not sure I can go back to the start now, and I don't want to lose my friend either.

I need to speak. I need to stop wringing my hands and losing blood from my face.

A toe touches my knee. "Kite, is it?" Kin dubiously asks.

Kettle runs his palm up and down in front of my face. "Are you okay?"

I sigh and sigh again; I forget to breathe back in and cough.

Kin's toe is still on my knee, and he taps it once. I look up into his dark eyes, the sun splintering through the branches of the willow behind us. They're stars. I blink. Stars caught in the net of rope-like branches. *Stars are like secrets. They need to fall. Let them fall.*

Kin squints and leans forward, his finger pointed accusingly at my nose. "I know you," he says and the stars start tumbling to the ground, burning holes in the lawn and singeing my skin.

I flinch.

Kettle glances at me sideways. Kin's finger still lingers in the air and I gulp, waiting for it to turn to a fist.

315

I close my eyes. Anger equals yelling equals violence. That's what I know.

I hear Kettle sigh deeply, exasperated. "Kin," he starts with a worn sound to his voice.

"You. You're the girl I was going to marry!" Kin exclaims, hands up in the air, like it finally all makes sense to him.

My eyes pop open. "What?"

Kin stands and we stand with him. He's laughing, holding his stomach with one hand, the other supporting himself on the chair. "That little girl you were with snapped my suspenders. Kettle, remember?" Kettle nods like he does remember. My mind tracks back to that day, and then I stare at Kin more closely. The memory unfolds. Inside is a box full of lightbulbs. One lighting up for every lie I've told and every truth-bearing word they utter. I remember him. I remember Kettle too. A voice rich and dark like hot-poured coffee.

I place a hand on my heart and whisper, "Oh."

"Yeah." He looks me up and down, smiling. His handsome face is painted with a new emotion I don't recognize. "Pretty girl like you... After our encounter, I thought I would seek you out... show you a good time... and then, you couldn't help but fall in love with me."

Kettle snorts and shoots Kin a look so dirty that he stumbles back a little and falls into his chair.

Relief doesn't feel as good as it should. They don't know it was me in the subway, but that doesn't ease anything. Not a thing. My hand goes to my throat, which feels hot and flushed like I've fallen into poison ivy.

Kin is still talking, a big, amused smile on his face, "We would have beautiful mixed race babies you and me. They'd look like Kettle…"

My head snaps to Kettle, who crosses his arms and snaps, "Shut up, Kin."

How do I make this better? How do I stop this strangling feeling?

Kin ignores him. "We'd be in the Times. High-society girl marries homeless Nisei," he teases, but I can barely hear him. I'm seeing that day through Kettle's eyes. Watching me being stretchered away while his brother lay dying on the platform. It's killing me. I've hurt the only person who's helped me.

His kindness will turn. It will turn.

"Kin, shut your trap," Kettle warns, his voice rising in volume.

The words written in my mother's will rise from the grass in smoky wisps of vapor. *Until I turn twenty-one or marry*, whichever comes first. That money could help us all. It is a clear solution. Marry Kin. Get the money. Take care of him, the boys, and Kettle. That would make it right.

"We could, you know," I whisper, my words as tiny as the dewdrops kissing the skin of my legs.

Kin stops laughing, confused. "Could what?"

"We could get married," I say warily and with regret.

More laughing from Kin. Kettle is silent but for his angry breathing mixing with the swish of the sad, sad willow branches.

"When I marry, I stand to inherit a great deal of money. It could help all three of us. It could solve a lot of our problems," I say unconvincingly.

Kettle takes a deep breath in. He's learning this all for the first time, and I can tell it's upsetting him.

I turn to him. "I'm sorry I didn't tell you," *I'm sorry I'm lying to you, all the time.* So. Many. Lies. But maybe if I do this, my father's identity won't be as big a deal. Maybe.

Kin's eyes light up. He puts a hand on his heart and says in a breathy, feminine voice, "This is all so sudden." Then more seriously, "Well, I do turn eighteen in a few days' time."

How did we get here so fast?

Kettle blows air through his nose slowly, and I count to ten. I don't know why we're both looking to him for permission but somehow, that's where we are.

"No," he says. "No way." There is a look being exchanged between the two of them, a silent conversation and an understanding. Kin shuts his mouth and tries to stop grinning.

Kettle faces me, looking like a disapproving father, tapping his foot and shaking his head.

"But it could be the solution to all of our problems," I say, only half-believing my own words.

He shakes his head again. From the kitchen, Miss Anna shouts, "Cookies!" Our heads all swing in the direction of the house and then fall back on Kettle.

Kin smirks. "Cookies sound good, don't they, Kettle?"

Kettle won't move. "You're not marrying Kin," he states flatly.

Kin's eyes go from Kettle to me, Kettle to me. "Well, well, well..."

I blink at Kettle and open my mouth to speak. He puts his hand up in my face, blocking my view of everything. "Don't look at me like that. You're not marrying me either."

I frown. He's being unreasonable. Not thinking it through. *Am I?*

The smell of chocolate chip cookies wafts over from the trays the women are carrying around the yard. "Well, there goes your chance to marry up in this world," Kin says to me with a wink, pointing to the sky.

Kettle snatches a cookie from the tray and snarls at Kin. "Don't wink at her. Just… don't."

It makes us both giggle, even though I know there's seriousness to come.

Kin and I take a cookie each and nibble at them, melted chocolate smudging our fingers. "Thanks, Tenpin!" Kin says with a smile.

Miss Anna giggles and slaps at him with her praying mantis arms. Then she looks at Kettle and me. "He has a nickname for everyone around here."

Kettle laughs, and I love the sound of it. "I don't doubt it."

The subject of marriage is dropped for the moment, although I can see it typing lines in Kettle's brain. We talk about the ladies who run the place, Kin's rehab, when he might come home. I observe them, saying little. Their interactions are easy. Brotherly. And my heart aches.

Frankie, I miss you so much.

"I can't come home. At least, not to that home," Kin says sadly. "Kettle, you know I won't be able to get around down there. If I came back to the city, it would have to be to a real apartment. Preferably Eastside, ground floor, great view, hardwood floors…" he jokes.

He doesn't mention my suggestion of marriage again, but I know he's thinking about it. He's hinting to Kettle.

"You'll be fine. We'll make it work, once you're better," Kettle says, lightly punching him in the arm. The action makes me flinch, and Kin catches my response. There's something in those dark eyes. They see more than his mouth lets on.

When it's time to leave, the ladies make us promise to visit again soon.

Kin manages to walk us to the door, taking a break halfway down the hall. It pains me to watch him struggle and to watch Kettle's reaction to that struggle. I might as well have kicked him in the stomach.

Kin leans his tall frame against the doorway and smiles.

"I'll come see you on your birthday," Kettle promises.

Kin looks over the top of Kettle's head and down on me. I blush. "And you? Will I see your beautiful face again, Kite?"

"I hope so," I say with a weird flutter in my voice.

Kettle stalks past us both, makes it to the first step, and then swings around. Quite suddenly, he rushes Kin, throws his arms around his neck, and hugs him tightly. I hear him sniff and then they break apart. "I'm glad you're okay," he says.

"I'll see you soon," Kin promises.

We turn and walk down the path. When we reach the gate, Kin shouts, "Goodbye, future wife!" He chuckles as the door closes.

Kettle's silence is unending. It eats at me, takes pieces and won't give them back.

The boys eat noisily at the card table. Kettle sits on his bed, hands clasped between his legs, just staring at the wall. The arch over him makes me think of an upside-down horseshoe, all the luck just tumbling out.

I find a drink in the grocery bag and take it over to him. It drips with condensation, and water slips from the bottle and onto the leg of his pants.

He grabs the bottle, muttering, "Thanks."

I sit down on the chest, the one full of all my mother's things, and sigh.

"I can't marry you," he says.

"I know." I stare at the floor. I don't really want this anyway. So I shouldn't be disappointed.

"It's just, it's not how things are done. It shouldn't be like this. If we were going to… I would ask… and…" I fill in all the missing words, but I find myself more confused. He flips the conversation. "That girl, the one who flicked Kin's suspenders, who was she?"

"My sister," I say softly, trying to close the door before all the lies come flooding out.

He sighs, disappointed. "You didn't need to lie to me about her. I kinda guessed she might be."

"If you knew, why didn't you say something?" I ask, my lies resist, but they're being forced open. One down, two to go.

"I figured you'd tell me when you were ready," he says. "Is she still with him? Your father?" He cringes when he talks about him. *Will that change?*

My voice is weak, cracked, "I don't know where she is. He took her away."

Kettle's dark blue eyes shine like the sun bouncing off the deepest sea. "I can help you find her. You helped me. Let *me* help you," he says, and my heart wants to reach for the hope he's offering, but I just can't. If he knows her name, my name, things will change. I now realize how stupid it was to suggest marriage. Once he and Kin learned who I was, it all would have evaporated. I'm the daughter of their defender, one of the men fighting for justice on behalf of the Japanese Americans who were interned during the war.

If I married Kin, there would be so many questions I wouldn't be able to answer. The truth about my father and what he's done to me could come out and the compensation case would be ruined.

I shake my head. "That's not necessary. You've done so much for me already. More than enough."

His hands are aflame, his eyes so earnest when they look at me. "Nora, what's going on? Why won't you let me help you? We need to find your sister and expose your father for the monster he is. The son of a bitch should be in jail."

"You don't understand. It's not that simple." My legs are matchsticks glued together. They buckle, they break.

"The hell it isn't!" he shouts, and five heads swivel in our direction.

The truth is pushing at the sides of my head, looking for cracks. And then there are the real cracks that my father made. Slowly, they are pulling apart. I clamp my hands on either side of my head to try and keep my head together.

Kettle falls to his knees in front of me and puts his hands over mine. He lifts my face to meet his and gently pulls my hands from my eyes. "Nora, tell me why you won't let me help you," he says, sighing, his gaze following the tears that drip into my palms and race down my arms. "Just tell me."

The floodgates open. "I was there. It was me. I'm sorry," I say into my hands. He won't forgive me. "I'm the 'rich chick', although I didn't faint from too many drinks. I ran away after the beating of my life. Kettle," I say, "I thought he was going to kill me. I had to run. Oh, but it didn't take too long for the great Christopher Deere to find me." I drop my head in shame. "I was free for barely an hour."

Realization smacks us both in the face, hard. I said my father's name. I want to shove it back in, but it's too late. My arms stretch out to him as I see his expression change. "Kettle, I'm sorry. I didn't want to tell you who my father was. I knew it would change how you saw me, how you felt about me, and I wanted a chance to make my own impression before that happened."

Kettle's anger grows. His fists tighten and his face contorts. "Jesus! I can't believe it! I can't believe... you." He points at me, and it's like a sword to my chest.

It's over. I stand and turn toward Kin's bed, to the only place I've ever truly slept. "I'm sorry. I'll go. I'll leave."

I'm shaking. I have nowhere to go. The mess I've made can't be cleaned up.

The boys have all stopped eating, mouths open,

staring at us from across the room.

Kettle makes a loud noise, a frustrated sigh. "Ugh!"

My limbs feel heavy. I knew it. He hates me. He can't stand me. I quicken my pace to gather what little I have and get out of here before he shouts at me some more, before it all descends into punches and blood and bruises.

His loud steps approach and I swing around. I lift my hands to my face and drop to my knees, bracing myself for the pain. I tense, ready for strong hands to tear my arms away from my eyes, for fists to seek out my soft skin.

I wait. Wait. Listen.

I drop my arms to the saddest face I've ever seen.

"Oh Nora," he says with breaking hearts and sorrow in his voice. "I'm not going to hit you."

Relief fills me from my feet to my head, and I cry out softly. I am ripped-up paper. I am stomped-up trash blowing across the sidewalk. I am so broken because of *him*.

"I don't want you to leave. I'm angry because you felt the need to lie to me, that you thought I'd turn you in, change my mind about you after I learned who you were. I'm not that guy. Your father is a bad man and no amount of money would ever make up for that. You hear me?" he says. "Christopher Deere is a bad man, and he needs to answer for what he's done to you."

These words are old and new. I know them, I've felt them, but for the first time in my life, I really listen. I open my ears, my eyes, and my heart. Kettle is right. Christopher Deere is a bad man and until I face him, this will never be over. It all leads back to him. This is all his fault.

I nod, sniffing, and trying to slow my breathing. Kelpie runs over to me, his face covered in sprinkles from the donut he just ate. "What's wrong with Nora?" he asks, innocently looking up at Kettle.

Kettle leans down and wipes the crumbs from Kelpie's lips. "Her name is Kite now."

I'm a King.

I think I can talk. A calm is settling over me. A resolution is solidifying inside. Kettle's warm expression extends over me.

"Kite—I like it. But it's not as good as Kelpie," Kelpie says proudly. "What was your name, Kettle, you know, before you became a King?" he asks, his eyes sleepy.

Kettle smiles. "I've had a lot of names. But I think my very first name was Hiro," he says it as if it's new to him too, like it's the first time he's ever said it out loud.

Hiro. It's perfect.

46

KETTLE

PRETEND

*THESE FEET DON'T GO ANYWHERE. SO HOW COME I FEEL LIKE
WE'RE FLYING? THAT I'M PASSING OVER THE WORLD, LIFTING TO
THE STARS... AND FINALLY TOUCHING THEM.*

Two sparks, almost simultaneous, growing to fire-
light dancing up the walls.

She sits up, the blanket curled around her like
ripples in a puddle, her hands planted on either side. I
can't sleep either.

There are so many things she hasn't told me. So
many secrets. She glances my way, her lips parted in
a sigh I've come to recognize. The one that means she
beating herself up. We stand and meet in the middle of
the room. A candle flickers by her bed and by mine, the
light arcing out in fading circles and nudging us closer
together.

I take a step. She takes a step.

"Can't sleep?" I ask. She nods, hair falling over her
eyes. I want to touch it and wind it carefully over her
ear, but with her, I never know what's too much, too
far. She grabs it herself and twists it together in one
hand, pulling it over her shoulder. In her silence are
words I need to find. Understand.

We stay in this never land between our two beds.

My eyes fall to the back of the tunnel, the pile of cracked stones and slabs of concrete. I don't want her in my room, or Kin's. We move to the neutral, broken space and sit down on the floor.

Her eyes lift to mine as if to say, 'Now what?' as she plays with the pearl button on her blouse, which is now un-tucked and hanging over a far-too-loose pair of my pants.

I give her a smile. "Tell me about yourself, your life," I say, slightly afraid of the answer. But I need to know.

"My sister, Frankie, was my life. After my mother died, I swore I'd protect her." She shakes her head, her eyes hollowing into deep pools of liquid amber. "I tried. But I didn't do a very good job."

"Does he…?" I glance up from my crossed legs.

"Once, when she was a baby. And *that* day, the day I was at the subway station with you and Kin, well, it was because he was about to hurt her again, and I stopped him. I was the shield. I tried to run away with her." She puts her hand to her head. "I was in no condition to run away."

I wince at her words, the honesty in them, the way her body goes rigid and yet shakes at the same time.

"Let me help you find her," I say again, leaning in, my hand wanting to touch her face, feel the blush under her skin on my palm.

She shakes her head. "No. He would destroy you, everything you've built here." She gestures around the tunnel. "Please, Kettle." Her eyes are rimmed with moisture, and I back off. Her heart is like a ribbon. I have to be so careful not to step on it, snag it, and disrupt the delicate rhythm of it rolling in. In and away from me.

"My life." She sighs the word like it's too much and not enough. "You want to know about my life. Well, the truth is, it wasn't *all* bad," she says, changing the subject, and I let her. There'll be time to discuss her sister later. "Some parts of my life were wonderful." She looks to the roof, dust instead of stars in her eyes. "There were friends, school, Frankie…" Her voice trails in sadness and she jerks away from the feeling. "And dances." She clasps her hands together and smiles. "Oh, I miss dances."

I snort, push my sleeves up, and lean back on my forearms. She watches me, her eyes on my bare skin, and I wonder what she's thinking. "Dances. Really? What's to miss?" My experience with dances was one forced event in the camps where we watched the grownups awkwardly shift in lines to scratchy music. It didn't look very enjoyable.

She releases the button she's been playing with and smirks. "Says someone who's clearly never been to one."

"How do you know that?" I say, raising an eyebrow and touching my chest, mock offended.

She laughs. It's starlight in a jar. I blink slowly. "Oh, I can tell just by looking at you, the way you move. You," she says, pointing at me accusingly. "Can't dance."

The candlelight twinkles like it's chuckling at me. "I can dance," I say, not sure why I'm lying to defend myself. I've never danced in my life.

She stands up and beckons me with her finger, and I think there's something wrong with my heart. It's hurting… but the pain feels good.

She looks like a pirate's cabin boy, shirt billowing around her small waist, ill-fitting pants rolled over at her hips to stop them from falling down. She points her bare foot at me. "Prove it!"

Shit!

I cough and stand nervously. I don't know what to do with my hands, so I put them behind my back. She giggles. Touches me. Runs her fingers lightly down my arms until she finds my hands. She grasps my wrists and I gulp as she places one on the small dip between her hips and her ribs, extending the other out like the bow of a boat. Her hand in mine.

I follow her small steps and we wind in circles, avoiding the clumps of debris, painting patterns in the dust.

I stare at my socks and her narrow bare feet, listening to the swish of them across the dirt. "You know, this is pretty weird without music," I mutter, looking up for a moment and suddenly losing my balance.

She exhales and brings us back to equilibrium. She starts humming softly. It's a song I've heard before, but I pretend it's the first time. Her voice is sweet, cracked and croaky, but in tune as she gazes at the ground and leads us up and down the back of the tunnel.

This moment is killing me. I don't want it, but I do. Because I know it won't be enough and it's all I'll get.

The end of the song is coming. It rises and rises and then softly peters out. We look at each other, understanding that something is changing between us, and we have to decide whether to let it. *Please, let it.*

She sings the last few bars. "And if you sing this

melody, you'll be pretending just like me. The world is mine. It can be yours, my friend. So why don't you pretend?"

Her voice is like the dust of a comet's tail. Full of a thousand things I don't understand but want to.

She stops and starts to step away. She's so fragile. Not on the outside. On the outside, her body is strong, tougher than it should have to be. It's inside that's very breakable. I'm scared to touch her, but I don't want to avoid touching her because of what she's been through. That seems worse.

So I do it, because I want to and I don't think she doesn't want me to. Her breath catches as I pull her closer. I just want to press my cheek to hers, feel her skin against mine. There is no music, just the rhythm of two barely functioning hearts trying to reach each other through miles of scar tissue.

She presses her ear to my chest and listens, then she pulls back to meet my eyes, her expression a mixture of confusion and comfort. She breathes out, her lips not wanting to close but not wanting to speak. She settles on a nervous smile and puts her arms around my neck. I inhale and look up at the ceiling, counting the stars I know are up there somewhere, and then rest my cheek in her hair.

I don't know how she is here. I don't know when she'll disappear.

We sway back and forth, and it feels like we might break. That we *will* break if we step apart from each other.

I can't let her go.

I think I love dancing.

47

A GIRL

There was this girl. She was battered, broken. Holding on but slipping. Because she was holding onto the wrong things. The things that can't support and can only cut her.

I'm not that girl anymore, and I know what I need to do.

48

KETTLE

GONE

I wake with a big, stupid smile on my face.
I stand up, stretch, and freeze.
She's gone.

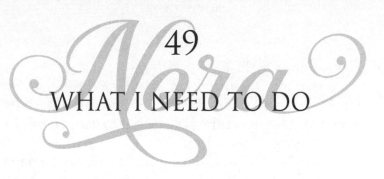

49

WHAT I NEED TO DO

I press the doorbell, the buzz shooting shockwaves through my body. I straighten.

My body that is strong and ready to fight.

If I can fly, I can do this.

I put a palm to my chest and wish I could cup a hand around my heart to calm it. It's beating loudly against my pleura like a warning.

Heavy steps approach, the boards cracking like a tongue wanting water, and I hold my breath until it opens.

Marie's face is worn and disappointed when she sees me. "Miss Nora, what are you doing here?" she whispers, her eyes darting back and forth along the empty street. She can't look at me.

"I'm here to see my father," I say, taking a step forward, one foot on the welcome mat, the other pulling me back so I'm straddling that divide between *in* and *out*.

Marie sighs and shakes her head. "Miss." She bows softly, but she doesn't move from the entrance. My hand goes to the doorframe, a wave of nausea slamming through me like a drunken ghost.

"Marie, let me pass," I firmly demand.

She steps aside, muttering under her breath, "Miss. Please. Don't." Three words punctuated with concern.

Signs written in the dust.

I step into the reception, the door closing behind me. Marie shuffles into the kitchen and puts up a barrier between herself and what's about to happen by closing the heavy kitchen door.

I stand on the tiles, staring at my feet. Am I a pawn on this chessboard? Am I small, insignificant, easily sacrificed? I move toward the base of the stairs with quiet, determined movements. *No, I am a King.*

The study door is ajar, a small triangle of light spreading over the landing. "Who's at the door, Marie?" my father's voice shouts impatiently from inside. I jump at the sound of his voice. So angry, so biting and dark. When no one answers, he stomps toward the landing. The door opens, the light pouring over the banister like a golden waterfall. The shadow of my father stops, painted on the stairs like it's glued down, and I realize he is the shadow. He is darkness swallowing the light, and he is everything I don't want. He grips the banister with both hands and leans over, smiling down on me. I catch a slight rise of his eyebrows like maybe he's surprised or impressed that I came back, but before I can hold onto it, it's gone.

"Nora," he says like a curse word. "You've returned."

He doesn't move. He won't come to me. He waits as I climb the stairs to meet him, always under his cold silhouette. It bends over every step, grabs at my ankles, as crooked as his own heart. He keeps his face neutral. He needn't bother. I know what's beneath the mask is thrashing and scratching to get out.

When I reach the top, I tip my chin at him. "Father."

He smiles sickeningly at me. "I knew you would come crawling back. You're not strong enough to survive without me." He looks at his watch, and then back up at me. "You didn't last much longer than a week." He sneers.

I close my mind to his words as they snap at my sides and try to take bites out of me. *I am, I am, I am strong enough* my heart stutters. I force myself to smile back and not respond to his comment. "I would like to speak with you."

He gestures for me to go into his study, lifting his hand to my back as we reach the doorway and pushing me inside, un-gently.

I resist a little, try to stand on my own feet, but stumble.

The door closes tightly like the lid of a chest, trapping me inside. No air, except his air. The room is filled with the smell of dusty books, leather and all of me, all the parts of me he took over the years. I pull them in, gather them in my arms, and reclaim them.

He stalks around me in a circle like a lion, knocking my shoulders as he passes. I don't move. I won't move. "I've missed you," he says in a stinging, point-of-a-dagger voice.

"I find that hard to believe," I say as he walks to the edge of his desk, folds his arms across his chest, and casually crosses his legs at the ankles. His vest is unbuttoned, his sleeves shoved up to the elbows.

He ignores my comment and goes for the kill, stabbing me with his words. "Your sister misses you too. Very much."

I plant my feet more firmly on the ground. *I'm a*

tree in a storm. He won't uproot me. "Where is she?"

He tsks and shakes his head. "I can't tell you that."

"Is she safe?" I whisper, wanting to scream, *Why? Why won't you tell me? What have you done with her?* But I'm trying to play his game.

His mouth twitches, a blanket of frustration whipping across his expression, fast like a bullfighter's cape. "She is... unharmed," he mutters, whatever that means. "And now that you are back home, I will consider sending for her."

I shake my head slowly. "I'm not back home."

The elastic of his skin tightens. His arms bulge as he wraps himself tauter. *How many punches are in there?* I wonder. *How many can I take?* My eyes flit to the corners for potential weapons. Golf clubs, umbrella, large, heavy law books that are already stained with my blood.

A bridge of a few seconds stretches between us, and then he laughs. "Don't be foolish, Nora, you have nowhere else to go, no money..."

I'm stuck on this rug, glued down. I pick up my feet, and then plant them again. "I will have money very soon."

He lifts from the desk and takes a step toward me. I take a step back. We're dancing. A horrible dance, a forced partnership I need to break. In his expression, I see fractured bones and purple flesh and then, abruptly, he turns toward his bookshelves and runs his finger along the spines like I'm boring him. He speaks to the letters, gold and black. "You plan to marry then? I can't imagine anyone would be willing to marry you."

I don't even know what I'm saying. "I do. I will be

married by the end of the week. Excuse me for not inviting you, but we wanted to keep the guest list small. Just close family and friends."

The corner of his eye twitches, but he doesn't turn. He pulls out a random book and flicks it open, holding it in one hand as he ruffles the pages. "I'll never let her go," he says, snapping the book shut.

My limbs wobble and try to uncouple. I swallow. "I'll give you half my inheritance if you tell me where she is. I just want your word that after that, you will leave us alone."

This is when he turns. Slow and fast. Made of molten metal and ire. So much anger that he might be on fire. "You are my daughters. *My* family. You belong to me, and I will never let you go. *Never.* I don't want your money. How do you think it would look if my only family ran away from me? Chose to live separate to me? No. I will not allow it. And I will not allow you to marry. I'll find a way to stop it from happening." He takes a sharp breath, his fists rolled up and waiting. "You Will. Not. Leave. This. House," he spits, slamming the book on the floor.

He shakes his fist as he screams. And I have crumbled. His shadow pins me to my place and I can't see, can't find a way out.

I will not, *cannot* stay here.

I step backward, mumbling, "My whole life…"

He pauses, smoothes his hair down, and stoops to meet my eyes. "Did you speak?" he asks with disgust.

"My whole life, I've been afraid of you. But not anymore." He's bent in at strange angles. Frozen by the fact that I'm finally standing up for myself. "Only a cowardly, cruel man hits a child, a mother... an unborn baby." He cracks, straightens like a puppet being put away for the night. He's not a real person. He is soulless, empty, and I hate him. I keep walking backward as I talk, "Do you know when the happiest time in my childhood was?" He is quiet and knuckle white, and my words slip from my mouth—venomous but true. "It was when you were MIA, and we thought you might be dead. I remember when we got the yellow letter. As she read it, I didn't see sadness in her eyes, I saw relief." There they are. My words. The truth. A tumble of letters on the carpet. We both stare down and back up. Our eyes are the same. Both filled with fury. The difference is what we do with it.

White turns to red turns to black, black, black.

I continue. "I will not stay here. And if you won't accept my offer, then so be it. I'll find her anyway. I'll find her, and then you will have nothing," I shout with my back pressed against the study door. "Nothing but the ghost of a wife who was terrified of you and an empty house!"

I turn my back to him to open the door. I don't even care how my words have affected him. I don't want to look in his furious, hurt, or suffering eyes. I want to go home. Back to the Kings, to Kettle.

My hand grasps the handle strongly. I think of Kettle and the boys and smile. I'll find Frankie and I'll make a life for myself. Then my hand slips from the door, my back inverts, my legs disintegrate, and my face hits the floor.

I DO BELIEVE IN FAIRIES

Muffled shouting pounds on the inside of the door.

"I will not let you go!" a man shouts. A mangled scream follows.

I'm too late.

I push on the door, and it opens. Black-and-white tiles shine under a chandelier. A creak to my left pulls my focus and a large woman lingering in a doorway sniffs, her eyes held upwards. "He's going to kill her," she says with little emotion. It's just fact—he will kill her.

I hear another thump, harder than my heartbeat but not stronger, and I race up the stairs that seem endless and towering. Stretching to the sky.

There's some part of me that doesn't want to go. Doesn't want to see what's in that room. I've never been so afraid… I think of the beatings, the blood, the shackles and suffering I've seen, and still… no. I have never been so afraid in my whole life.

"Stop! Please," Nora's small, wet-sounding voice comes from behind a dark, oily-looking door. Another noise like someone batting dirt from a rug and she screams, though it sounds like a scream beneath a mountain of cloth, like she's buried.

I grab the handle, turn and push, finding it hard

to get inside because something is blocking the door. "Nora," I yell through the small gap.

I glance down and my throat tightens. Tears form, burning rings around my eyes, because the 'thing' blocking the door is Nora... and standing over her is a wild, furious man, holding what appears to be a hat rack snapped in half.

Oh Jesus.

I don't have time to be gentle. I shove the door and Nora inward, put my head down and charge at the man. Christopher Deere—defender of civil rights and monster.

I drive him toward the desk, holding the wrist that's still clutching the coat rack and smack it down on the tabletop. He won't let it go, and I have to smack it several times before it clatters to the ground.

"Kettle," Nora wheezes, pulling herself up to an almost sitting position. She holds her stomach, her face a frighteningly pale, gray color that terrifies me. She coughs, and I'm watching her instead of him. I am rewarded with a book to the side of the head.

I fall to the side and roll onto the floor, clambering up to my knees, but he's already got a boot to my stomach. My insides compress, flooding with pain.

Nora screams, "Leave him alone!" and starts dragging herself toward us.

I put a hand up to stop her, but he slams his foot down on it. "Is this him?" He laughs. "Oh Nora, you really can pick them," this cold, dark man with Nora's eyes shouts as he laughs sardonically.

There is silence. Air moving in and out of the room like a lung. Something shiny and silver catches the corner of my eye. Another blow hits my ribs and pain flares. I grab at his legs but I can't gain an advantage from the floor. He grabs my collar and jerks me up so I'm hanging from my clothes, choking.

A metallic click like a lock sliding into place stops him dead. We hear a sliding sound and turn toward Nora at the same time.

A flash of white light.

I wait for the loud bang, for him to fall…

And then I am released.

He grunts. All his anger is pooled at the tip of a sharp, silver letter opener in his hand, poised ready to run me through. It drops to the floor, and I scramble away. I look up at Nora, who's holding a large Polaroid camera to her chest. It seems to terrify her father.

"Kettle," she manages in a crushed-to-pieces voice. "Run." He takes a threatening step toward her and she bolts, with me following behind but slower as I try to block his path.

"Nora, stop!" he thunders, but she doesn't listen. She grips the camera like it's the most precious thing in the world and runs down the stairs.

Breathless, she shouts, "How will it look for you, Father?" as she takes the steps two, three at a time, a giddy, hysterical edge to her words as she laughs. "The great Christopher Deere caught beating one of the very people he's been trying to defend."

She skids on the carpeted stairs, grips the banister, and turns her face upward. *Slow down*, I think.

"Tell me where Frankie is or I'll give this photo to every paper in the city," she threatens, holding the heavy camera up to the light. She cracks open the back and peels the photo out, her eyes lighting up when she sees it. Swinging the camera back, she lobs it onto the landing. Her father jumps back as it smashes, the flashbulb sending splinters of glass everywhere.

She starts moving again. I'm a few steps away from her, but she's moving too fast. Her father stays at the top, his face rippling with fear, glass dusting his expensive shoes.

"You wouldn't dare!"

"Yes I would!" she yells, stomps her foot, sways, and then loses her balance. And I think, *now. Now I have never been so afraid in my entire life.*

Nora

This seems almost funny. I must be bouncing around inside a shell. Because I hear the cracks, the sharp shattering of things, and I think, *This has all happened before and it can't be me.*

It's fast. The fastest. My face is split black and white by the cool tiles seeping into my skin. I breathe out and try to decide whether I should breathe back in because it would be easier to sink. Join her down there.

KETTLE

I run, doing the same stupid thing that she just did, taking two steps at a time, not holding on. Bounding, breaking, my heart is breaking. *Why doesn't she move?*

Why does she hug the floor like she wants to disappear beneath it?

I launch from the last step and skid to a halt beside her body, falling to my knees. Carefully, I run a hand down one of her arms. She doesn't move. *Move.*

Her father hasn't moved either. He's frozen in some sort of branched-out horror, his hands clenching the banister, his face giving away nothing. No expression at all. If he cared that he's killed her, he doesn't show it.

The large woman still stands in the doorway. She has taken to moaning and swaying back and forth in the space, like she's trapped there. I eye her and then look up at Mr. Deere. "Don't you move a goddamn inch!" I shout, my hand up. He says nothing. He is stone and soon, I forget he's there. "Oh, Nora. Nora. Nora. Get up. You can't stay here. Please don't be dead," I whisper, moving closer to where her face lies cheek to cheek with the tiles. "You have to come home. You have to come home with me." My hands are shaking as I brush her hair from her ear. This can't be happening.

So many feet, marching, turning, and kicking up splinters on the whitewashed floor.

"He's under the bed," the gruff voice I've learned how to avoid grunts. "He's always hidin' under the bed. I always find him though."

Upside down, brown eyes blink at me. "This is Hiro Jackson? He's only a little kid. How old is he?"

"Yessir, that's him. Bout five, I think."

Is that my name? Thick hands grab around my middle and drag me out like a possum under the porch. I kick and scratch like one too.

I'm scared. I'm always scared.

I don't know what's happening, but I give up quickly. Wherever they're taking me, maybe it's better than here. I relax in the large arms.

"Here's the order," the soldier holding me to his hip says, showing a piece of paper with black writing on it that starts off big and gets smaller and smaller like an eye test.

The man who's been looking after me for two years peers at it for a second, tracing his finger along the larger words. Then his hands drop and he looks away from the paper and from me. "Don't care. Just take him."

Down the stairs, past the staring eyes of the other children.

I don't get to say goodbye.

The soldier places me gently in the backseat of a large, black car. I shiver and pull my legs up to my chest and he sighs, giving me his jacket.

"Yeah, this one must be a spy," he says, laughing. The other men laugh too, only for a second, and then they are quiet.

"All right, Hiro Jackson, time to take you to your new home."

The car pulls away from the gray shingle house and I look out the window, thinking of clouds, and where she is, and why my name is Jackson.

"Nora. You have to come home with me."

I'm so close to her face that my lips brush hers, scratched and perfect. A puff of warm air reaches my skin, and I shudder with relief. She's alive.

Tiny splinters of words reach my ears.

A ghost of a kiss.

"Nor... rah... Nor... rah," they whisper. Gentle fingers press into my shoulders and shake, nudging me to life. Reminding me to live. "Kite," he whispers. I pull my legs up. I could be a kite. Wind punching me through, colors and shredded tails. I could fly away. Live in the sky...

Reel me in.

The sharp corner of the Polaroid digs into my chest. Words scrape my lips like sand. "Tell me where she is," I whisper, hoping someone can hear me.

Kettle reaches under me, his hands bumping things he shouldn't be touching, but it doesn't matter now. He rolls me over, sits me up, holds my face in his hands, and tilts it from side to side. Those dark blue eyes hold me together. I see an emotion I don't recognize in them, a feeling I want to learn.

He takes the photo still pressed to my chest, stares at it, and then shouts up to my father, who is spilled concrete, splattered all over the landing. Unable to move. Kettle's voice rumbles and fills the space. "Where is Frankie?" He waves the photo back and forth in the air and then stills. The image is a scar on paper. Christopher Deere about to stab a Japanese boy with a letter opener. It's clear. My hands were so steady in that moment. I could almost laugh, if my ribs weren't pinching my lungs.

A number and a street name tumble from the sky, slide under my flattened body and lift me up.

I will get up.

I'm a miracle about to happen. I'm a star that refuses

to die.

Leaning heavily on Kettle, I get to my feet, slipping on the splash of red marking the pristine tiles.

I glare up at my father. "If the address doesn't check out, you'll regret it," I say firmly, my bones made of steel, my leg dripping blood.

He nods. Nothing else. He doesn't try to stop me. Doesn't threaten me.

It's over.

Kettle's arm wraps around my waist as he half drags me across the threshold, across the common area, and into the cool, autumn air, the sun hitting us with pale gold light. I stop on the step, straighten my clothes, and smile.

"I'm okay, Kettle," I say, turning to his warm, copper-colored face.

He looks down at my leg and then back to my face. I'm radiating something new. I'm a solar flare. I'm heat and determination. He releases me, a hand hovering at my back, just in case.

"You're better than okay," he says, smiling, pushing my heart in at funny angles until it hurts to breathe. "You're a King."

I'm a King.

I wear his crown. Wear the blue of his eyes, the kindness in his voice. I want more. More words, more time, more light shining on dark places. I want *him*.

It should, but this change growing between us doesn't throw me off balance. It doesn't take up space that should be Frankie's. It opens me up and anchors me. It sinks roots to the ground and stretches up to reach the sun. It is good. Nourishing and pure. It is things I never thought I could have.

I take his hand, hold it tight, and together, we step down and away from the brownstone. I picture my father standing, static on the landing just once, and then he becomes fire-cracked clay, an ornament easily broken. In my mind, he will be frozen that way forever and my brain flicks his image to the side, toppling his wooden likeness as if he were the chess piece. All the power he had over me... gone.

My bones crack, my skin splits, my leg drags behind me, but the pain seems to shatter and shed from my body the further away we get and the closer we become, until it evaporates into the clouds. I look up and watch the bad parts of me shrinking to dots in the wide blue.

We're going home.

Together, we write words across the sky in giant, messy script, full of mistakes and crossed-out letters. And I am filled with hope as I watch them dance and clash and poke at my fears, because although I know I can do this on my own, now I am sure I don't have to.

Frankie, we're coming.

Acknowledgements

This book is primarily about love and survival. So I want to thank the people who taught me about these two things. The way they work together. How they are inextricably linked in times of adversity.

Love comes in many forms as everyone knows. Romantic love, love of family, of friends, and of oneself. To me, it is the backbone of getting through, the thing that holds us up when the world is trying to pull us down to the dirt. And even if we do fall, I think it somehow stops the dirt from clinging.

My inspiration for this novel came from two people who survived some of the most appalling conditions during their internment during World War Two, my grandparents, John (Grandad) and Jeanne (Nanna). During the Japanese occupation of Malaysia, they were thrown into two separate internment camps in Singapore. Grandad was beaten severely, starved and forbidden from seeing his wife and baby. Nanna, still nursing her young infant at the time, was forced to eat rodents and insects just to survive. They were just nineteen, newly married and in love, facing conditions no one should ever have to face.

But they got through, and if you asked Nana how, her answer, in her very vibrant and animated way of speaking, was love, the hope she would see Grandad again, and that they would get out, make a life for themselves, and never look back on the muddy, razor wire-surrounded grounds of those camps again.

They did get out. They had another child (my father) and went on to live fulfilling lives—ones full of love, grandchildren, color, and laughter. But they were shortened lives, which makes me even more thankful that they shared their stories with me.

There isn't much I would wish for in this world, but to have them back, to have had more time with them than I did, would be my biggest one.

For surviving, for your love, hope, and beautiful souls, thank you, thank you, thank you.

I wouldn't be here without you.

About the Author

Lauren Nicolle Taylor lives in the lush Adelaide Hills. The daughter of a Malaysian nuclear physicist and an Australian scientist, she was expected to follow a science career path, attending Adelaide University and completing a Health Science degree with Honours in obstetrics and gynaecology.

She then worked in health research for a short time before having her first child. Due to their extensive health issues, Lauren spent her twenties as a full-time mother/carer to her three children. When her family life settled down, she turned to writing.

Author of the best selling Woodlands Series, she is also a 2014 Kindle Book Awards Semi-finalist and a USA Best Book Awards Finalist.